FLIGHT OF THE ALBATROSS

FLIGHT OF THE
ALBATROSS

Deborah Savage

Houghton Mifflin Company
Boston   1989

Pages 177 and 246: From "Fern Hill," by Dylan Thomas
Page 255: "Song for Te Hauapu," by Noho-mai-te-rangi;
translated from the Maori by Rob Dyer

Library of Congress Cataloging-in-Publication Data
Savage, Deborah.
   Flight of the albatross / Deborah Savage.
      p.   cm.
   Summary: Sarah goes to New Zealand to spend the summer with her
mother and becomes involved with a Maori boy and his cause.
   ISBN 0-395-45711-4
   [1. New Zealand — Fiction. 2. Maoris — Fiction.]   I. Title.
PZ7.S2588F1   1989   88-36880
[Fic] — dc19   CIP
                          AC

Printed in the United States of America

P   10 9 8 7 6 5 4 3 2 1

To my friend Leif,
with thanks
for knowing that the albatross was perfect

and to my parents
Richard and Judith Savage

and to Cynthia, Martha, Richetta,
Norma, Sandy, Joan—with love and thanks.

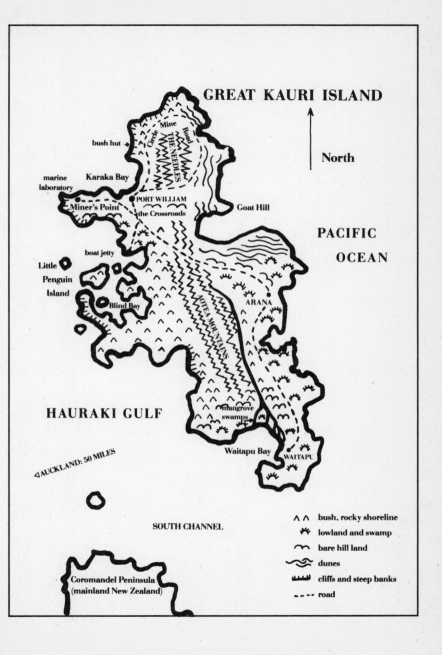

GREAT KAURI ISLAND

North

Mine

Road

Circle

bush hut

THE NEEDLES

marine
laboratory

Karaka Bay

Miner's Point

PORT WILLIAM

the Crossroads

Goat Hill

PACIFIC

OCEAN

boat jetty

Little
Penguin
Island

Blind Bay

AOTEA MOUNTAINS

ARANA

HAURAKI GULF

mangrove
swamps

Waitapu Bay

WAITAPU

◁AUCKLAND: 50 MILES

SOUTH CHANNEL

∧ ∧   bush, rocky shoreline

⋎⋎   lowland and swamp

⌒   bare hill land

~~   dunes

⊥⊥⊥⊥   cliffs and steep banks

- - - -   road

Coromandel Peninsula
(mainland New Zealand)

CONTENTS

I pass, like night, from land to land;
I have strange power of speech;
The moment that his face I see,
I know the man that must hear me:
To him my tale I teach.
THE RIME OF THE ANCIENT MARINER
Samuel Taylor Coleridge

PROLOGUE

Two people first saw the tiny seaplane breaking through the storm clouds tumbling in over Great Kauri Island. Each stood alone, many miles apart from each other, neither knowing of the other's existence. The boy stood on the deck of an old fishing boat, arrested for a moment in his job of coiling lines and ropes into neat piles. Some trick of light, some memory of sun long since disappeared into the rising storm, flicked the wingtip of the plane as it began its spiraling descent into Karaka Bay. The boy stood transfixed, for the plane was changed by that trick of light into a brilliant, shimmering sea bird of a sort he had never seen before.

Miles up the coast, where there was no longer any human habitation, an old woman watched also. She stood on the beach of a wild little cove, bordered on both sides by rock-jumbled headlands. Behind her, dunes rose sharply into low cliffs, ending in a tangle of forest. The old woman had been gathering wood along the shoreline, but now she stood intently staring into the sky. She had not moved for several minutes. It had been a long time since she had felt such fear, longer still since she had been caught with such exultation.

The emotions came over her with the same blinding swiftness as the light on the wingtip of the little plane. She, too, saw a sea bird in the instant of a single breath . . .

By the time the plane had bumped down on the bay and taxied unevenly to the wharf, the boy had finished coiling his lines. There was no one else on the wharf, or on the dirt track that led up to the road. Even the pub in Port William was closed. The storm hung just off the coast, gathering itself, and the islanders stayed in during winter storms.

The pilot swung down from the cockpit, greeted the boy cheerfully, and pulled from the plane the usual cargo of mail sacks and parcels, a few boxes and some sacks of grain.

"Hope they get to these before she breaks!" he said, humping the last heavy mail sack onto the splintered wood of the wharf. The boy shrugged in reply.

"You'll be having a few days holiday, eh!" The pilot grinned, indicating the little boat bobbing fitfully against the tires hung along the edge of the wharf. "Can't take her out in this."

"Too right," said the boy flatly. The pilot turned then, but instead of climbing back in the cockpit, he opened the door on the passenger side. The boy glanced up, his face flickering briefly with interest. A passenger? On a day like this, in winter?

A girl scrambled awkwardly from her seat in the cramped cockpit, tugging at two bright green backpacks. The wind twisted her hair into a black tangle as she dropped the packs close to the edge of the wharf. She shoved at them impatiently with her foot, her eyes already searching the road up into the little town. She hardly turned to wave at the pilot as he climbed into his plane.

"Got to get straight back!" the pilot called out, looking past the girl to the boy on the fishing boat. "This blow'll do us both in, eh! Tell Mike I'll be back straight after it clears, OK?"

The boy nodded with a short jerk, and stopped in his work to watch the pilot maneuver the plane out over the chop before beginning to taxi down the open bay. The girl stood next to her packs, looking up the wharf without once acknowledging the presence of another person. She shifted her weight from foot to foot. The wind battered her with spray, dashing her long hair in front of her eyes. She moved her head to get the hair out of her face, and with that movement, her eyes and the boy's met. For a startled instant, each was held by the dark eyes of the other, caught in a strange stillness like the eye of a storm.

The girl blinked and moved, stumbling slightly against one of her packs. She scuffed the wharf with her sneaker, once again staring impatiently up the road. She turned completely away from the boy, holding her thick hair in her hand so she could see.

A Land Rover swerved off the dirt road above the wharf and skidded to a stop just short of the first pilings. A tall woman ran down the wharf toward the girl, her voice clear and high in greeting. The girl smiled nervously but did not make any move or say a word. The boy, forgotten, watched this from his boat.

"Look at you! Oh, *look* at you!" cried the woman, holding the girl now at arm's length. She pulled the girl into a hug, and for a moment, the dark hair snapped and tangled with the blond hair of the older woman.

"I just can't *believe* you're finally here!" laughed the woman, grabbing one of the green packs and throwing it lightly over her shoulder. The girl lifted the other pack almost reluctantly and followed the woman, who was still talking brightly. They threw the packs in the back of the Land Rover and drove off, the dust behind them whirled into eddies by the wind. The boy was left alone again, with only the insistent tug and bump of his boat against the wharf and the low keen of the coming storm.

Many miles north, on the wild beach by the forest, the tide was flinging itself before the storm as it raced in over the rocks on the headlands. Froth already snapped at the pile of driftwood the old woman had been collecting all morning. She stood without moving, staring into the sky from which the seaplane had descended forty minutes earlier. Her reason had long since told her that it *had* been a plane — the ordinary silver seaplane that came in three times a week to Port William from Auckland, fifty miles west across the Hauraki Gulf.

But she could not shake from her eyes the image of a great white bird, circling at the front of a storm, holding the last light of the sun on its slender wings. It filled her with foreboding and with an almost unbearable excitement. She could not reconcile these emotions, and so she stood, her old face tense and distant, with the water lapping over the toes of her worn rubber boots.

The plane . . . a silver bird . . . what was it? It had something to do with her. She knew this. Something . . . something . . . She swallowed sharply, caught on the edge of a thought. Could it be? She shifted her weight in the wet sand. Could it be? She faced full into the storm, feeling the wind lace her old skin with sand and salt.

Her face tightened into intense concentration. Yes! Yes! She was sure now. Her eyes glittered with the keen satisfaction of understanding. She knew now: Two people had just met, two people who did not know her or each other, and soon now, everything she had been waiting for all her life would begin.

"Soon!" she whispered, her voice cracked and fierce. "Soon!"

She gathered the pile of driftwood into an old sack, her movements quick and short. She climbed the dunes with strong steps, and disappeared into the wind-torn trees of the bush.

1
THE ARRIVAL

On the stove in the kitchen, the teakettle began to whistle. Sarah sighed, put down her book with a thump, and leaned back on the sofa. She had been perched uncomfortably on the edge of the cushions as she read; the sofa had long ago lost its springs and was now a lumpy mass permeated with the same smell of old damp that hung on everything in her mother's flat.

The fire spit feebly in the grate, but the room still ached with cold. The girl jammed her shoulders into the moldy couch, trying to draw some warmth from the rough fabric. She stared around the dull room, wondering how many times she had done this in the three days since she had come to the island. There were no pictures on the walls — couldn't Pauline at least have found some bird pictures from magazines? Anything was better than this. The girl's eyes strayed to the windows, curtained in limp polyester lace, but outside the storm still lashed at the gray-green grass on the hills. She could see no farther than a marshy paddock fenced with sagging wire, for the rain clouds lay almost at ground level. She tried to stare beyond the grayness, to discover some relief in the awful dullness that was Great Kauri Island.

The teakettle was screeching now, and Sarah stifled a desire to scream herself in boredom and frustration. She sat stubbornly on the couch, finding a perverse pleasure in letting the kettle fill her ears with its piercing whistle. The corner of the book she had been reading dug into her hip, and she threw it to the other side of the couch where it fell, one page bent under. She couldn't stand to read another word of it — but what else was there? She couldn't write letters — what would she write about? Even her flute, lying gleaming and slender in its velvet-lined case, did not entice her.

With a jerk, she flung herself off the sofa and padded into the kitchen. Her sock caught on the broken edge of linoleum on the floor and suddenly her eyes burned with tears. She yanked the kettle off the flame and leaned against the sink, looking out the window at the storm-battered yard with its clothesline and the few straggly fruit trees.

"This is just great, Sarah Steinway!" she muttered aloud, pouring the boiling water into a teapot already filled with soggy leaves. "You don't even *like* tea!" she continued to herself, finding unexpected comfort in the sound of her own voice. She reached for her mug and slid the milk bottle closer to her. There was no refrigerator here — who needed one, she thought darkly. Subtropical, indeed! This island was about as "subtropical" as Lincoln Center Plaza in January!

Sarah sat at the little kitchen table and held her hands around the mug. The steam warmed her chin and her fingers lost their stiffness. For the hundredth time, she wished her mother would come back from the laboratory for lunch.

"You'd think she could just take an hour, for God's sake!" she said to herself, hating the whine in her voice. She shuffled idly through the pile of papers, old mail, and magazines that

Pauline always left sloppily on the table. She found an official-looking letter addressed to her mother at Miner's Point Marine Research Laboratory, Great Kauri Island, New Zealand. It had been sent recently — the postmark was June 1. It was probably from some scientific foundation, she thought, offering Mom money or something — everyone offered you money, when you were as famous as Pauline. She held the thick envelope up to the light, but could make nothing out through the paper. It had an Australian return address. Maybe, after her year of research in New Zealand, Pauline would be invited to study some rare bird in Australia.

Well, she sure won't get me to visit her *there*, that's for sure! Sarah thought. It'd be a desert, and just as awful as here. I can't *believe* I let her talk me into spending my whole summer here! And I don't even get a summer — it's winter!

She picked up a magazine dated almost two months earlier, and leafed through it. It was *Royal Forest and Bird*, and she stared at the bright photos of bush and beach that were supposedly New Zealand's North Island. Great Kauri Island lay fifty miles off the coast of North Island, but so far nothing Sarah had seen looked anything like these pictures of lush woodland and tropical white beach. An article caught her eye: "The Storm Petrel of Great Kauri Island." She scanned the paragraphs and sure enough, Pauline's name was mentioned several times. Pauline was doing some revolutionary research on the rare bird that had only recently been discovered on the island.

She tossed the magazine back on the pile, and as she did, something fell out from between the pages onto the floor. She looked down at it before bending slowly to pick it up. It was addressed to Pauline in Sarah's own handwriting — it was the letter she had sent her two months ago from home, telling Pauline that she would come to stay the summer with her.

Sarah ran her finger over the New York City postmark, and pulled out the pages.

". . . been practicing the flute a lot, but Dad thinks I could afford to take the summer off before school. I'm really excited, Mom! You haven't seen me in two years — I'm really different! I'll be sixteen in August! I'll bring the flute so you can hear me play; I'm good . . ."

Sarah sighed and put the letter down. So far, Pauline had just looked at her flute when she had showed it to her and laughed apologetically when Sarah offered to play.

"I'll have lots more time in about a week, sweetheart," she'd said, on her way out the door. "And I'd *love* to hear you play!"

Pauline had a way of silencing you, thought Sarah. I mean, the flute's the most important thing to me in the world! I'm good, and I'm going to be world-class — you'd think she'd have a minute. It's not as if I've been a real drag on her — she left Dad when I was six, for God's sake!

She looked down at the letter on her lap, remembering the excitement she had felt when she'd written it. To not only get to stay with Pauline for a whole summer, but on a lovely, subtropical Pacific island — it sounded so romantic! No electricity (except what was created by small windmills and gasoline generators), dirt roads, tiny hamlets, and real old-fashioned crank telephones! It was going to be wonderful.

". . . next fall, when I go away to school," she continued reading. "I really love the school; it's in the Berkshires, and has a great music department. Also, Dad's letting me have a private teacher for extra lessons — but it's worth it. I won't know anyone there. Stephanie and Marjory are going somewhere else in Connecticut — but that's OK. I'll be pretty busy with my music. Anyway, it's just *perfect* to be able to spend the summer with you! I thought Dad would mind, but he seems pretty happy about it. He decided, since I'd be gone, to spend the summer at some library in Europe — I guess to bone up on his physics!"

Sarah folded the letter carefully and slid it back into the magazine on the table. She wished she'd gone to Germany with her father. Anything but this godforsaken island where it was *winter*, and where Pauline left early in the morning to go down to the Point, and didn't come back till evening. And in between — nothing. Nothing but rain-lashed windows, incessant wind, and dim walls. No TV, no people except the landlords in the other half of the house. And the flat wasn't even in Port William! It was two miles out of the tiny hamlet, at a place called the Crossroads, where four muddy tracks converged, coming (it seemed to Sarah) from four different swamps . . .

She wandered through the living room into her bedroom, and plopped down on the springy bed. The books she had brought were lined neatly on the dresser, her clothes packed carefully away in the drawers. A notebook with a pen and some refills lay in front of the books. On her bedstand was her music; her sleek flute case lay next to it, protecting the silver instrument. She reached in the drawer, took out her portable tape-player, and slipped a tape in. The room filled with the sweet notes of a flute played by a master. Sarah closed her eyes and for a moment, the storm and cold and desolate landscape were forgotten.

A hesitant knock on the door leading from the flat into the hallway made her jump. With some curiosity, Sarah moved stiffly to open the door. The hallway was dark, but at the far end, the door into the landlord's flat was open. Backlit from that light, the child standing before Sarah seemed very dark and tiny, her eyes so black they showed no expression. She looked up at Sarah.

"Hi," said Sarah, trying to put a brightness in her voice she did not feel. The child stared up at her, speechless, until Sarah's smile relaxed her.

"Mum says come to tea," she said finally, so softly Sarah had to bend down to hear. With that, she turned solemnly and padded back down the hall into her flat. From the bright doorway a wave of warmth hit Sarah, the smells of cooking food and the sounds of pans set on the stove top making her ache for home. She hesitated.

She had met her mother's landlords Mike and Mari Harris when she first arrived, and once Mari had come over to the flat to ask if everything was all right. She liked Mari. She was tiny, almost absurdly small beside the giant of a man Mike was, with his huge voice and full red beard. Mari moved with quiet, quick movements, her eyes dark and full like the eyes of her three little girls. But she was so reserved Sarah was self-conscious around her, and with Mike she was nervous. He had such large ways of moving, and his voice, though friendly, was too loud.

She shuffled her weight in the doorway, feeling heavy and clumsy as she always did around strangers. Did she want to spend an entire evening with these people? But there was the warm golden light from the open doorway, the smell of food — still she hesitated. Maybe Pauline would come home early this evening . . . She found herself straining to listen for the sound of the Land Rover over the continuous lashing of wind against the tin roof.

From the kitchen down the hall came the sound of an oven door being opened, the rasp of a heavy pan being pulled out. She could hear the babble of the children and the drone of the television clearly — before, they had only been low sounds through the wall. She hadn't really thought of the Harrises before this — that they were a real family, in a warm, comfortable home.

Mari Harris appeared in the lit doorway. Sarah blushed, knowing it looked rude for her to be standing in the hallway, as if she had been listening. But Mari rubbed the soft dark hair out of her face with her arm and smiled.

"Did you get my message, then?" she asked, with a curiously flat but friendly voice. "Mellie begged to be allowed to get you, but she gets all shy when it comes down to it."

"Oh, yes! I mean, she asked me . . ." Sarah stumbled over her words, hating the way she went stiff around strangers. All she really wanted, she realized, was to be in that comfortable kitchen, enveloped in the heat and glow of a family. Pauline, she knew, would have accepted immediately with her bright bubbly way, laughing, putting everyone at ease . . . but then, she was not Pauline. It was hard to imagine, sometimes, how she could even be her daughter, so unalike were they.

"Your mum called, love; she's going to be late back from the Point, so we want you to have tea with us. Mike says there'll be a good film on telly later, if you like," Mari said, smiling again and moving back into the kitchen. Sarah was suddenly aware that Mari somehow *understood* her hesitation, and was allowing her to be alone. It was this realization that made up her mind. She wanted to be around Mari, who was calm and quiet and moved with such reserved purpose. Her body ached for the heat from the kitchen. When she walked through the doorway, she almost groaned aloud in relief.

"Just take a chair from one of my helpers," said Mari, busy scraping carrots over the sink. The three little girls stared at Sarah from their chairs, so reserved she wanted to laugh. The sparkle in the three sets of black eyes gave away their excitement over having a visitor. They were all miniatures of their mother, and Sarah wondered how the great red Mike could be their father.

Mari must be Maori, she thought, remembering poring over the huge atlas in her father's study. A brief passage had described the native people of New Zealand as being "of Polynesian descent, arriving some five or six hundred years ago in huge, seagoing canoes. They called the land 'Aotearoa' — Land of the Long White Cloud — which the Europeans later called New Zealand." It had said little that Sarah could remember, and she had assumed that Maori lived in certain parts of the country, and that she would never see them.

"Here, love, put these on the table for me. Ta," Mari was saying, handing her a stack of dishes warmed in the oven to place around the table. The warmth was dissolving all the chill in her, and to her surprise, she felt more relaxed.

"It's very nice of you to have me to dinner," she said carefully, so that she would not trip over her words. She had said almost nothing since she had come in, but the tense knot of loneliness and anxiety was melting inside her. Mari moved around her with such ease — as if I'd been here a hundred times, thought Sarah. She watched her gratefully. Mari was leaving her alone to find her own place within the kitchen.

She wondered if Mari noticed that Pauline was never around. She took a plate of meat from Mari and put it near the head of the table. Had Pauline ever gotten to know this family? She doubted it — she was never here. She watched Mari from the corner of her eye. The woman moved with a perfect economy of motion, her body almost condensed in the small room. Does she feel sorry for me? Sarah wondered, but immediately put the question from her head. There was nothing of pity in Mari's manner.

"Well!" said Mari now, again brushing her hair from her face and sitting in a chair. "I can take a break, eh. They'll all pile in when the news is over!" She smiled her quiet smile at Sarah.

"You'll be getting cold and lonely over there by now, eh," she said. It was unexpected, this statement of fact — not a question. Sarah found herself smiling back into those alert dark eyes, and when she answered, it was not with the self-pity she had been feeling all day.

"I'm pretty bored," she admitted. "But Pauline — Mom — is really busy. I guess some new data came up and she has to work overtime till she gets it processed. She's got a lot of responsibility," she finished proudly. Pauline was one of the leading marine ornithologists in the world, and much information about the sea, weather patterns, and pollution was gathered from the study of sea birds. It was an important job.

"She has more energy than me," laughed Mari. "When she first came here, we worried the island would get to her, eh. It's so isolated — not many Americans would like it. But she set right to her work — Mike says it puts him to shame!"

Sarah smiled happily at the older woman. The cold flat at the other end of the hallway was forgotten.

"What does Mike do?" she asked.

"Oh, he's a fisherman — got his own business, eh. When we first came, he only had one boat, but now we got two, and Pita . . ." She frowned slightly, and paused for the space of a breath. Sarah waited, curious.

"Pita — that's my older son — he fishes now, too. It's a real good business for one person. No good for commercial fishermen anymore, the gulf is all fished out, but if you know where to look, eh, you can make a decent living." Mari stood abruptly and went to the door into the living room. Her manner seemed to have suddenly closed — when she mentioned her son, Sarah thought. But she had no time to muse, because Mike Harris burst into the kitchen carrying all three of his daughters on his broad back. The whole kitchen had to expand to accommodate his size and energy.

"Sit down, love, sit down!" he boomed at her, grinning, holding out a chair for her with one hand. Sarah sat with a thump, subdued in his presence.

"Here you are, love, have some kumera," he said now, passing her a plate piled with a rootlike grayish pink mass. She stared at it in dismay, but Mari came to her rescue.

"Don't tease her, Mike," she admonished. "She can't know what it is, eh . . . they won't have it in America, I reckon." She turned to Sarah. "It's sweet potato. It was a staple Maori food, but Pakeha eat it too. Only try it if you want."

"Pakeha?" asked Sarah, trying the word on her tongue.

"Pakeha means white European. It's common usage," said Mike, who seemed quieter once he'd eaten a bit.

The family ate silently for a few minutes, the little girls glancing every now and again at Sarah. When she looked at them, they giggled so softly it was more a whisper, and ducked their heads. Sarah felt unease tugging at her in the silence. Oh, why can't I be more like Pauline? she cried to herself. She always knows what to say to people; she always seems so interested in them. No wonder everyone loves her!

"You'll have to come for tea whenever your mum works late, love," Mari was saying now. Sarah nodded; her mouth was full, and she blushed with embarrassment. This time it was Mike who came to the rescue.

"Ah — she'll not be sitting around the flat forever!" he cried, grinning again at her. "She's got a whole island to explore. Can you ride?" he demanded suddenly. Sarah choked on her carrots, her face still hot.

"You mean — horses?" she asked, confused. Of course he meant horses, stupid! she yelled at herself. What else would he mean?

"Sure, horses, love!" he laughed at her. "Don't you have them in America, then? Everyone with a flash new car — "

"Let her be, Mike," smiled Mari. "She comes from New York! Where would she ride a horse in a big city?"

"But I *can* ride!" She surprised herself, answering so quickly. She wanted them to like her.

"My dad taught me to ride — in Central Park," she explained, the words coming in a rush, wanting to tell them about home. "We live pretty close, so I went every Saturday for a while. My dad teaches at Columbia, but in the summer he has time, so he took me riding. It's neat! Is there a horse here I could ride?" She finished out of breath.

"She can ride Whiskey," said Mari, looking at her husband for affirmation. "Celeste is too big — besides, she's really for work, eh. And I'll draw you a map — not many roads, eh! You can't get lost if you stay on the road."

Sarah felt the first stirrings of curiosity. After all, this *was* an exotic South Seas island! If she had a pony to ride — who cared if Pauline worked all day and couldn't show her around! So what else is new, she reminded herself wryly. I'll just have a good time on my own.

"Will the storm be over soon?" she asked. It had not let up for a moment, day or night, since she had arrived. The one time she had ventured out in her thin plastic parka, the wind had torn it from her and she had been soaked to the bone. It had taken her an hour to get enough of a fire going to feel it — she wasn't going out again until the rain cleared!

"Oh, another month or so — " Mike began, but seeing her stricken face, laughed and said, "It should be clearer tomorrow, love — not a good welcome to the island, eh! But she'll be right, soon enough." Turning to his wife, he continued: "After this rain, we'll have to take the boats out further, till the shore water clears, eh. Snapper should be running now, and trevally — but no flatfish or crayfish till the silt calms. Better call Bob tonight."

He left the table with the three girls trailing after him. Sarah watched him go, liking the way his children were always being held or touched. They probably didn't see him much, if he fished all day and got home after they were in bed, she realized.

"You met Bob — he's Mike's partner," said Mari, clearing the dishes into the sink. "He owns the seaplane, and he flies the catch to Auckland twice a week. He's a good man."

She scraped the leftover food into a plastic bucket. With a wince, Sarah realized she hadn't touched the grayish root they called kumera. Seeing her expression, Mari laughed.

"No worries!" she said. "The girls eat it cold. It won't be wasted, eh. Now, here's the tea towel — you can dry."

She helped dry the dishes silently, listening to the murmur of the children in the other room. "Pakeha," "kumera" — two words of a strange new language; how far from home she was! For a moment, she was overcome with homesickness, missing the comfortable New York apartment, with its book-lined walls and classical music on the stereo. How different the Harrises were from her father's friends and colleagues, physicists like himself, or painters, or musicians . . .

"Your mum says you play the flute," Mari said, breaking into her thoughts. Sarah looked up, startled. Pauline had told her that? She flushed happily.

"I love it," she said, almost shy. Would Mari understand about being a musician? Would she understand how it was to *know* what one was born to do? To want to be the best? She wanted to explain to this quiet, somehow *wise* woman —

The sound of a truck coming to a slamming halt outside the house interrupted her thoughts. Her eyes flew to the hallway door, thinking it might be her mother, but it was the outside door to the house that banged violently open, and almost at once she heard angry voices in the living room.

Mike's voice, loud as ever, was now harsh and unfriendly. Sarah shifted uncomfortably. She looked toward Mari, but the older woman's face had gone flat and expressionless, closing her out. The warmth went out of the kitchen, and once again Sarah was acutely aware that Mari was a stranger, that this was not home. She felt her own face take on a familiar, sulky expression, and she wanted to be back in the empty flat next door. As unobtrusively as possible she edged toward the door.

Mike had stopped yelling in the other room, and now there was another voice, one that caught her, made her want to listen. She hesitated in the doorway, trying to hear what was being said. It was a low, strong voice, not loud but somehow more forceful than Mike's, more intense. She strained to hear the words.

In that moment of hesitation, as she looked back over her shoulder, she saw a huge black dog appear in the doorway of the living room. So sudden was the animal's coming it was as if he had materialized from the shadows. Too surprised to speak, Sarah gazed at the dog, taking in the great broad forehead and short strong muzzle, the dense black fur, and eyes even deeper black that gazed calmly back at her.

"Oh," she cried softly, without intending to. He was an amazing animal, a wild animal, but she was not frightened of him. She realized this with some wonder; she did not like dogs much, especially the silly, pampered apartment pets she had seen. But this was not just a *dog;* this was something more, something utterly *beautiful.* She wanted to touch him, to know how that fur would feel . . .

When the boy appeared in the doorway next to the dog, she thought at once, They look alike! His hair was thick and dark like the dog's, his body had the same compact leanness. But his black eyes, unlike the animal's, were not calm. He glared into the kitchen, wide mouth half open over white

teeth, breathing hard. She had never seen such intensity concentrated on a face as she saw on this boy's.

She stood in the doorway, half in shadow, staring at him
in fascination. But it was not until he turned and saw her,
and she met the full force of his glare, that she recognized
him as the boy on the fishing boat the day she had arrived in
Port William. Once again, there was a stillness as they looked
at each other. She was repelled by the ferocity of that stare.
She glared back. Don't you stare at me like that! she said
inside herself. Don't you dare! Who do you think you are!

The boy curled his lip and dropped his eyes as he turned
toward the counter. For the first time, Sarah noticed that his
hand was buried deep in the fur on the dog's neck.

"You know I don't want that dog in here," said Mari, speaking for the first time. The boy muttered under his breath as
he reached across the counter for some food.

"I just want my tea, eh," he snapped, but moved back out
of Mari's way. The woman put her hand on his arm, forcing
them to stand closer. She reached up and brushed the long
hair off the boy's forehead. He bent his head in a gesture that
seemed to Sarah pleading, but still somehow proud.

"I'll be off, then," he said. "I want to check the boat's still
fast." He stuffed the food in the pocket of his black denim
jacket. When he turned, the light glinted on an animal-tooth
earring. Once again, he looked over at Sarah; this time it was
a bolder, more calculated look, filled with curiosity.

She felt drawn into those eyes. Her hands clenched; she
was angry. He had ruined the evening! She glared at him.

Mari slipped between Sarah and the boy in a strangely
deliberate move. Sarah let out her breath softly. She was
suddenly very tired; she blinked her eyes. The boy and the
great black dog were gone into the night. In a moment, she
heard the truck roaring to life.

Sarah stood in the doorway, uncertain what to do. Mari was a stranger now; nothing was comfortable anymore. As if she had said it aloud, Mari turned toward her with a gentle smile, putting her hand on Sarah's arm as she had on the boy's.

"It's all right, love," she said reassuringly. "It sounds worse than it is, eh. That's my son, Pita — he and Mike don't get along so good. Maybe . . ." She paused, sighing, then continued. "He doesn't want to be here. He was in Auckland until two months ago; my sister couldn't handle him, and Mike gave him a job on the boat. He's so wild — doesn't even like his name, eh; calls himself 'Mako.' "

So the boy wasn't Mike's son. The memory of those black eyes came back to her and she pursed her lips in dislike. He came from Auckland — wild — probably some punk street kid who hung out listening to a blaring radio. She dismissed him from her mind.

Mari smiled at her again, and some of the warmth filtered back into the kitchen. But still, she wanted to be alone.

"I have to go now," she said, hearing the stiffness returning to her voice. Mari smiled a little sadly, as if she knew how the evening had been changed for Sarah. All Sarah had to do was stay now, talk a little more, but she could not. She could only stand woodenly in the doorway. She could almost see the hard little wall she had put up. She wanted to cry.

"Come by, then, love, if you want company," said Mari kindly. "The storm'll break by afternoon; you can go introduce yourself to the pony, eh."

Back in her room, Sarah sat stiffly on the edge of the bed. She could not cry. What had gone wrong? She had just begun to feel at ease, and then . . . then . . . the boy had come in. He was the one who had made her close up inside, close into her hard, untouchable self. She punched the bed with her fist.

I liked them! she cried silently. I *liked* them — and they liked me, and then he spoiled it! She stalked into the bathroom and jerked on the light cord. When she saw her face in the mirror, she stopped.

"For God's sake, Sarah Steinway!" she said aloud, staring at her face in the chipped glass. "What in the world is the matter with you! You always get like this with people — as soon as you like them, you get — I don't know — all screwed up inside. Whose fault is that?"

She studied her face in the glass, putting her hands against her cheeks and trying to pull them taut. How different she was from Pauline! How could Pauline, slim as she was, have a daughter who was overweight and clumsy? She assessed herself without mercy. She liked her eyes; they were large and direct. Her brows, too, were strong and dark — but her face! She put her hands down in disgust.

"I don't care!" she said, scowling at the image in the mirror. "It doesn't matter what you look like, as long as you are the best at what you do. And I'm going to be the best!" She lifted her arms in the familiar motion, flexing her fingers, as if she were holding her flute. When she played, she was perfect, she was no longer overweight, no longer ill at ease with people. She would play in front of thousands!

She held her breath, caught in her own stare. Her dark eyes reminded her, unbidden, of the boy's. She looked away, flooding the sink with cold water and scrubbing her face roughly.

"Who cares!" she muttered, not knowing quite what she was referring to. "Who cares, anyway!" She wished her mother was here, so she was not alone in this cold flat at night. She shivered, wanting to cry again. This time, she felt the anger at herself.

She sat defiantly on the bed, taking out her flute from its

velvet case. She held it in her hands, drew it along her cheek, feeling the cool perfection of it on her skin. Just holding it made her feel strong. *This* was the most important thing in the world — what did it matter that Pauline was late, as usual? What did it matter, the problems of the family next door, people who had nothing to do with her? And the boy — what did he matter? Whoever he was, whatever his problem was, it was no concern of hers. Nothing, *nothing* could get in the way of the concentration and discipline it took to *be the best*, to play the flute so that the world would listen. Calmer now, she put the flute back and went to bed.

2
DAPHNE

Although she had not come home until late the evening before, Pauline was up early. The familiar whine of the teakettle made Sarah grimace; she jumped out of bed and ran shivering to the bathroom. Pauline called cheerily out to her.

"Did you have a good time last night, with Mike and Mari?"

Sarah replied, her answer muffled with toothpaste. How could Pauline be so energetic at this time of day, for God's sake! She hurriedly yanked the comb through her hair, grunting. She stopped a moment, stood listening; no sound. She cocked her head; a shiver of excitement ran through her. No wind — no rain! The storm was over.

She ate breakfast sitting on the edge of the stool, so she could look out the window. It was still gray, but the clouds had lifted and the landscape already had changed . . .

"What?" she said, catching the tail end of something Pauline was saying. She dragged her eyes away from the window and looked at her mother. Tall and slender, her face classically graceful with strong bones and clear tawny skin, Pauline leaned back easily in her chair, idly picking at the formica tabletop. She wore loose clothes that somehow did not hide her body, and her hair, tied casually back from her face, looked nevertheless as if it had been styled for the cover of a magazine. Sarah felt the familiar wave of pride, and something else . . . something that stung a little and made her feel tight inside; she shoved the thought from her mind. Pauline was great! She had dedicated her life to her profession, and there was nothing Sarah admired more than that.

". . . some important breakthroughs, and I have to put it together before I do anything else. This batch of university kids I have now aren't the best I've had . . . Have to talk to Gordon about that . . ." Pauline was saying. Sarah nodded, still unable to catch the gist of what Pauline was telling her. Pauline didn't seem to notice.

"So, anyway, you don't mind, do you, sweetheart? I mean, you brought things to do, didn't you?"

Oh, she means she'll be busy, and I won't see her all day — what else is new? thought Sarah, twisting her face into a reassuring smile. Actually, it *didn't* really matter, not now. Outside, the fresh cool smell of the island came to her, made her restless and excited. She wanted to be out in it, to ride the pony and explore the wild, exotic hills and beaches . . .

"It's OK, Mom — really! Mari and Mike said I could ride their pony. I'll be fine, don't worry," she said.

Pauline flurried around the flat for several more minutes. She chattered as she gathered her things, telling Sarah about the petrels, the nests they had found just the other day in the mountains that ran down the center of Great Kauri Island, and how the whole world was excited . . . Sarah leaned in the doorway, trying to be interested. She felt herself struggling inside, so that her heart raced and her face felt hot. What on earth is bothering you? she asked herself, watching Pauline blow her a kiss as she finally went out the door. Of course Pauline was busy! Did you think she'd take the whole summer off just to entertain you? Shaking her head angrily, she went out onto the verandah.

She could clearly see the hills beyond the low paddocks now, raggedy and scrub-covered in the hollows, but becoming sheep-cropped as they rose clear of the marshland. Here and there, dense clusters of trees with slender trunks covered the slopes. The paddocks themselves grew in clumps of rushes and little hummocks of pale yellow grass, fenced with wire tacked to worn posts.

The mist had lifted enough so she could see the mountains, the mountains Pauline had talked about. She stared at them a long time, fascinated. They looked like impenetrable walls of black rock, their jagged tops piercing the sky like crazy needles. Could there be roads through those massive things? Did animals live in them? She wrapped her arms around herself, chilled in the damp air. From the other side of the house, she could hear voices and the squealing of children.

"Come have a cup of tea, love," said Mari, behind her, making her jump slightly. This time she did not hesitate, but followed her gladly into the house. Mari spoke over her shoulder. "I thought you might want to meet some real islanders," she said with a smile. "The nurse is here, eh. She'd be happy if you wanted to come with her on her rounds — she gets a bit lonesome, driving all over by herself!"

This last she directed to the woman sitting on the sofa with the three children, a woman who filled the room with her presence. She turned to Sarah with the widest smile Sarah had ever seen. It was impossible to remain self-conscious, and she found herself grinning back.

Daphne Spenser, the district nurse for Great Kauri, seemed to Sarah like a brilliant sailboat in full sail, spinnaker and all. She radiated about her a feeling like the wind in one's face on a sunny day, and Sarah found herself holding her head back as if to catch it full on. The woman was dressed in a skirt of bright material, with scarves and sashes wrapped around. On her fingers she wore rings of stones, and on her arms bracelets of copper and ivory; everything on her seemed to clink or billow or glitter. Thick rubber boots peeked out from under the long lavender and green skirt. She was a large woman, tall, with long hair worn in a thick braid down her back. Sarah could not help staring, utterly bewitched. Daphne Spenser was like no one else in the world.

"So — you'll keep me company for the day, eh!" she said, after Mari had introduced them. "Only if you want — but it'll be good fun! I've the whole north bit today — some real characters. Hope Elsie doesn't pick today to go into labor; she refuses hospital, and I can't force her." She laughed happily, throwing back her head.

"You see — we couldn't get on without Daphne," said Mari, with her quiet smile. Sarah watched them together. How different they were, one big and expansive, the other small and contained.

"I'd like to go," she said. Her answer surprised her. Spend the day with a complete stranger? I don't think I'd do it in New York, she thought. Something attracted her to the big woman. She's beautiful! she found herself thinking, startled. But she must weigh two hundred pounds! And she laughs and everyone feels easy — but it's not like Pauline at all, it's not the same . . .

"The kids are perfect," Daphne told Mari. "Clean bill of health, the lot of them. Must be the fish — not like some of 'em here, feeding their kids roots and seaweed and what-all! They think if they pour brewer's yeast on everything, it'll be right." She made a face and Mari laughed with her. Daphne leaned toward the smaller woman and gave her a quick hug around the shoulders.

"I don't know what I'd do without *you*," she said, her voice suddenly soft. She picked up her huge black bag, stuffed the stethoscope inside, and hugged all three girls before going toward the door.

Daphne's truck somehow suited her, old and bouncing, once red, with bulbous fenders and a grill-grin that made Sarah smile.

"They'd have given me a flash new one," laughed Daphne, as she threw the truck into gear and spun out onto the track. Everything about the truck was vocal; they had to shout when they spoke. "But there's a lot of miles in her yet, and I like her," continued Daphne, patting the dash.

They jolted at great speed down the road through Port William, Daphne waving at everybody they passed. Each wave in return was one of happy recognition; everyone, it seemed, knew Daphne's truck.

Port William was no more than a few nondescript buildings set in haphazard fashion along the road; Sarah saw a tiny shop, a gas pump near a low cinderblock building with a red phone kiosk out front, and a verandah-bordered structure that seemed to be a bar. The road ran on the high ground curving along the bay. Trees with snake-like branches and glossy leaves twisted out over the ground and curved down toward the water.

"Pohutukawa," said Daphne, seeing Sarah look at them. "Great for climbing in."

Sarah imagined Daphne climbing those weird, twisty trees with her sashes and skirts . . . It amazed her.

"Don't look so shocked!" Daphne grinned. "I'm not above climbing a tree now and again!"

Sarah flushed. She realized she'd been rude, to stare at this woman — but she couldn't help it. Daphne didn't seem to mind being overweight at all — in fact, she seemed to revel in it. She felt a rush of admiration, and with it, a familiar attack of self-consciousness. She pressed her face to the window and watched the land jolt by.

They had left Port William behind and were climbing steadily up from the bay, until the water could no longer be seen. The hills had become steeper and the patches of dark, scrubby bush more frequent. In the swampy ravines, along the sides of the road, island cattle grazed. They were bony and lean, with scraggly coats of mottled gray or roan or dun. The wide sweep of their horns made them seem wild and mournful.

"Don't you climb trees?" asked Daphne suddenly, after minutes of silence. Sarah opened her mouth, but could think of nothing to say.

"There . . . there aren't many trees in New York," she stammered at last. Climb a tree? she'd feel foolish — stupid! Anyway, she wasn't athletic, and it would embarrass her to get stuck . . .

"I'd look dumb," she blurted, without intending to. Daphne looked down at her frankly, her eyes clear with understanding.

"And someone might laugh at you?"

"I don't ca — Well, it's not that; it's just not what I *do*," said Sarah, finishing hotly.

"What *do* you do?" asked Daphne, jerking the truck over a cattle grid.

"I play the flute," Sarah said. She hesitated. "I'm — I'm good. I mean, I want to be the *best*. It's really important to me. Music takes your whole life! It's not that I don't climb trees — it's just that there're more important things . . ." She had begun earnestly, but her voice trailed off. Daphne smiled at her.

"Maybe here you'll climb a tree," she said. "No matter what you do, there's always *something* more important. But the most important thing is to be yourself, and not be scared."

Sarah did not know what to say, so she turned toward the window again. Scared? She wasn't scared; what was there to be scared of?

The road wound up through the hills and they were now on a rough plateau. The land banked down on one side into thick forest, hung with creepers and ropes of vines, huge swaying ferns growing among the massive trees. Daphne swerved the truck off the road and stopped, turning off the motor. The sudden silence was almost deafening; Sarah rubbed her ears, and Daphne chuckled.

"Here, get out, eh," she said, creaking open her door. "I always stop here, for a breather. It's real lovely . . ."

They stood leaning side by side against the warm fender. Up here, the wind buffeted the tall tussock grass, whining in an eerie hum through the lonely stretches of telephone wire. There were no sign of other human beings; even the few sheep looked wild and fierce. Sarah could see the forest more clearly now, especially the umbrella-like spread of tree ferns that grew out along the edge, bobbing in the wind.

Sarah became aware of a high, clear-trilling sound. "There — can you hear her?" whispered Daphne, leaning closer to her. "I wanted to wait till you heard it." She pointed into the sky, but it was several seconds before Sarah could make out the tiny bird hovering high above them, suspended in the sun.

"It's a pipit. They sing like that all day, just hanging way up there in the sky. I always stop here, so I can hear them. If I was to die and have a choice, I'd come back as a pipit!" said Daphne, closing her eyes, throwing her face back to the sky.

Sarah swallowed, her throat tight. How she liked this woman! How amazing the wind felt on her face! She wanted to fling her arms open to take it all in. She shifted uncomfortably against the truck, tugging at her jacket, which seemed suddenly constricting. She stared down at her sneakers, covered in a fine dust kicked up by the wind.

"What are you thinking about, love?" asked Daphne. Once again, Sarah was startled. She took a deep breath.

"That I like you . . . that I wish . . ." Her throat was dry, but she was determined to continue. "I wish you liked me."

"But I *do* like you," said Daphne softly, a puzzled smile on her face. "I like you just the way you are!" She grinned, and Sarah jabbed the toe of her sneaker against the tire, smiling too.

"I guess I'm a little lonely here. I mean, Pauline's really busy, she's in the middle of some important stuff . . ."

"You don't have to explain yourself, eh," said Daphne, as they climbed back in the truck. "It's always hard opening up. We all have silly ways of defending ourselves against other people — but it's all in our imagination, that we have to. I guess that's why I like being a nurse, eh. People sort of — let down the barriers, I guess." She tossed her long braid over her shoulder with a chuckle, winking at Sarah.

"Love, just don't let me babble on too long, or I'll never get to my patients! We need to hustle."

Daphne pressed the accelerator of the old truck and it flew crazily over the track, jolting Sarah until all she could do was hold on and laugh. They passed through a series of cattle grids and gates, which Sarah lugged open and closed behind them. She couldn't imagine that people lived out here. It was an unreal landscape where the wind and sky were as tangible as the rugged, clay-scalped hills and the forest. The smell of the forest bit into her with heavy, pungent force, and overlaid on it was the sweet clear tang of the sea.

Daphne's first patients were not the simple farmers Sarah had expected would live here. They entered a patch of bush bordering the track, and within a few minutes, Daphne swung the truck off the road and up a rutted trail that hardly seemed wide enough to take them. The ferns and creepers brushed the sides of the truck, and the forest closed around them with a cool, filtered dimness.

And then the forest ended abruptly in a clearing. Sarah said "Oh" in a small voice, and could say nothing more. It was as if they had been transported to a gentle nineteenth-century English garden, complete with bordered paths and roses, and a tiny whitewashed cottage of stucco and thatch. The roses were in bloom, the colors swimming together like a soft old watercolor in a book of poems. The only things out of place were the carefully pruned trees heavy with lemons and oranges. An old terrier, fat and defiant, came waddling down to greet them, and behind him, equally old, came the elder of the two Wentwood-Smythe sisters.

"That's Margaret," whispered Daphne, as she climbed down from the truck. Sarah followed slowly, looking around her.

"G'day, love!" cried Daphne, and the old woman pushed back her straw hat and pulled off her gardening gloves. The terrier worried Daphne's ankles.

"Get on with you, Timmie!" she said to him. "How are you keeping, you two?" she continued, smiling at the old woman and her sister, who had appeared in the door of the cottage beyond.

"Oh, Mabel and I are both fine, just fine," answered Margaret Wentwood-Smythe, her voice as prim and laced-up as her clothes. "Who's this you've got with you, Nurse? Can't see properly these days — come closer!"

Sarah stepped nearer the woman and met the old eyes, pale and deep-set in the weather-stained face. The introductions were formal and quietly elegant, and Daphne carried them

out with perfect, sincere grace. Sarah glanced from the corner
of her eye to see if Daphne was smiling — this was so unreal!
No one was like this!

They were ushered into the cottage for morning tea. The
rooms were dark and cluttered with ninety years of life, and
the lives of their family before them. The couch was hard and
brocaded, and the walls were hung with sepia photos in gilded
frames. Fragile china dishes lined a glass-fronted hutch, and
velvet drapes hung heavily at the windows. The whole place
smelled like an antique store.

Even before she was handed her tea in its paper-thin cup,
Sarah could feel the weight of clumsiness stealing over her.
These old women did not seem real to her, nor did even the
ancient terrier wheezing under the mahogany chair. She sat
nervously on the edge of the couch, sure that with a single
turn of her body she would shatter the china bell at her elbow,
or knock over the painted porcelain lamp with its crystal-
dangled shade. She hardly dared breathe in the cluttered
room, sliding her eyes around without turning her head. She
was suffocated, and wished more than anything to be away
from this place.

"Sugar, my dear?" inquired Margaret. She held the silver
bowl in a hand as thin and translucent as the china.

"Thank you very much," said Sarah. Her voice cracked with
nervousness. She could not look at Daphne. How could
Daphne stand it in here! Everything was breakable and old,
and these sisters — so unbelievable!

But Daphne was completely at ease, inquiring discreetly
after the sisters' health.

"Well, Nurse, we *could* do with some of that tonic — you
know, that you brought last time?" Mabel coughed delicately.
"And of course, those wonderful little pink pills — they *do*
help, my dear. Of course, I could do without them, but — "

Daphne reached over and held the old hand. Sarah watched, fascinated. The light filtered through the heavy lace and velvet at the windows and gleamed softly on the bracelets hung around Daphne's wrist. One narrow-boned finger traced the jewelry gently.

"Such lovely trinkets you always wear, Nurse," said Mabel brightly, looking (thought Sarah) like a tiny brown sparrow about to eat a crumb.

"Are you quite finished with your tea, my dear?" said the other sister, reaching to take Sarah's cup and saucer. Forgetting to move carefully, Sarah hastily turned to give it to her, and the cup toppled to its side on the saucer. She saved it just in time, her face burning and her body tense and sweating. No one seemed to notice.

Daphne poured some thick brown syrup into a plain bottle, which she labeled carefully before handing it to the sisters. She counted out the pink pills, which were promptly transferred into a silver pillbox with little clawlegs and a domed top.

The sisters and the terrier stood watching as Sarah and Daphne walked back to the truck. The dog wagged his tail in stiff disapproval, and the sisters waved together with their gloved hands.

It was a while before she could speak, and by that time the truck was passing again through lower marshland and ravines of rushes and strange trees that looked to Sarah as if they had come straight from Dr. Seuss.

"They weren't *real*," she finally said, still caught in the curious time warp of the little English cottage.

"Oh, they're real, all right," said Daphne firmly. "You've got to look a bit deeper to see it, though. They aren't as pathetic as they seem! They've been there eighty-some years, forty on their own. Their daddy cleared the place, farmed it his whole life, and the whole family's tough as nails." She paused, musing. "What's amazing is, they keep their ways, eh. They dress for dinner, they wear gloves, they observe the 'niceties.' "

Sarah remembered the shock of the teacup falling off the saucer. She slumped in her seat.

"Well, I thought they were silly," she muttered. Imagine doing all that English stuff, all alone out in the woods! For what?

Daphne looked at her sharply.

"Oh, not really silly," she said mildly. "It's important to them — that's what counts." Sarah looked at her, catching the change of tone.

"You like everybody," she said slowly, wondering. "You like yourself."

"Don't you like yourself, then?" asked Daphne, her voice softer now, curious. Sarah blushed. Daphne continued smoothly, giving her more time. "I don't always like everybody, anyway. But I try real hard to accept them for who they are. I have to, being a nurse, eh!"

"I don't know — I wish I was more like Pauline," said Sarah, saying the words in a rush before she could stop herself. "I wish I wasn't so clumsy and *big;* I wish I could be charming and witty like Pauline. Everyone likes her."

"Do you trust me?" asked Daphne. The unexpected question startled Sarah.

"Yes, I think I do," she answered truthfully.

"Then you should trust that people like you, that *I* like you — it's a good step toward liking yourself. Why do you want to be witty and charming? That's not you, eh! You're curious, and serious, and determined. Those seem good qualities to me," Daphne said, smiling. Sarah leaned back in the seat, studying her knees. She was still thinking about the Wentwood-Smythe sisters.

"They have beautiful roses — like an old watercolor," she said softly. The roses had been real. Daphne reached over and squeezed her close around the shoulders.

"They have the most magnificent roses," she agreed.

The next people on Daphne's list were Bob and Fiona Grant. The truck bounced down into a ravine. The air was close and still, unlike the hills with the wind racing through them. Here the bush clung like sticky clothes, damp and clammy.

"These are different people than the sisters," explained Daphne. "My 'brewer's yeast' patients — back-to-the-landers. There's a lot of them about on Great Kauri. Land is cheap here. They're hard patients — a lot of them don't hold with medicine, eh. Into natural things. It's hard . . ."

They were walking into a clearing littered with animals and children, old machinery and broken crates, empty feed sacks, piles of compost and manure. At the far edge of the clearing a black-bearded man in a torn T-shirt was driving a tractor. Between his knees stood a child, holding the huge wheel. He waved energetically to Daphne without stopping the machine. A billy goat bleated, skittering off and glaring at them from yellow eyes. A flock of straggly chickens pecked nervously in the dust.

"I tried reading a bit about herbal medicine, after I got here to the island and saw what I was dealing with," said Daphne. "It's not all hogwash, eh. But no matter what, sanitation is important whether you take pills or eat weeds." She waved her hand around the clearing, shrugging. Sarah realized suddenly that Daphne was not of this place, either; she had come from somewhere else. Why had she come? What drew her here, taking care of odd people like the old sisters, or this hippie family?

A child sat in the dust at the edge of a plot of bare earth that Sarah saw was a poor garden. He was clad only in a dirty shirt. Daphne scooped him up and he chortled at her, grabbing her braid. She swung him so he was sitting perched on her arm.

"Whatever you do, treat Fiona with dignity," Daphne said suddenly, in a low voice, before descending a steep path from the clearing down into the bush. Before Sarah could respond, they had come upon a shack set in a rough cleared space. The bush was so dense here no light warmed the moist, uneven ground. Moss grew on everything, tree trunks, rocks, rotting logs. Tree ferns brushed thickly against the hut, their steaming black trunks repulsive. Every tree was overgrown with vines slithering down the branches. When her eyes had adjusted, Sarah saw the little hut more clearly through the blue haze of smoke from the open fire.

It was patched together, a dwelling place open at one end, made from rusted sheets of corrugated iron gone black with mold and rust, palm fronds woven roughly into mats, fitted with bits of grain sack and the slats from broken crates. The frame was fashioned from raw tree trunks and lashed with rope. The fire burned sullenly in a little circle of stones, and a young woman squatted near it nursing a baby. Another child played quietly near her in the dirt. When the woman saw Daphne, she stood quickly, with a timid, childlike smile of welcome.

When she saw Sarah, however, the woman froze. Her long blond hair hung limply around her face, accenting the thin bones and huge dark eyes. The child on Daphne's arm squalled and the woman turned, her hands reaching in an almost automatic response.

"Saw Bob up there, busy as ever," said Daphne easily, as a way of greeting. The woman's eyes flew between Daphne and Sarah nervously. Daphne bent to examine the baby, looking up offhandedly. "Oh, this is my mate Sarah; she's here on holiday, and a bit bored . . . How's he eating, then?"

The woman seemed to relax, and squatted next to Daphne by the baby. When she spoke, her voice was a total surprise to Sarah: clear and even, with well-educated tones.

Daphne knows how to be with everyone — how can she keep it all straight? Sarah wondered. There was a great difference in greetings and introductions between the two old sisters and this young mother, yet Daphne had handled it all with perfect ease.

Sarah sat quietly and out of the way on a log near the fire, while Daphne examined each child, speaking in low tones to Fiona. The young mother nodded several times, and once she listened through the stethoscope that Daphne had placed around her neck. It seemed the children all had worms — worms! thought Sarah, careful to keep her face quiet — and the herbal dosage Fiona was treating them with was not working.

"It could just be a problem with the plants, Fiona," said Daphne seriously. "I think the growing season wasn't as good this summer — not enough rain. So the plants won't be as strong, eh. Next year, it'll be better, I reckon. So let's just dose them with this stuff till you get the garden going again, OK?" Smoothly, with perfect diplomacy, Daphne persuaded the woman, and each child was promptly dosed.

"I'll be back next Tuesday, to do it again." This time, Fiona nodded meekly, without a single protest. Daphne shot Sarah the subtlest glance of triumph.

They had another cup of tea, but this time there were no delicate china cups, only thick white mugs gone gray with use. Sarah studied the dwelling place. Inside, the walls were patched with sagging cardboard and bits of newspaper stuffed into crevices. A pile of mattresses lay in one corner, gray-striped and lumpy, and on these the two older children crawled, half-naked and grubbily blond, playing like puppies. The food supplies were stacked in tins and wooden crates near the entrance, and along the roof beam, with bark beginning to shred from it, a line of giant ants were making their way into an open box of sugar.

"How's Bob doing, then?" Daphne was saying.

"He can't get work — he's tried. I know he tries, but there's just no money," said Fiona, sighing, fiddling with the corner of her shirt. She lifted her chin, her glance taking in Sarah this time.

"He's getting the house done, though," she said, defiant and proud. "It only needs the roofing material, then we can move in. He works so hard . . ."

Fiona led them up the bush trail, a narrow-shouldered, pale girl-woman, her bare feet making no noise on the soft earth. She showed them her garden with pride mixed with worry, and Daphne examined the wormweed with interest. To Sarah, the plant looked lifeless.

"*Why* does she stay there with him!" cried Sarah, after they had driven the truck back onto the main track.

"She loves him," said Daphne, simply. She shrugged. "There's lots like that here, hidden back in the bush. They come full of dreams and ideas, wanting the 'simple life.' But this place isn't a friendly place — it's been torn and ravaged and doesn't give much back, for all the sweat put in. It's not a peaceful land . . ."

This seemed a strange thing to say, and Sarah tilted her head slightly, wondering if she would explain. But Daphne changed the subject.

"Fiona's bore two babies down in that hut," she said, suddenly fierce. "Bob's got her all convinced that the natural way is best. She almost died after the last one, and him creeping around during it like a whipped puppy. I could have killed him then!"

Sarah laced her hands around her knees, imagining that tiny, fragile woman giving birth in the bush, on those grimy mattresses. She shuddered.

"What does he do — Bob, I mean?"

"Oh, he's a jack-of-all-trades, I guess — couldn't make it out on the mainland, so he trucks the whole lot of them here, with big ideas of building a house. Well, it's been four years in the building, eh, and still not even a roof."

Daphne's voice was strident in her anger, and Sarah shrank from talking about it anymore. Bob Grant was not a human being Daphne had succeeded in accepting.

They stopped twice more on the way back, and it was evening when they roared through Port William. Sarah sat curled on the seat, her head almost touching Daphne's shoulder. They hadn't spoken for half an hour, both of them exhausted by their day.

Though Sarah was tired, thoughts were racing through her mind. So much to think about — so many people, such strange, *different* people! She closed her eyes, and without warning she found herself thinking about the boy of the evening before. She hadn't thought of him all day. She wondered if his truck would be in front of the house, if she would see him . . . Angrily she snapped open her eyes, just as blinding headlights roaring up behind them forced Daphne to swear and swerve the truck to the side of the track.

Sarah sat forward and stared after the truck, her breath caught sharply in her throat. In the back of the truck, balanced perfectly against the jolting ride, was a huge black dog.

"That was Mako!" she cried, eager and disdainful at once. Daphne snorted good-naturedly.

"Bloody rotter!" she said. "He's a pain in the butt. Someday, eh, I'll run the nasty little piece off the road!" She laughed out loud, looking over at Sarah, curious. "You've met him, then, love?"

"Oh — not really — just last night . . . I had dinner, I mean tea, at the Harrises . . ." she stammered, suddenly mortified that she had even mentioned him. She didn't want Daphne to think she *knew* him! The last thing she wanted to do was talk about that horrible boy, or even *think* about him, with his know-it-all looks and ignorant manners.

"I like him," said Daphne frankly. "He's a bright little devil, nasty and a rotter, for all that. But there's something different about him — he's got *something*, that one. I don't know what; just have a sense of it, really, eh. But he'll need to get rid of the chip on his shoulder or he'll just waste himself back on the streets . . ."

"Did he grow up in Auckland?" asked Sarah cautiously, despite herself.

Daphne nodded. "He's a city kid — like you. He's about your age, too — seventeen, actually, Mari told me. Came here a couple of months ago when Mari's sister kicked him out for causing trouble. Dropped out of school last year; there isn't much of a future . . ." Her voice trailed off, as if she was thinking, but she continued after a second.

"Mike's his stepdad — I reckon it's hard for him, his mum getting married to a Pakeha. He only just met his real dad — never knew him. He's some sort of Maori activist, pretty well known, Mari told me. He walked out on her when Mako was a baby, and last year he just waltzes in an' presents himself to the kid, sweeps him off his feet, so to speak. Mako worships him — why not! He's loud and colorful. So the kid quits school, hangs out on the street with the gangs — wants to be just like his daddy."

Sarah experienced an unexpected sympathy for Mako, feeling an unwanted kinship with him, with what he was going through. *It's sort of like me with Pauline,* she thought . . . but then she remembered his eyes as he had looked over at her across the kitchen, how he had thrown the whole house into turmoil, how he had marched in and then out with an arrogance that made her grit her teeth.

"Well, I can't stand him!" she said passionately. Daphne looked over at her and smiled.

"He's a bit of a hard case," she admitted. "But he might be worth getting to know. There's more to him than meets the eye — he's not really the punk he seems, I don't think."

"Why would I want anything to do with him! He wouldn't know *anything.* I mean, he probably can't even *read!*" It was a snotty, bratty thing to say. She sat stubbornly looking out the window. Once again, she found herself caught in a bewilderment of emotions. What on earth was the matter! She'd hardly met the stupid kid, and there was no reason why she had to have anything to do with him. But why, why did she *want* to see him again?

"He could use a friend," said Daphne softly. "I don't think he's close to anyone his own age here. He gets along with Russell, Mari told me — Russell owns the bar in Port William — but he's older. Anyway, I see he's made you angry somehow, so maybe it doesn't make sense . . ."

Sarah bit her lip, frowning. She wished she could express herself better, especially to Daphne.

"He didn't really *make* me angry," she said slowly. "I just *feel* angry. I guess I just had a weird day yesterday . . ."

Daphne had pulled the truck up to the house at the Crossroads. She turned and enveloped Sarah in a warm hug.

"It's hard, opening up to people," she said. "I know . . . it took me a while."

Once again, Sarah was reminded that Daphne had come from somewhere else, had a whole life behind her. She found it hard to imagine her any other way but as she was now — warm and intelligent and *loving*.

"Maybe," Sarah began slowly, looking at the lit windows of the house where Mari and Mike lived with the children, and the dark empty windows of the other half, "maybe I'll see him around. He must be busy, fishing and all, but maybe . . ."

Daphne grinned and started the truck up again.

"Take a risk — what the hell!" She laughed. "I got to go, love, I'm all done in, and I've still got to get back to Waitapu tonight. You don't want to find me in a ditch somewhere, eh!"

The truck roared off. Sarah climbed the steps onto the verandah. The black dog was lying alert and silent on the ground, watching her. He was invisible but for the light reflected in his eyes. She wasn't sure, but she thought she saw the slightest movement of his tail.

3
THE ALBATROSS

Sarah leaned on a fence post and watched the two horses grazing along the edge of the wire. She had been standing like this for almost an hour, the sun like a warm hand in the middle of her shoulders. Every so often she flipped her head back, catching the breeze that butted through the tussock, bringing with it the smell of the gulf.

She studied the pony. He was swaybacked with age, his short legs hung with fur; his ears twitched continually as he moved slowly along the fence. Occasionally he would lift his blunt head and stare back at her, half-chewed grass dribbling from his mouth. The other animal was different.

Celeste was a lanky, raw-boned horse, her neck and hind-quarters knotted with muscle. Her head was long, with a distinct curve in the muzzle, and her eyes were not the languid, bored eyes of the little pony. Instead, they gazed from time to time into the wind, violet-dark, secretive, alert. Her coat was a rough mottle of white, gray, and rust, and along her withers Sarah could make out scars where a harness had rubbed for many years. She was of immense stature and bulk, only her lankiness suggesting she had anything but draft blood running through her veins.

It was the way the mare constantly assessed the wind that touched Sarah's heart. She was far from beautiful, but a *spirit* surrounded her, something big-hearted and free. Sarah imagined riding her, galloping without fear straight into the wind, racing along the wild beaches at the edge of the waves.

But they had told her she could ride Whiskey, not Celeste. Once again, she studied the pony. He was fat and lazy. She held on to the fence post with her hands and swung back, deliberating. The day filled her with a reckless exuberance. After all, last summer she had completed the intermediate class in riding; if she had stayed in the city this summer, she would have been in advanced. She jumped back from the post, her mind made up.

The saddle lay in a disorganized pile in the shed where Mike had told her it would be. She lugged it out into the sunlight and squatted next to it, studying it. She picked at a few straps, then, grunting with the effort, she tugged it over a rubbish bin so everything hung down in the general direction it was meant to go. It was like no saddle she had ever seen — a stock saddle, Mike had called it — but eventually she thought she had it right.

Getting the blanket and saddle on Celeste was more of a struggle, but the horse stood surprisingly still, the result of years of patient waiting while she was harnessed up. Letting the stirrup down to its fullest length, Sarah scrabbled her way into the saddle.

The huge mare gathered herself, twisted into a corkscrew, and skittered off sideways down the paddock. Before she had a chance to be afraid, Sarah was thrown off, falling against a clump of tussock. The breath was knocked out of her. She lay where she had fallen, seeing the mare standing a few steps away with her head down, blowing softly at her.

Sarah slowly sat up, smudging dirt and tears from her face. She glowered at the mare, feeling betrayed. Frustration filled her. She didn't want to ride that stupid pony! She wanted to scream at the mare, hit her.

"She can't stand the saddle, that one. She's an island horse; she wants to be ridden bareback."

The voice startled her so much she didn't move, her eyes glued to the mare. A hand touched her shoulder for a single instant, and Mako walked around so she could see him. He looked down at her, his hand buried in the thick mane of fur around the black dog's neck.

"I was around the front," he said, his voice as flat as the expression on his face. "But Kikiwa saw you, so I came." He reached out and ran his hand down the mare's sinewy neck.

"She just can't take a saddle, eh," he said again.

Sarah struggled to her feet, trying not to wince. She brushed off her jeans furiously, tilting her head down so the wind blew her hair across her face, hiding it. But Mako showed no sign of leaving.

The dog shifted almost imperceptibly, and she felt just the barest touch on her leg. He made no other move. Without thinking, her hand dropped and rested on the broad head. Under her fingers, the fur was so thick and warm it was almost electric.

"Kikiwa likes you," said Mako. There was a slight change in his voice that made her lift her head and look at him. For a moment, she had thought he'd said, "I like you." Now that she was looking at him, she didn't know how to back away, and stood helpless.

"I'll unsaddle Celeste for you," the boy said, still with that curiously flat voice. "You'll want to get back on her, eh. Or you'll lose your nerve, and she'll know it."

She was regaining her composure. There was no way she was going to get on that horse again! Mike had told her Whiskey, and if she'd had any sense at all, and not got all caught up in her silly fantasies, she would have listened to him. And anyway, who was this kid to lecture her!

She turned her back on him and walked toward the paddock gate.

"The pony isn't the right one for you. He's lazy and stupid. He doesn't like the wind, eh; he won't run on the beach."

She caught her breath, and stopped. For a moment she stood, unnerved. How was it he had known to say that?

"It was dumb of me to try riding her in the first place," she said haughtily. "Mike said I could ride Whiskey, and he was right."

"It wasn't dumb," he replied softly, rubbing the mare's nose. "This is a strong horse. She's smart, and brave. Why wouldn't you want to ride her? She loves the wind — besides, Mike don't always know what's what, eh."

She could find no answer to this. She frowned stubbornly at Celeste, tugging at her heavy sweater impatiently. Reluctantly, she walked back, touched the muscled neck with the tips of her fingers. Celeste dropped her head and snuffled softly.

"She *wants* you to ride her," said the boy.

"How do you know?" she challenged.

He didn't answer her, but reached around to unbuckle the heavy girth strap. The saddle slid easily off into his arms, and he threw it over the fence. Sarah stood uncertain, stroking the flat bony forehead of the mare. Celeste seemed to lean into her hands, and Sarah felt again a yearning toward the animal. It had been her fault, after all — the poor horse had been more scared than anything. She probably had never worn a saddle.

Mako was watching her. She flushed angrily. Why couldn't he just go away now and leave her alone? With horror, she realized he was waiting for her to get back on the horse. He had moved back and was standing so close his denim jacket brushed her arm. She felt she was suffocating.

She squared her shoulders and moved carefully away from him with all the dignity she could muster. Over her shoulder, she said, "I don't want to ride her now."

She was not going to make herself look pitifully ridiculous by trying to clamber on that huge animal without a saddle! Obviously, Mako was enjoying making her feel uncomfortable.

"Then let me," he called after her.

"Go ahead — she's your horse," she snapped back, still walking toward the house.

"I need help getting on, eh. Give me a boost up."

Defeated, she stopped, looking at him. There was nothing on his face but puzzled friendliness. She walked over to him, and he showed her how to cup her hands with her fingers laced together. She had to stand very close to him. He put his foot in her hands and with the slightest lift from her, he vaulted over the mare's back. For a moment, unbalanced, he lay sprawled and clutching. He grunted and pulled himself straight.

"Crikey!" he cried, looking down at her. "You didn't need to throw me, eh!"

She stared at him with her mouth open. She'd hardly moved her arms! He'd looked so funny sliding all over the horse's back; she clamped her mouth shut, to keep from giggling.

"Have your laugh — go ahead!" he muttered at her, but his face had opened good-humoredly. She thought, If that had been me, I'd be dead with embarrassment. The giggle came out in a stifled sneeze. They grinned at each other.

Mako turned the mare in a circle to quiet her, and then slipped off next to Sarah. It was her turn now. She stepped tensely in his cupped hands. He butted her with his head.

"Relax, or you'll end up like me," he directed.

To her surprise, she pulled herself up smoothly and was settled in the middle of the broad back before she knew it. She looked out of the corner of her eye; had he noticed how heavy she was? But he was only brushing off his hands. She took the reins and walked Celeste in a tight circle, as she had been taught at her riding class. Mako pushed her leg with his hand, so that it hung further forward.

"You can balance better that way," he said, cocking his head up at her.

"How come you're so good at this?" she shot at him, although she no longer felt the sharpness of her challenge. But what a know-it-all he was! "I thought you grew up in a city."

"I did," he grinned at her. "I'm just good at fakin' it."

He opened the gate for her and she tapped Celeste with her heels, feeling a little unsure with no saddle to hold her. But the horse moved smoothly and calmly into the yard. Before she could direct the mare out to the road, Mako reached up and caught hold of the reins.

His eyes shimmered, liquid as burnished satin. The sunlight moved strangely within the dark pupils. The wind lifted the mat of hair, and Sarah noticed how brown and clear his skin was, and how strongly defined the bones of his face.

"I like hearing you play your flute," he said, his voice so low she could hardly hear him.

Her hands tightened on the reins, and she looked away. She wished he had not told her that. Her practice time with her flute was her alone time. She could feel her stomach churning inside her, and a shiver of anger went through her. Twice now, this boy had shattered a peaceful time with his arrogant, presumptuous manner!

"So?" she said coldly. He continued to watch her, but his eyes went suddenly flat again. She was sorry now.

"You smile when you play," he said, letting the reins drop from his hand. "I've never seen you smile — only heard you."

"It makes me happy, to play," she whispered. He smiled at her, and she found she could smile back. He threw back his head, clenching his fists.

"If it was *my* flute, I'd make it bloody toot!" he cried, jerking his head passionately. "I'd make it toot *mad!*" He bounded toward his truck, Kikiwa moving at his side. His abrupt outcry was more than she could fathom. She tapped Celeste and headed out onto the road.

The wind and sun and the smell of the sea chased all disquieting thoughts from her. Sarah threw back her head and breathed the air in great gulps, thrilled. The horse moved easily under her. There had never been any day as glorious as this one! She passed through Port William and was all alone on the track.

She lost all sense of time. She recognized the plateau where she and Daphne had stopped the day before, and she pulled up the horse so she could hear the pipit. Very soon, above the wind, she made out the trilling song. The hilltops were all eroded, the deep clay-ocher scars dry. The wind flashed over them, rattling its dusty way through the bleached white grasses. It was such a clear day she could see the mountains in the distance.

Eventually, Sarah's legs, unused to riding, began to ache. She chose a spot where the forest grew close to the track and slid off the horse's back. For a long time she leaned back against the mare's side. It was wonderful — it was life itself! — to be able to stand this close to another living thing, to breathe in the same breath, to share the same love of the sea-filled wind! She buried her hand deep in the coarse mane, and the mare leaned into her arm. How perfect she was! What an *alive* creature!

She knew, suddenly, what Mako shared with the black dog, why he would stand as she was now, holding deep to the fur as if to be part of the same blood and bone and muscle. She leaned her forehead briefly against Celeste's neck.

She left the horse tethered by the bridle reins to a fence post near the forest's edge. Pushing aside the tangled creepers and feathery brush of ferns, she slipped into the coolness of the bush. At once, she was in a fairy realm of tree fern and brilliant moss, so plush it almost unbalanced her to walk on it. She plunged her hand into the moss, smelling the earthy dampness of it.

She was in a living dimness of green and shadow, trees with trunks and branches so massive they were like ancient monsters hulked over the sprites of fern and palm. Squatting on the limbs were parasitic growths that looked like cabbages gone mad. Vines snaked and climbed over everything. The trunks of tree ferns were repulsive to her, their black fibers looking as if they had just pushed their way clear of some primeval muck.

She discovered a narrow path, and felt a faint surprise at this sign of human touch. She walked cautiously along it in the dappled light. Something crashed quite close to her in the trees; she jumped, and froze. After all, what sort of animals might live in a place like this? But it was only a huge pigeon, with feathers of iridescent grays and greens and lavenders.

The path sloped steadily down, and she wondered if it eventually ended at the sea. She thought she could hear the roar of waves, but as she came closer she found the path curved

along the side of a stream. The stream dropped sharply and
became a series of waterfalls, swollen with the recent storm.
Once or twice, above the deep rock pools, a stray shaft of
sunlight sliced down through the trees, illuminating mist and
insects.

The unbearable magic of the place filled her until she could
not contain herself; with a little cry, she threw back her head
and bounded down the path. She felt as weightless as the
sunlit mist. She felt as if she had left something terribly heavy
behind, something she no longer had to carry.

When she stopped, out of breath, she had arrived at a crude,
swaying bridge made of supple vines woven skillfully into
ropes. Gingerly, she stepped onto it. It held her weight, and
she slowly made her way across and continued down the path.
Soon the land leveled briefly, and it was there, in a thicket
of ferns, that she saw the hut. It looked deserted, the slabs
of corrugated iron rusted and corroded. A stovepipe stuck
above the roof, but no smoke issued from it. She pushed
through the ferns and peered closer, but decided not to go
in to explore. Perhaps, she thought, it was a hut used by
hikers in the summer — that would also explain the path.

No change of light told her she was coming to the edge of
the bush. Suddenly, without warning, she found herself in
the bright glare of sunlight, at the top of steep dunes that
swept down to the sea. She looked out over the vast expanse
of the Hauraki Gulf.

The dunes were covered in places with an odd hummocky
shrub that was springy to her touch. Tentatively, she leaned
into one and found it supported her weight like a mattress.
Laughing, she threw herself into it, leaning back so the sun
beat down on her face, sheltered from the stiff breeze coming
from the water. She studied the little cove. It was a miniature
place, a tiny curve of white sand bordered by a tumble of

rocks on either side, the water so blue it bit into her eyes. Later, she thought — later, I'll go down there. Right now, she could not keep her eyes open.

She lay comfortably in a half sleep, feeling everything in her relax. Gradually she allowed her thoughts to calm, and the people and images of the past few days overcame her.

At first, she dreamed of Pauline, gliding in and out of her half dreams, saying something to her Sarah could not quite hear. And then Daphne filled her mind, and she snuggled deep into the hummock bush, smiling. Flitting images of bush and the rose gardens, of the little seaplane, of a fishing boat . . .

Again, the boy intruded on her thoughts. She stirred uneasily. She felt she was drowning in the depths of those strange, compelling eyes. He puzzled her, he angered her, he excited her more than she could stand —

She came out of her half sleep grappling with a sense of losing control. Somehow, she knew, she had to sort out these feelings! She didn't like this *not knowing* what she felt. She wasn't used to it.

"Get hold of yourself, Sarah Steinway!" she growled. She put her hands behind her head and looked up at the sky.

"You *like* him, that's the thing," she continued, her voice full of scorn as she berated herself. She knew this was true — something about Mako attracted her, and at the same time filled her with a violent dislike.

She forced herself to think rationally. It wasn't that there was anything wrong with liking a boy. She fully intended to marry someone someday, after she had become successful — an oboist, perhaps, or a violist . . . They could form a duet, tour the world. But now there was really no time for boys, or for anything of that sort. Now was the time for discipline, practice, dedication. Look what had happened to silly Marjory, after she started seeing Steve. It had been *awful* — and her cello practice? Forget that! It had all gone down the drain. Not that the school orchestra had suffered much from the loss . . .

She slid down the dune on the seat of her pants and walked along the beach. What was it like to really know someone? she wondered. It must take so much time . . . How could there be time for anything else? But what would it be like? What would it be like to know what Mako thought about, to know why his eyes looked so far away, to know why he changed from calm to fury in the flicker of an instant? And then, would he know her as well? Know how important her music was, really *know*, as she knew? Or care?

She frowned, and shook her head. She had reached one end of the beach and was climbing out on the rocks of the headland. It was better not to let oneself in for hurt. Pauline, she realized, had made that discovery years ago — and she had been right.

Something white was bobbing in the water just off the tip of the headland. She glanced at it, thinking it was a bit of sail cloth or a plastic bag of rubbish. She tilted her head, squinting. Curious, she scrambled as far as she could out on the rocks.

Floating in the swell was the largest white bird she had ever seen. At first it seemed lifeless, but she caught a glimpse of a small black eye, and that eye was very alive. She held her breath in excitement.

It took careful maneuvering with her sneakered feet wedged between rocks for her to grasp a wing and pull the bird toward her. She could hardly lift it from the water.

She hauled it as carefully as possible up onto the dry rocks, feeling its defiant fear under her hands. It tried feebly to snap at her with its half-open beak, and she quickly moved her hand back.

She arranged the bird as comfortably as she could and knelt, looking at it. She guessed it might be a gull of some sort, but larger than any she knew of. The wingspan had to be at least six feet! It had feathers of the purest white broken in places by a mottling of brown. The beak that lay panting open in the sun was pale yellow, sectioned and creviced with intricate lines. The bird's eye watched her under a distinct brow, which gave it a stern, fierce gaze.

She examined it, staying clear of the beak. Neither the wings nor the legs appeared to be broken, but at last she found, at the base of the neck and around one leg, a section of fishing net stiff with salt. It had tangled and bitten deeply into the flesh so that the feathers were broken and the skin raw and infected. The leg was swollen, and when she tried to tug at the net, the bird snapped at her with a hiss.

Pauline would know what to do with this bird, she thought. They were always doctoring gull chicks and injured ducks at the Point. But when she lifted the bird in her arms, keeping the head away from her, she knew she would never manage to carry it all the way back. She would have to get help, and in the meantime find a place to leave it safely until she could come back.

She ran her hand along the cool smooth feathers on the bird's back. How alive was the eye that stared at her! How strong and perfect the wing felt under her fingers! The bird was graceful and powerful even in this agony, and she imagined it soaring over the open ocean. She imagined the fierce eyes gazing out through winter storms, imagined that great span of wings against the sky. She wanted with all her heart to see this bird in flight, to set it free above the ocean and watch it spiral higher and higher until it was a glint of light against the darkness.

She had to do something quickly, because it was getting

late in the afternoon. She realized, too, that she was tired and extremely hungry, and she still had to climb back through the bush and ride to the house. Her mind raced. She couldn't leave the bird out in the open — she was sure there would be predatory scavengers around. And it might even manage to struggle away. She remembered the little hut in the bush. If she could get it that far, it would be safe until she got help.

She almost did not make it. Her legs burned with effort, and her arms felt like lead with the weight of the bird. Climbing the dunes was close to impossible. She was sure she was causing the bird agony by the way she had to clutch and tug it. Finally, whimpering with exhaustion and frustration as she made her way up through the bush, she came to the half-hidden hut.

She pushed open the door with her foot. In the dim interior she could make out only a pile of rubbish, a broken crate, and empty tin cans. The hut was obviously deserted. She arranged the bird as well as she could in one corner, near the grimy window where there was a faint light. Once more she tried to remove the net, but soon gave up. It would take a knife. Outside, she blocked the door shut with a rock and hurried back up the path.

Celeste was grazing calmly where she had left her, and Sarah saw guiltily that the little area the reins had allowed for movement was cropped completely clean. She was too tired to even try climbing on, so she began to walk, leading the mare.

So tired and lost in thought was she, she did not hear the truck until it was almost beside her. Celeste wickered.

"Thought you got lost, eh!" said Mako, leaning out the window. "Mum sent me to find you. It's five o'clock!"

She was too tired to be surprised.

"I didn't get lost," she said. Then, suddenly, "Mako! I found something!" The words tumbled over her tongue. *He* could help her get the bird, with the truck! She came closer to the truck in her excitement.

"I found this amazing bird! It's huge — really big. I don't know what it is, but it's hurt and I couldn't get it back by myself . . . but it might die, Mako! It's so beautiful; it's the most beautiful thing I've ever seen!"

He had stopped the truck now, and she tugged his arm.

"I left it down there, in the woods. Help me with it, OK? Will you?"

"You're daft — a *bird?* What're you going to do with it?" He frowned at her, impatient. He'd been in the middle of cleaning the truck when his mother sent him out to look for her. He got out of the truck and walked around to her, watching how the wind blew her hair across her cheek. She was looking at him with such intensity — he was distracted by her eyes. And the way her hair was . . . he wanted to touch it, to see what it felt like.

"I'm not going to do anything with it! It's hurt, and I want to get it to my mother, so she can help it." She saw him hesitating.

"Well, then, *don't!*" she snapped. "Just help me up on Celeste and I'll find someone else."

She was shaking with frustration and exhaustion, and Mako saw her legs were trembling as she stood. Ah, crikey — what the hell had she been doing all day, saving some bloody bird . . . It was probably a sea gull!

"Crikey!" he said, more softly. "Where's the damn bird?"

She gestured back toward the path, and they tethered the horse once more, to the tailgate of the truck. Kikiwa bounded silently from the back and followed them.

"It'll have gone off by now, I reckon," he muttered at her.

"No, it won't have — I left it in an old shack. It's not far — "

He stopped in his tracks and looked at her, alarmed.

"You left it in a shack?"

"It's OK, Mako — it was really a pit. It's deserted. That's why I left it there, so nothing would get it." But she had caught his alarm and felt a flutter of fear.

"I'm sure it's OK," she whispered. "Really — there wasn't anything in it but some old rags and stuff."

"That hut belongs to Aunt Hattie," he said quietly. "I heard about her from Russell, eh. She has a shotgun, and she'll shoot your head off. If you left your bird there, it'll be stew by now. I sure as hell ain't going down there!"

He had stopped on the path stubbornly. He knew this was a dumb idea — silly Pakeha chick! No sense — but she was not coming back with him. He waited impatiently.

"Go ahead, then. I'm going myself. I can't leave her, Mako — I have to help her," she said, her voice low and determined. He could see she was scared. He gave up.

"Let's go," he muttered, avoiding her eyes. He couldn't let her go down there alone. Anyway, what did Russell know? Just some dumb story of his, he reckoned . . .

"It's like I was *meant* to find her! She's so beautiful," Sarah said. "I want . . . I want to see her fly. She belongs out there . . ." She held her head back, as if to an open sky. "Don't you see, Mako? Don't you see?"

He mumbled something she could not quite hear.

"What?" she whispered. But he only shrugged, looking over his shoulder with a half smile. At first she thought he was reaching back to take her hand, but he was only holding a branch back from snapping in her face.

In that whisper of sound, the boy heard the echo of his own words, the words Sarah had not been able to hear — "You are the bird . . ." His mouth was strangely dry, and he swallowed. Why had he said that?

Mako walked stiffly down the path in front of the girl. Everything in him told him to turn back, and he did not know why. Kikiwa glided in the dimming light just ahead of him, and it seemed to Mako as if the dog was leading them. He shook the thought away. He was glad the dog was with them. He hated the bush, the way it was clammy and cold and closed around him. He'd take a city street, any day!

They hadn't spoken for a long time, and still had not spoken by the time they reached the little hut. And almost at once, they saw a trickle of bluish smoke coming from the stovepipe.

They had no time to think what to do. Sarah saw Mako's back tense in front of her, and she felt his alarm. They stood without moving.

The old woman came at them through the ferns. She was an apparition in shapeless clothes, her face hidden under the brim of a greasy hat. She was shorter than either of them, but to Sarah, she seemed to fill the forest.

"You have left a bird in my home," said the woman, in a voice more powerful than her tiny body would suggest.

Sarah took a deep breath. This, after all, was her doing. She moved forward, away from Mako.

"I'm sorry," she said steadily. "I thought the hut was deserted, and I couldn't carry her any further. She's hurt . . ." She stopped, tongue-tied.

"You are frightened of me, and you must not be. You must stop being frightened. Stop!"

This extraordinary command carried such force that Sarah found herself obeying immediately. She was no longer frightened. The old woman stepped closer and stared fixedly at a place just beyond Sarah's shoulder.

"You are standing in the shadows, boy. I cannot see you, and I want to see you. Come out."

Mako stepped closer to Sarah, touching her arm with his

own. The old woman leaned forward. She peered intently into his face, as if searching for something. Startled again, Sarah pressed against his arm, half protecting, half sheltering. But Mako had dipped his head away from the old woman's eyes, averting his gaze deliberately.

"She is the bold one," the old woman said, not taking her eyes off Mako's face. "You still stand in the shadow." She paused and then, as if having come to some decision, she nodded her head twice.

"Yes," she said firmly. "Come!" And they could do nothing but follow her through the ferns to the front of the hut.

Lit now by two kerosene lamps, Sarah saw that the pile of rags was a crude bed, and the crate was a table. The cans had been picked up, and the bird lay in a wooden fishing crate on a pile of moss. The light from the lamps flickered warmly on its feathers.

Mako knelt immediately. "An albatross!" he said softly. "You found an albatross!"

Sarah knelt beside him, clasping her hands together.

"An albatross!" she breathed. "Isn't it beautiful? See — see?"

They stroked the glossy wing, and this time the bird only watched them and did not snap. Sarah felt along the neck and saw that not only had the netting been removed but a salve had been smeared into the torn flesh.

"Oh!" she cried, turning to the woman behind them. "Thank you!" Her eyes were bright. "Is it going to be all right?"

"She will live, and she will fly," came the answer. "You will help her."

Sarah knelt again by Mako.

"It's a *wandering albatross*," he said. "They live so far out on the sea, no one ever sees them. They fly for years. She must have dived into a broken net after fish, and then got washed up by the storm." He stroked the smooth head, and stood up.

Sarah turned once again to the old woman, who was busy building a fire in her grate.

"I have to get it back to my mother. She'll know what to do — she's an ornithologist. I'm sorry about coming into your house. But *thank you* . . ."

The old woman was not listening to her. She had once again moved toward Mako, who was standing meekly with his eyes turned away. The woman walked slowly in a circle around him.

Sarah's arms prickled coldly. Maybe the woman *was* crazy! Maybe she did have a shotgun . . .

"You are frightened of me again!"

So abruptly did the woman stop in her pacing that Sarah gasped, stepping backward and stumbling.

"I am not crazy, and you must not be frightened."

The girl and the woman stood facing each other. Sarah licked her lips.

"Of course I'm scared; what do you expect!" she cried in a low voice, forcing the defiance to come. She felt the blood rushing to her face. Why didn't Mako do something, for God's sake, instead of just standing there!

"And stop doing all that stupid voodoo stuff to Mako. Of course you're scaring us!"

The old woman threw back her head, bellowing with laughter. She stomped her feet in their huge rubber boots.

"Ha ha ha, boy!" She stood with her hands on her hips in front of Mako. "This one will pull you from the shadows! And you, girl," she continued, swinging back to Sarah. "You will leave the bird with me. She is not for your mother. *You* found her; she is yours. You did not find her by chance — you do not believe you did. You will care for her here. She is yours, and you will help her fly free again. That is what you want."

It *was* what she wanted. She knew it suddenly, without question. And it was true — she *had* felt she was meant to find it.

"But . . . doesn't she need real help? I mean, I don't know what she needs . . ." Sarah protested weakly.

"Food. Rest. Care. Love. That is all she needs. She doesn't need more. Then she will fly."

And she was hers. She would not be one of Pauline's brilliant studies, tagged and inoculated and studied and written up in a research paper . . . No!

"The boy will fish for you, so you can feed your bird," the old woman said now, looking calmly over toward Mako. He had moved back until he stood just in the doorway, and beside him stood the massive form of Kikiwa. Where had the dog been all this time? Sarah wondered, her thoughts disjointed. The last she remembered, he'd been trotting ahead of them down the path — almost, she thought, as if he knew the way . . .

"That is his anger-companion," said the woman, in such a low voice Sarah leaned closer to her. "He feels strong because of his anger. But there are other strengths he does not know." She jabbed her finger at Sarah.

"Will you let him, girl?"

"Will I let him — fish? He fishes all the — I mean, I don't care. I guess; it's the only way I can get fish," she said. She was avoiding looking at Mako; it made her nervous, to see him standing so . . . so *meekly*.

"Good. He will fish. You will come with fish for your bird, every day." There was smugness in the woman's tone.

Every day! She opened her mouth, but the woman silenced her with a look.

"He needs you," the woman said now. Sarah blushed. "You like him. You love the bird; you need her. You will come here. Now. It is getting dark. You are hungry, so go."

They went. This time Kikiwa trailed behind them up the path. The sun had gone down by the time they reached the truck. Sarah was so tired she felt sick to her stomach, and her legs would not stop trembling. She wished she could touch Mako, just to feel another person. But he had been as frightened as she.

"Was that Aunt Hattie?" she said at last, to break the silence. What did it matter?

He shrugged, his eyes blank.

"What is she?" As soon as she said it, she wished she had not asked. He glared stonily down the road.

"How would I bloody well know?" he snarled. Almost involuntarily, he blurted, "She has *mana*."

"Mana?"

Again he shrugged. "It's her — *self*. Inside. Around her . . . I don't know, for Christ's sake! I can't explain. *Presence* . . ." He gritted his teeth.

"You were frightened of her." The girl gazed up at him, and it seemed to Mako her face was as soft as the evening light on the hills around them. He couldn't think straight, with her looking at him like that. He couldn't think . . . he hadn't wanted to go down there! The girl had made him go.

"I wasn't scared, you dimwit!" He lashed out at her, his face twisted with wrath. "Why would I be scared of a bloody old crone?"

The shock on her face at his attack made him angrier. Silly little twit! What was she, anyway — just a Pakeha chick; you could never trust them.

"I knew I shouldn't have listened to you!" he said furiously. "What a waste of time! This whole bloody place is a waste of

time! If I have to be here I'm not going to waste my time
with some dumb Pakeha chick and crook bird!"

Sarah had recovered from the shock enough to set her face
in disgust. She turned and untied Celeste, beginning the walk
back the long road toward Port William. It would be completely dark by the time she got to the house.

The boy watched her go. Before the dusk obscured all de-
tail, he saw her raise her arm once in a jerky little gesture,
and he knew she was rubbing the tears from her eyes. He
wanted to race after her, grab her, hold her until she stopped
crying.

Bloody hell, what was happening! He got in the truck and
leaned his forehead against the steering wheel. It hadn't been
her fault — he just didn't want to be here. And that daft old
woman, talking such rot! He choked on a wave of homesickness. He was trapped here; it was the only place he could
make money. There were no jobs in Auckland for dropped-
out Maori kids who got into trouble . . .

And he had to have money! It was the only way he could
buy his own boat, anchor it off the Coromandel near where
his father lived. Henare Mokutu, his father — that's where
it was all happening! He was at the heart of it, all the exciting,
new ideas . . . a Maori New Zealand! Aotearoa!

He leaned back in the old truck and closed his eyes, flushed
with the force of his pride and excitement. He fingered the
shark's tooth he wore on a gold circle in his ear, never taken
off since the day last year when his father had given it to him,
after their first meeting.

"It's from the mako shark, boy," his father had told him.
"That's the fighting shark. That comes from your ancestors,
from son to son, all the way back to Tawahi, the greatest
fighting chief of the Ngati Niwha. I live on our ancestral land,
boy, and someday you'll come with me . . . Much is happen-

ing! This is *our* land: Aotearoa! It was stolen by the Pakeha; they killed the land with their sheep and axes and stupidity. But we will have it back; we have only to wait, and prepare!"

He had listened then, only half understanding, but filled with the sense of it. He'd watched his father's face, painted with the blue-lined *moko* of the Maori warrior. He'd pondered things all this last year, leaving the stupid Pakeha school where all he learned was pap. He knew he was meant to follow in Henare Mokutu's footsteps, listen to him speak, learn from him all the knowledge that had been passed down from Tawahi, chief of the Ngati Niwha, his people.

He was not sure how to go about it. His father had disappeared one day as quickly as he had appeared, although Mako now knew he lived on the Coromandel peninsula. Mako had spent the year on the streets with a gang of boys, getting into trouble — how boring it had been at times, just waiting! Not knowing what he was waiting for — and now! Here he was, working for his hated stepfather — a *Pakeha* — because it was the only work he could get. But inside, he nursed the infant idea, the kernel his father had left for him: Aotearoa! A Maori New Zealand. The Pakeha would leave, dissolve back across the sea, disappear in the infinite span of ancestral time, and the Maori would be waiting to take back the bruised land.

But that was all he had — an idea, no more. And here he was, alone. He pounded the steering wheel with his fist, impotent with rage. He had to get out of here! And the last thing he needed was to get mixed up with some silly American girl who obviously came from someplace as posh as Remuera, with all the same snobby ways! He stomped on the accelerator and sped down the road, passing her in a shower of dust.

4
"KA TAPU TE TAMAITI!"

The sun had just begun to brighten the sky over the Needles. Sarah leaned in the doorway looking out toward the mountains, smelling the cold freshness of the wind and knowing the day would be beautiful. Her whole body ached from yesterday, but it was a good ache, comfortable. She watched Pauline jamming some papers in a bag as she got ready to go down to the Point.

"You'll really have to come down soon, sweetie," she tossed over her shoulder to Sarah. "I want to give you the royal tour!"

Sarah sighed and pushed away from the doorjamb with her shoulders.

"I'm ready when you are," she said, knowing it sounded flip. But Pauline did not seem to notice. A truck rumbled by down the road from Port William. In the back, two cows jostled together, held fast with ropes.

"Some of them start early, the day the barge comes in," said Pauline. "The barge doesn't leave again till after dark, but some of the farmers have to make several trips all the way to Waitapu, before they get all the stuff they're shipping off the island down there."

Sarah sighed again. She was anxious for Pauline to leave. She wanted to get Celeste bridled and ride to the bush to see the albatross, getting back by two so she could go to Waitapu with Pauline. Some expensive equipment her mother had ordered for the lab was coming in on the twice-monthly barge from Auckland.

"Maybe you'll get some good practice time in before I come back to get you," Pauline was saying, and Sarah started, a thump of guilt in her stomach.

Her flute! She hadn't practiced since the first day or two in the flat! Automatically, she wiggled her fingers — were they getting stiff? She turned her face away from her mother. What would she think of her! Pauline would never be so lax in her own work. How on earth could she expect Pauline to be proud of her, if she so easily forgot what was important?

She waved goodbye to Pauline speeding off down Circle Mine Road toward the Point. The day seemed to have lost its promise. A knock at the kitchen door made her sigh again.

Mari stood smiling on the back step, a basket of washing under her arm.

"I didn't hear you come in last night," she said. "But my son said you were OK — said he found you riding back from Port William, eh, so I knew you'd just had a good long explore."

What a liar that punk is! thought Sarah in disgust. She smiled wanly back at Mari.

"I'm hanging up the wash — keep me company?" asked Mari. Sarah nodded and ran back to her room for her pack and heavy sweaters. May as well get out, she thought.

The wind blew in through the open door from a sky as high and bright as the wings of a sea bird. She thought of the albatross, lying healing in its bed of moss. She imagined holding the great bird, feeling the cool feathers against her cheek, feeling the heart pounding down into her own heart, and then . . . then she imagined opening up her arms, imagined the weight of the bird taken from her into the opening wings, the slow beating, the lifting, and the freedom!

She ran back through the flat, grabbing a bird book from her mother's desk and stuffing it in her pack as she went, cramming some cheese and apples beside it from the kitchen counter.

Mari struggled with the heavy sheets snapping at her in the wind. "It's why I only wash them twice a month!" she called to Sarah, grinning.

Celeste was standing near the gate, and Sarah had her bridled in five minutes. She left her tethered in the yard and went over to Mari.

"So she's OK for you — not too big?" asked Mari, looking with some question at the big horse.

"She's great! Except . . ." Sarah blushed, remembering the morning before. "I can't get on her by myself." Somehow she didn't mind Mari knowing how clumsy she felt.

"Oh," laughed Mari, clothespins in her mouth. "There's a trick to it, love. I'll show you, eh. I rode ponies all my life."

Sarah looked at her quizzically. Where had Mari come from? It was strange, meeting new people and not knowing anything of where they came from. It wasn't like that at home. Everyone she knew had basically the same background as hers. But here: Daphne, Mari . . . Mako — and Aunt Hattie! Where on earth had Aunt Hattie come from? She couldn't imagine her anywhere else but in that shack in the forest.

"Didn't you come from Auckland?" she asked. Mari hung up a tea towel and then sat on the kitchen step. Sarah sat next to her.

"I only shifted to Auckland after I was married," she said, her eyes unreadable. "My sister was there. I came from Northland . . ." She gestured vaguely with her hand. "Near the Bay of Islands. It's all country up there. But I came to Auckland with . . ." She had stopped and was gazing off in the direction she had gestured toward.

"Mako's father? He wanted to live there?"

Mari nodded. "And then, after he left, when my baby was just a year old, I stayed on, because my sister was there, and my mother had died." She smiled softly over at Sarah. "You call him Mako, too, then?"

Sarah flushed and opened her mouth to speak, but Mari shook her head and went on. "It's OK, a boy can decide his own name. It's good, his father came for him last year. He was not good to me, but maybe, to his son . . ." She paused again before continuing. "Mako doesn't have family, like I did. He's just a city kid, eh. No *marae*, no brothers. The gang's his marae, I reckon. I had to work all the time, when he was little. But he did good in school, eh, until two years ago, and then last year, he just left. He is all anger now."

Sarah traced a pattern in the dust at her feet with a twig. She wanted to know more. She wanted Mari to go on talking about Mako.

"Why?" she asked, almost in a whisper. "Why is he so angry?"

Mari looked at her, and Sarah caught a flicker of a change in the calm dark eyes.

"He is angry . . . he is Maori," answered Mari firmly. "He does not know where he belongs, and many things shut him out." With this, she stood up and picked a shirt out of the wash. Sarah held the clothespins for her, saying nothing. Maori. Pakeha. Two cultures, two races, caught together on a tiny island nation. She wished she knew something of the history. Had there been wars? Were there race riots, like there were in America? What was it like for Mako?

She was still thoughtful as she rode up through Port William toward the bush. As she passed through the first cattle gate, she jumped down off Celeste to open it, rather than struggle with it from the mare's back as she had the day before. Mari had showed her, as she'd promised, how to get on Celeste bareback. A push with the legs, a spring, a levering with the arms, and she was on, slightly out of breath but triumphant.

The day had fulfilled its promise, full of sun and the cool wind and the smell of the sea. Sarah rode easily, finding herself still thinking about the things Mari had told her. Mako had screamed "dumb Pakeha" at her yesterday — she was Pakeha to him. She frowned. He hated her! But still, he had left a parcel of fish on the verandah; she carried it wrapped in newspaper in her pack. She wasn't sure when he'd brought it — he must have gotten up before dawn.

Did he hate her for being Pakeha? She shifted her weight nervously on Celeste's back, and the mare flicked her long ears. Still, she thought stubbornly, he doesn't have to be a total idiot! He doesn't have to fight me . . . *I'm* not the enemy, for God's sake! She felt her face go hot, remembering the way she had snapped at him.

Maybe he'd thought . . .

She had reached the section of road where the bush came near to the edge, and she had to concentrate on finding the right place. It all looked the same. She searched for the fence post she'd tethered Celeste to yesterday, and at last picked it out against its backdrop of ferns and trees. This time she had a long rope with her, allowing the mare a good area for grazing. She rubbed her cheek against Celeste's nose and left her, checking her watch as she did. It took exactly an hour to get from the house at the Crossroads to the path in the bush.

The bush was even lovelier and more magical than it had

been the day before. It was cool and airy, the breeze making all the ferns and dark glossy leaves shimmer with light and whispers. Two tiny birds followed her to the bridge, twittering and flicking their long tails. They hovered near her in the air, sometimes hopping from twig to twig, bright-eyed and bold. She talked to them as she walked. Once, she stopped, startled at a raucous screaming above her, a thrashing of leaves. Three black parrots scolded her, tumbling around in the upper branches. When she stopped, they paraded above her, stripping bark to shower down on her, hanging upside down by their beaks, gabbling incessantly.

"You're clowns!" she said, laughing at them. The parrots flew noisily with her until she reached the hut.

Aunt Hattie was sitting near an open fire on the packed earth of the clearing. She sat with her legs stuck out in front of her, smoking a pipe made of white clay. When Sarah came through the ferns, Hattie pushed back her old hat and looked up.

"The kakas told me you were coming," she said.

Sarah looked up at the parrots still chattering above her. Well, *that's* no big deal, she thought — anyone would hear those birds a mile away! She felt uncertain now that she was here. The old woman made no move to get up or greet her. The face she could clearly see for the first time looked like an old paper bag, brown and weather-worn and crinkled. She was browner than either Mari or Mako — but her eyes! They were *blue*, blue-green, like the underside of a sea wave shot through the sun. Although the face was tiny, almost wizened like some animal's, those eyes filled Sarah's own as if they were larger than life.

"Do you always stare at people like that?" snapped the old woman at last, taking the pipe from her mouth. Sarah smiled sheepishly.

"I guess I was just looking at your pipe. I never saw a woman smoking a pipe before," she said.

"There's much you haven't seen," Hattie grumbled, tapping the pipe on the earth and standing up. "Learn to watch without being seen." She jerked her thumb toward a sagging structure of wire and wood stuck off to one side of the hut. "Your bird is in there."

Sarah dropped her pack and went over to the pen. From the dim, fern-shadowed interior the albatross watched her, nestled in its bed of moss. She knelt in the dust, rapt. The light dappled on the feathers, sparkled in the alert eyes. Everything — the graceful curve of the neck up to the dome of the head, the lovely pale yellow of the beak, the way the feathers lapped over and over each other down the folded wing — everything about her was perfect! She was spellbound. The old woman stumped up behind her.

"Nothing is broken on her," she said. "Her feathers were rubbed away by the net; they have to grow back. She needs to be strong."

She turned and dumped the contents of Sarah's pack on the ground unceremoniously. Pushing the other things aside with her foot, she picked up the parcel of fish.

"The boy got this." She looked sharply over at Sarah. The girl averted her eyes and the old woman hissed softly.

"Aha, girl, you don't look at me. You hide from me. But I know: the boy makes you angry. Right? Right?" Hattie nodded her head matter-of-factly, pleased. She continued smoothly, as if enjoying Sarah's discomfort: "He touches you, eh. He hurts you." She nodded again, unwrapping the fish and sniffing it.

Sarah stumbled awkwardly to her feet, slapping the dust from her jeans. She angrily grabbed her pack and put back the contents Hattie had dumped out. What game did this old witch think she was playing? She was so annoyed she nearly broke the zipper. None of this was any of her business!

"Look!" she said finally, challenging the old woman's eyes with her own. "What is your thing with him, anyway? Just forget about him — OK? If he wants to get fish, fine; I don't care. I don't know why you want me to keep the bird here, but you may as well leave *him* out of it. He's a total bore, totally rude — he's just a punk kid who hangs out on the streets!" She actually stamped her foot on the hard earth in her agitation. What a dumb idea this was! When she saw Pauline this afternoon, she'd just get her to come down here and take the albatross to the lab where she belonged.

"That's right, you stomp around, you get mad!" Hattie said, her old mouth twisted into a pleased grin. "You don't like *him*, you don't like this one, that one . . . you don't like *you*. Nobody is the way you think they should be. That's OK," she nodded. "OK. Someday you like yourself. The boy likes you. OK."

"He hates me," Sarah said stonily. This woman didn't know so much.

"He likes you. You play your little flute, he hears it, he don't feel so angry, eh."

"How do you know about my flute?" she cried, stung. Hattie squatted, pounding the fish into a gray paste in a dented tin can. Sarah could no longer see her face.

"Maybe you told me yesterday," said Hattie. Sarah still stood looking down at her. I didn't tell you anything at all, she said to herself.

"You come here. You are cold," said Hattie. Sarah found herself obeying, kneeling beside her and watching as she mashed the fish. The little fire seared her face. She peered from the corner of her eye at the old woman, feeling calmer.

"I'm sorry I yelled," she said softly. "It's just that Mako is really a pain, and I really don't want to waste my time with him. I have to start practicing my flute again, anyway, or I'll lose my touch — and that takes a lot of time." She stopped, fiddling with some pebbles.

"I *do* like him," she admitted, daring the old woman to cut her with a remark. But Hattie remained impassive, concentrating on her task.

"But I don't have the time — you know? I'm going to be a great flutist! It's what I want more than anything in the world. It takes total dedication."

The old woman put down the can and the sticky spoon. She sat back on her heels.

"Then, that is not music you make, girl," she said smugly. "No music comes from shutting out the world. Who taught you this? Your mother?"

"No one taught me!" cried Sarah, stung. "And anyway, if you know so much — look at my mother! She's tops in her field. Everyone respects her! Do you think she got that way by staying at home and raising kids?"

The old woman snorted, poking the fire to make it burn. The sea-blue eyes seared the girl, hotter than any flame.

"She left you."

The statement was so unexpected, Sarah had no time to control her response. She felt the tears branding her cheeks as if they were boiling hot. She glared into the fire, not speaking, not even brushing her eyes. The old woman stood up.

"Your bird is very hungry. You must feed her. She is too frightened to eat on her own!"

There was nothing to do but comply. Sarah held the bird in her lap while Hattie began to force the fish mash down its throat with a blunt stick. They worked in silence. The breeze dried the tears on Sarah's face. The bird strained in her arms.

Hattie's hand, gnarled and broad, brushed over Sarah's arm

and gently probed the injured neck. They continued with the bird in silence, finally getting a good portion of the fish down its throat.

"She's so beautiful," sighed Sarah, standing up and putting the albatross back in her pen. "She's so *perfect*. I want her to fly! It's so sad, she can't even see the sky here . . ."

"Your sadness is good," said Hattie, breaking her prolonged silence. "It is good you see how beautiful she is, even when she is hurting. Because that hurt will go; it will be as if it never was. But the *perfectness* — that is always there, in all living things." She turned toward the door of the hut, and Sarah thought she heard her say something else.

"You are the bird . . ." Was it only her imagination? And why did it feel as if she'd heard the words before?

Sarah had her pack on her back and was ready to go, when Hattie came up to her and held her strongly by the arms. For a long moment she stared full into the girl's eyes.

"I like you, girl," Hattie said, her voice gone strangely quiet. "You come here, you feed your bird. Maybe you play your flute for me. There is music in you. Someday it will fly free like your bird . . ."

They were standing very close. The kakas had stopped their screaming. The ferns hung heavy and unmoving in the stillness. The old hands held her firmly.

"I will tell you this," said the old woman. "I will tell you. The boy is important. He is important to me. *Ka tapu te tamaiti. Me mataaratia. Kua kite mai ahau i te ariki paerangi. Ka tapu te tamaiti.*"

The voice became a thing apart, a thing alive and throbbing. She heard the words without understanding them. They came inside her and became part of her, so she could hear them in her thoughts and repeat them with her voice.

"*Ka tapu te tamaiti . . . Ka tapu te tamaiti . . .*" The words were a chant in her blood, a chant like the chant of her heart. She swayed against the old woman. The hands held her firm, and the blue eyes bore into her.

"I tell you this, but I cannot tell you more. You must trust me. You are strong; you will turn lives with your music. This I can see." Still the hands would not let her go, and she did not want them to let her go.

"You have come here by accident," the voice went on. "I did not expect you. But you are here. Your life only touches his for an instant. His life touches you for the softest of moments. You each have your own path, but your paths will be brighter because you have touched each other."

The voice was carrying her somewhere she could never come away from. But she was listening.

"You cannot choose what you touch, or what will touch you," said the old woman. "Whatever comes to you, you *must* let come to you with all your being! You must! You must allow yourself to be touched. You must put out your hand and touch. *That is life*. Do not turn away. Do not turn away!"

The voice stopped. Somewhere, deep in the bush, a bird called with a sound clear as the notes of a flute. The softest of breezes brushed against Sarah's face; she could smell the sea. She stepped back from the old woman, put out her hand and touched the coarse cloth on her arm.

"Thank you for helping me with the albatross," she said softly. "I will come again tomorrow."

She stopped halfway up the path to wash her face in one of the pools, letting the mist from the waterfall cover her with coolness. She gasped at how cold the water was.

The words she did not understand ran though her head. *Tapu. Tapu. Ka tapu te tamaiti.* She struggled to remember. A voice . . . a voice had spoken them . . . the old woman's voice. She shook her head. What did they mean? *Tapu . . .*

sacred? A sacred person? No . . . a person who must be . . . untampered with, left to *be*. How could it be that she *knew* this? How could she know these words were Maori?

Like a kaleidoscope, her thoughts tumbled around inside her. She paused at the top of the trail, looking back down into the bush. Tomorrow, she must come back, bring the fish, feed the albatross . . . She must come back.

With faint surprise, she saw by her watch that she would be back before Pauline came to pick her up. The big mare moved smoothly under her, almost trotting, eager to be back in her open paddock. Sarah rubbed her hand down the flat hard withers, and the mare blew softly through her nostrils in reply.

She turned the mare loose in the paddock, and walked slowly into the flat. No one was about. Mari must have taken the little girls to the store in Port William. She went to her room and sat on the edge of the bed.

She took her flute out and held it lightly in her hands. She ran it across her cheek and over her lips. *You will turn lives with your music* . . . The words touched her lightly, cool as the barrel of the flute. *Your music will fly free like the albatross.* She lifted the flute to her lips and the first notes rippled over her like the liquid song of a bird hidden deep in the bush.

5

THE TRIP TO WAITAPU

It was the second week of June, and the early winter chill blew in through the windows of the Land Rover. The road from Port William, running by the Crossroads and continuing over the Aotea Mountains south to Waitapu, was little more than a dirt track. Within two miles of the house, the road began to twist and zigzag its way up into the mountains. The island was thirty miles long, no more than eight wide, but travel was slow and settlements few; Port William seemed a long distance from the little village of Waitapu.

The Land Rover skidded on a sharp curve, and Sarah tensed, looking at the drop down into a cascade of tree ferns and palms thirty feet below. The mountains were dangerous, a maze of volcanic outcrops and cliffs, scored deep with gullies and choked in rain forest. The road wound around up the cliff, a narrow line of ocher-yellow against dark rock. Up here, the mist seemed to sit in wait for them, lifting from the dripping forest interiors and swirling unevenly over the road.

Sarah didn't want Pauline to notice her nervousness, so she concentrated on the road. Finally, to take her mind off the drive, she asked her mother cautiously what she knew about albatrosses.

"There's a protected colony for the royal albatross on the Otago Peninsula, in the South Island," said Pauline, her eyes sparkling as they always did when talking about sea birds. "I wouldn't mind being invited to study there for a while! It's quite an honor."

"Would they have wandering albatrosses there?" asked Sarah, keeping her voice low key. Even so, her mother glanced at her with raised eyebrows, and Sarah felt a shiver of anxiety. No one must know about the albatross — or Hattie! It was *her* secret.

"Have you been bird-watching?" joked Pauline. Sarah smiled, relieved.

"I borrowed your bird guide one day, 'cause I saw a few birds down by the water. I just thought the picture of the wandering albatross looked so . . . so amazing."

"They're incredible," said Pauline, lost in her subject again. "They're really rare . . . and hard to spot. The albatross can fly for seven years without once coming to land! They rest on the sea, and they nest on remote islands."

She smiled again at Sarah, putting out a slim hand and patting her knee. Distracted, Sarah thought, It's the first time she's touched me since I got off the plane.

"I don't think you'll see a wandering albatross, sweetie . . . Even I haven't seen one, ever! But there are a lot of other interesting species all around in these Gulf islands; I'll take you out in the launch someday soon, and give you a tour."

Sarah sat back in the seat. All these promises, she thought. I've been here more than a week, and this is the first thing we've done together — and that's only because she has to get her stuff off the barge.

She shook the sour thoughts from her head angrily, looking

over at her slim mother handling the treacherous drive with ease. Pauline knew what she wanted in her life, and she pursued it with determination and charm; Sarah wondered if she had inherited the same drive to achieve.

"How's your father?" asked Pauline. Sarah jerked her head up. Pauline stared steadily ahead through the windshield. It was the last question Sarah would have expected from her.

"He's fine," she answered dubiously. What was she supposed to say? Pauline glanced at her with a look Sarah could not fathom. They said nothing for several minutes.

"Is he . . . glad about your music?" asked Pauline at last.

Sarah thought of her tall, bearlike father with his easy ways and enveloping hugs. He'd come to every performance, every recital she'd ever been in, and he had spent as much time and care as she had on researching which prep school had the best music department. Glad?

"He thinks I'm good," she said, knowing her voice had taken on its tight, closed little tone. "He gives me a lot of space . . . you know?"

Pauline nodded, again looking in that strangely sad way over at Sarah. What had she and her father been like together? Sarah wondered. She had been six when Pauline had left; she barely remembered them as a family. Of course, there had been visits with her mother off and on, quick, elaborate visits — a trip to Disneyland, Christmas one year in South America — and short, bubbly notes full of promises that went flat as months would go by afterward with nothing.

"I'm sorry, sweetheart," Pauline said after a long pause. Sarah stared at her mother, horrified; she wouldn't be able to *stand* it if Pauline cried.

"Did you know that?" Pauline continued softly. "I wish it had been different. I wish I hadn't felt so suffocated . . . I wish . . . I just want you to know that," she finished, her voice taking on the familiar lightness. Sarah sat tense in her seat.

"Mom, it's OK!" she said quickly. "It's not so bad — I mean, I see you lots! It's better than Marjory's mother and father, fighting all the time . . . you know? Besides . . ."

"Besides what, sweetie?"

"Well — you *had* to go!" she answered, turning to Pauline eagerly. She *did* understand — she really did! And everything had really worked out well, so it didn't matter.

"I mean, you had really important work to do! You're the best, one of the best in the world! If you have something that you're really good at, that you could be great at, that you *have* to do, you just can't waste time dealing with relationships, and stuff . . ." She finished a bit lamely, but continued to look at her mother, her eyes shining.

"Oh, Sarah," whispered Pauline, "I wish there had been another way . . ."

She didn't want to hear it. She turned from her mother stonily, staring out the window. It was just that Pauline was having a bad day — maybe being with *her* was stirring up things better left alone. She wished she had opted not to go to Waitapu; if she'd stayed at the Crossroads, she would have seen Daphne again, coming by on her rounds.

They had bounced down off the mountains and the land had become marshy and low around them. A signpost next to the road read: ARANA 4 km — WAITAPU 32 km. A man leaned against the signpost, smoking a cigarette. Near him in the ditch a pickup truck was parked, with the hood up.

"Ta," he said laconically when they stopped, opening the door and sliding in next to Sarah. He wore the common clothes of the island — rough trousers, bulky woolen sweaters, and thick rubber gum boots. Sarah shook her head when he offered her a piece of sticky candy pulled from a pocket.

"Barley sugar," he urged, friendly. "Real good for energy." She took it reluctantly and put it in her mouth; it was very sweet.

"I reckon I'm obliged to you for a ride to Waitapu, eh," he smiled over at Pauline. "Ute broke — the bloke in Arana's down to the barge by now, I reckon. Got a dozen sacks of sheep nuts comin' in on the barge — sure as hell hope they didn't get soaked, eh!" He shook his head, chewing on his cigarette. "Worse summer since I can recollect, it was that dry. No grazin' left . . ."

He grinned at them curiously. "You're the American lady stayin' at Mike Harris's," he said, tilting his head. "You the one that studies them birds, the ones that live underground?"

Pauline laughed and nodded. She seemed perfectly at ease with this mud-spattered farmer, and he took this as an invitation to ramble on. Sarah squeezed herself as carefully as she could away from him, trying not to appear obvious. She folded her arms straight around her knees and watched the landscape through the windshield.

". . . and I haven't seen Mike in more'n a year. You'd think this place was the size of Australia, the way you don't get to see folks. He's a good bloke, Mike is, eh. Hard worker. No one thought he could make that fishin' business go, but he wasn't so daft! He's got the right idea, him an' his mate with the plane."

They rattled through Arana, and Sarah had only a glimpse of a low cinderblock building on one side of the road, and an older, wisteria-covered stucco building on the other. A gas pump stuck out of a cement slab near the road, and a crooked clothesline swayed with a full load of laundry. The road leveled

out by a wide, shallow river and once again they were traveling
through marshy hummocks and clumps of thick rushes and
tall, feathery grasses.

"Toi toi," commented the farmer, pointing to the grass for
her benefit. He lit up another cigarette. Sarah concentrated
on the scene outside the window, watching the straggled
groups of wild-looking cattle. They stood half hidden in the
grasses, and on their backs perched small pure white egrets
pecking the insects from the shaggy coats.

". . . too bad for Mike, eh," the farmer was saying now.
"That boy's no good . . . wouldn't have expected any different, though. Pretty decent of Mike to take him on. But he's
no good for the island . . . a troublemaker. Hear he's a school-
leaver, eh. Most of 'em are, though. Just can't take the work,
I reckon . . . And then it's the gangs. Well, that's his people.
Like I said, can't expect more."

Sarah peered at him from the corner of her eye. He was
talking about *Mako!* She was incredulous at the tone of smug
self-satisfaction in the farmer's voice.

"You know, in my day," continued the farmer, nodding,
"we just didn't have such trouble from our Maori. They were
a good lot, for all they're a bit lazy. But there's a few of these
radical types now, stirrin' things up with all sorts of rubbish . . . Worked with a Maori chap up in Whangarei,
once — *he* was a good bloke, but his sons went to Auckland,
came to no good, eh, with the drink an' gangs . . ."

Unbidden, the words pulsed in her head: "He is important!
Ka tapu te tamaiti!" And over them, softer voiced: "He is
Maori . . . he is angry." She squirmed closer to Pauline, no
longer caring if the farmer noticed. She couldn't bear to be
near this man and his repulsive opinions!

". . . some fool notion it's sacred, or something," the farmer
was saying. She caught her breath. "Been here forty years

now, and no Maori'll go south on the island past Arana. Never
go to Waitapu. Course, keeps trouble out of the place, eh,
especially for the summer people."

Maori wouldn't go south of Arana? Why? She caught her
breath. Why? Her fingers tingled. She shook the premonition
from her.

They had come down off the hills into Waitapu. The street
was lined with twisty pohutukawa, and in the bay a clutter of
boats bobbed in the winter sun. The town of Waitapu was
clustered around the tiny bay, a hodgepodge of drab cinderblock or patched wood buildings, roofed with corrugated tin.
The buildings meandered along the dusty street, one or two
extending up into the low hills above the bay. Every building
had a tiny garden straggling near it, but the plants were with-
ered or bare in the winter cold. A few lemon trees were hung
with fruit, and some dwarf azaleas bloomed where they could
steal the sun from the giant pohutukawa.

There was a hotel in Waitapu, catering to the summer crowd
of yachters and hikers. It was a sprawling, graceless place with
unadorned windows, and a wide sagging verandah over which
hung generations of wisteria in thick ropes. Behind the hotel,
the only school on Great Kauri sat on a slight rise, overlooking
the bay. There was a post office and gas station combined, a
generator shack, and a store that carried everything from frozen sausages to gum boots, chicken feed to dried milk powder.
Waitapu on barge day was a bustling center of activity.

Pauline parked the Land Rover on a dusty patch near the
wharf. The farmer lifted his hat to them and went off. Sarah
looked around her in astonishment. Everyone on Great Kauri
must be here! she thought. Crowding the wharf and the dusty
street was an extraordinary assortment of vehicles. Jeeps and
Land Rovers of indeterminate age and encrusted with mud
and dust jammed up against motorbikes rigged with elaborate

systems for carrying supplies, old cars in various stages of disintegration, shaggy island ponies harnessed to wagons or tethered bareback to the fenders of the nearest truck . . . Even Bob and Fiona's tractor was parked at a crazy angle at the edge of the harbor beach.

The wharf was busy with farmers and sheepmen collecting livestock and supplies, yelling to the barge crew or to the milling pack of dogs that were used to herd sheep and cattle from one place to another. Among the farmers were the other residents of the island: a barefoot woman with a tangle of white-blond children following her, also barefoot and brown-skinned; a number of bearded men wearing clothes that reminded Sarah of photos of hippies in the sixties; a stout British-looking woman dressed in tweeds, carrying a walking stick and followed by an equally stout Labrador dog; a thin boy about her own age wearing a huge pack and gum boots several sizes too large on his bare legs. Waitapu had about it the atmosphere of a carnival, complete with eccentrics, herds of children, recluses, ladies, farmers — the people that made up the island. The hotel had its door open even in the winter chill, and a new vehicle entering the town from down off the hills would blare its horn in greeting as it rumbled down the little street.

Sarah wandered into the store. It was dim, jostling with people who all knew each other, all joking to the owner or to each other. She selected a drink labeled "Lemon and Paeroa" with curiosity, and paid with the heavy, large coins of New Zealand currency. She had left Pauline to organize the unloading of her lab equipment.

Idly, she leaned against a truck and watched the activity on the wharf, sipping the tangy drink. A group of men had just unloaded a group of bulls that threatened to break loose on the street. Three massive dogs harried them, barking on the command of their owners, plunging in to snap or growl. When the bulls were loaded onto a trailer, the dogs crouched tensely, staring through the slats at the animals. The dogs were dark, and their broad thick heads and deep eyes reminded her of Kikiwa. She shifted against the metal fender of the truck, putting the can of juice down on the tailgate.

She jumped back as if stung, looking at the truck. A few wooden crates that needed mending piled in the back, a familiar black denim jacket tossed over the seat in the cab — Mako! He was here somewhere in this milling crowd of people. She looked around. Again she was filled with the uncomfortable tightness, and again the strange words from the morning pounded through her.

But why was Mako here? Hadn't the farmer just said no Maori went south of Arana? She stood tensely by the truck, a confusion of thoughts running through her. *Tapu* . . . *tapu* . . . the words poked at her. Wai*tapu* . . . What did it mean? She shook her head, annoyed. This was all so crazy! That farmer was so ignorant, anyway — what would he know? Of course Mako could come here if he wanted!

When she spotted him, in the midst of a restless group of boys, she shrank into the shadow of the trees. He leaned with the others against the railings of the hotel verandah, surveying with disdainful nonchalance the activities in the street. Some of the boys had cans of beer in their hands, and all of them shared the same darting, boldly restless look.

His was the only dark face. He mimicked the movements and expression of the other boys perfectly, but even from this distance, it seemed to Sarah that Mako was acting a part. Too late, she realized she had stared too intently. He turned and saw her, and she dropped her eyes immediately, breaking contact. The last thing she wanted was to deal with him and his group of nasty friends! She snorted at herself in disgust.

Why would he want to see *her,* anyway? Not with all his friends around, he wouldn't! She stared stonily out toward the wharf.

"Did you get my fish, then?"

She jumped. He had moved up behind her soundlessly, Kikiwa at his side. She glanced nervously at the other boys, who leaned grinning against the verandah, watching.

"Yes, thanks," she said, lifting her head defiantly. He had his hands in his pockets and was kicking at the dust with his foot. Their eyes met for a moment, briefly, and he looked away. She softened.

"She ate it, too," she said. He smiled quickly.

"You here with your mum?" he asked. Sarah nodded.

"She doesn't spend a lot of time with you, eh," he said now, flatly. She bristled.

"She's busy! She's in the middle of some important — "

"Don't bite my head off, eh," he said, so mildly she closed her mouth in surprise. They considered each other for a few seconds. *Your life will touch his for only an instant . . .*

It was true. There were only a few months. After that, she would be a world away, a hemisphere away, in the crisp autumn of a Berkshire prep school . . . And Mako? Where would he be?

She shrugged, grinning a half grin at him in apology. "I guess I get sort of defensive," she said. "I haven't really been around her much since I was six, so it's kind of awkward. She keeps *promising* to spend some time with me, like she wants to make up for something, you know? But she never does . . ."

"I reckon she needs you more than you need her, eh," he said. She cocked her head.

"I guess . . ." She'd never thought of that. She remembered Pauline's words in the Land Rover on the drive down, about wishing it had been different. She shrugged again.

"I reckoned it was like that with my dad," Mako said now. "He needed to see me, to see who I was, eh? An' we didn't know each other, either . . ." He wanted, suddenly, to tell her about his father, how it had been, to meet him for the first time . . . how it had been, to hear about his ancestors, about the great warrior Tawahi . . . He opened his mouth to speak, sure she would understand.

Two farmers with dogs passed quite close by, and they looked sharply at Mako. Sarah bit her lip. No expression passed over the boy's face; his eyes had gone as flat as the sea on a foggy night. The men walked on up the street.

"We gave a ride to a man coming down, and he said Maori didn't come to the south of the island," she said. "He was totally obnoxious. I couldn't stand him."

"So?" he answered, without expression. She met his impassive eyes with determination.

"Why did he say that, then?" she asked stubbornly.

"How would I bloody well know!" he snapped at her. "Bunch of rubbish! I go where I want. No old stupid stories are going to stop me, eh."

"I don't see any other Maori here," she pursued, possessed with some strange recklessness of her own.

"Oh, bugger off!" he yelled at her. The group of boys on the verandah were listening now, laughing.

"Hey, Mako!" they called. "Maybe you shouldn't waste your time with her, eh!"

One or two moved slowly toward them. Kikiwa rose softly without a sound and stood near her; she could feel the rough fur on his head stiffen under her fingers. She leaned toward Mako, the rush of anger and disturbing excitement caught in her low voice.

"I'm sick of talking to you!" she said angrily. She could feel the eyes of the other boys on her. She clenched her fists.

"I'll just ask Hattie!" she taunted, so low only he could hear. "*She'll* know why Maori won't go south of Arana." She did not wait to hear his answer, but stalked away toward the wharf. Behind her, she heard the sniggers of the other boys.

"Eh, Mako!" they were saying. "She's a silly chick! You don't want a Pakeha chick, do ya?"

Her face was stinging with hurt and anger, and something else she could not define. Shame? But it was not her shame — it was shame for him! The boys were as derisive of Mako as they had been of her; she could hear it in their voices even now as she walked away. Why did he let those stupid boys shame him with their voices, their suggestive looks? Why did he even choose to hang out with them?

She wished she could find her mother. She searched the wharf with her eyes. Pauline was arguing with a man on the barge.

"Hi, sweetie," Pauline said distractedly. "Having fun? Look — you don't mind looking around a little longer, do you? The whole shipment is in a mess — they let sea water get on the boxes, and they've left a whole section of it back in Auckland." She turned back to the barge man, and Sarah sat slumped on an upturned crate.

"Pull yourself together, Sarah Steinway!" she said to herself. She looked around her at the disarray of crates and boxes, then over at her mother. It wasn't *her* fault the order had been messed up. This was Pauline's work; she had to put it first.

"How else do you think she got to be so good?" she told herself fiercely as she walked back up to the street. She scuffed her feet in the dust, a wave of loneliness and misery engulfing her. She found herself at the far end of the street and was about to turn back when a neatly lettered sign caught her eye.

"DISTRICT NURSE. SURGERY HOURS: 4 TO 8 P.M. WEEK-DAYS," she read under her breath. Without thinking, she turned up the path and pushed open the door into a tiny waiting room.

Daphne's bright skirts were half concealed by a long white jacket, and the light from the window glinted off her stethoscope. She exclaimed joyfully when she saw Sarah, pushing back her chair and wrapping the girl in a warm embrace.

"What a grand surprise!" she cried, holding both Sarah's hands. "I just was wanting a good chat and a cuppa, and here you are, like magic!"

She swept into the tiny kitchen adjacent to the waiting room and clattered the kettle on the gas.

"Let's see — none of your boring Kiwi garbage for us, eh!" she laughed, poking through the boxes of tea. "How about Mystic Mint — or Lemon Zinger?"

She unwrapped a package of cookies with a flourish and yanked a tray from under the counter. She set the tray on a table and looked over at the girl.

"You're crying," she said calmly. Sarah stood in the doorway with her hands clenched, unable to step in any further.

The nurse took her by the shoulder and led her to a couch. She locked the door coming in to the surgery and sat down next to Sarah. Her hands were so big and warm Sarah wanted to drown in them. She took the tissues the woman handed her and scrubbed at her face.

"I'm sorry," she whispered at last, sniffing. She picked the disintegrated tissue off her hands with jerky movements.

"I hope it's only the tissues you're sorry about, because you've sure made a mess of them," said Daphne softly, putting her cheek for a moment against Sarah's. "I have a feeling you didn't just come in here to hide. I think you came to see *me*. What's up?"

"Everything," said Sarah, her voice so small she hardly recognized it as her own. "It's just that . . . I want to *like* someone — I mean, I want to like *people*, and then they just . . . they just . . ." She shook her head in misery, studying her hands. Daphne got up to take the kettle off the burner.

"They just don't act the way they should?" she asked. Sarah looked up a moment, then nodded.

"I know that sounds awful," she whispered miserably. "It's more that it never turns out the way I think . . . I mean, I was just *talking* to him, and he turns around and gets really horrid! And then Pauline — "

"Him — you mean Mako?" asked Daphne, straining the tea into the cups. Sarah nodded again, not looking at her.

"You like him, don't you?" Daphne said softly, and then, without waiting for an answer, she continued: "He's got a chip on his shoulder a mile deep, that one. Nothing will be predictable with him. You won't be able to expect *anything* from him, Sarah; you'll have to let him be himself."

"Well, what about *me!*" Sarah cried, stung.

"*You* must be *you* — that's all anyone's responsibility is," smiled Daphne. "Here I go, lecturing you again! Look, I have an idea: go find your mum, and tell her you'll stay here the night. We'll turn on the generator and watch a good bit of telly, eh! A real mushy film — and I'll make us a pavlova! How about it?"

Sarah hesitated, thinking of Pauline on the long drive back over the mountains. Maybe they'd really get a chance to talk, since all the worry over the equipment would be done with . . . She looked around the little waiting room, decorated with Daphne's warm touches — the thick yellow curtains, flowered couch cover, brightly braided rug . . . She wanted this warmth and brightness! Pauline could just drive back alone! We wouldn't talk anyway! Sarah thought fiercely.

She'd be all preoccupied with where the stuff was going in the lab or something . . .

"It would be real nice to have a good long chat," said Daphne, watching the hesitation. "Talking always helps sort things out, eh. Pauline can do without you."

She sure has done OK without me this long, thought Sarah, a stubborn determination filling her. She *wanted* to stay with Daphne! She ran out the door and down the little path.

It was almost dark now, and the wharf was lit with flickering bulbs run by a generator. You'd think it would be cheaper just to set the place up with electricity, thought Sarah.

Pauline was still busy, loading her boxes with the help of several men into the Land Rover. She had a little frown on her face that only seemed to enhance her looks. She stopped a moment when she saw Sarah, brushing back her blond hair.

"Well, sweetie, I don't know where you'll fit," she laughed. She glanced at her watch. "Looks like we won't have any time to spend together here, after all — but that's OK! Tomorrow you could come with me to the lab and we could have some time there while I set this stuff up." She gave a brief direction to a man with a heavy box. He deposited it in the passenger side of the Land Rover with a grunt. Pauline laughed.

"How good are you at balancing on the top, sweetheart?" she asked Sarah, looking with exaggerated dismay at the boxes. "That one *has* to go on top, Tom!" she called. "There's no room for my daughter otherwise!"

"Pauline — " Sarah said. She swallowed. "Pauline, Daphne — you know, the nurse? — asked me to stay over. She can bring me back in the morning. You'd have more room — "

"Oh, sweetie!" Pauline said, relief and worry apparent in her voice. "But — all night? You don't mind?"

Sarah shook her head, numb. It doesn't matter! It doesn't

matter! she said to herself. But as she stood on the wharf watching Pauline drive off, she thought she would faint from the lump in her throat. For the second time that day, tears burned at her eyes. She thought of Pauline driving back alone over those dark mountains. Maybe, in the dark, they could have talked about things, things mothers and daughters were supposed to talk about. Maybe she could have told her about Mako . . .

Mako! She dashed the tears from her face. It was his fault she was so miserable! Pauline couldn't help it that her order got messed up — it was Mako with his stupid friends! She stomped up the street, stopping by the steps into the hotel.

She hadn't intended to do this. She didn't even know if he was still here, but his truck was parked where it had been, and the bar at the hotel was lit up. It was just the sort of place he *would* be. She climbed the steps quickly, but hesitated in the open doorway. The bar was full of men and smoke and music.

He saw her from his table in the corner. He got up and came toward her without speaking to the two boys who sat with him. When two people leaving the bar jostled her in the doorway, Mako reached out to steady her.

She pulled free of his hands, and the shock of her look went through the boy like scalding liquid.

"Why don't you just *grow up*," she said fiercely. "You act like a baby — everyone has to pussyfoot around you so you won't get *offended!* I'm sick of you. Why don't you just grow up!"

Their faces were barely three inches apart, and each felt the breath of the other. Their eyes were locked. The light in his eyes reminded her of the old woman. Her breath caught and she swayed slightly toward him. He had to hold her to keep her from losing her balance.

"I have a message for you," she said, her voice like a voice from a dream. "I have a message. *'Ka tapu te tamaiti. Ka tapu te tamaiti.'* "

She was not in control of this. She knew it. But the words that had pounded through her all day had found their way to him. Somehow, she was meant to say them; he was meant to hear.

The face of the boy had gone pale, and his hand on her arm trembled.

"From Aunt Hattie," she whispered. Daphne would be wondering where she was. She turned and went down the steps.

6

A PENDANT OF GOLD AND GREENSTONE

Daphne stopped the truck in Arana and they had a cup of coffee from her thermos while the gas was being pumped.

"Can you check that noise, Peter?" Daphne said, leaning over the open hood and peering into the engine. "You know I can't make head or tail of this!"

Peter Brown grinned and wiped his hands on his jeans.

"What noise would that be, now?" he teased. "For we all know the vocal talents of your fine machine!"

Daphne swiped at him with the old towel she was using to clean the windshield, and Sarah giggled. Being with Daphne on this bright morning made her feel like dancing with open arms on the dunes above the Pacific. How could she have been so miserable yesterday? Last night they had watched a rerun of *Dallas* and eaten the incredibly sweet confection of whipped fruit and sugar Daphne had made. And before that, they had talked.

She didn't want the drive to the Crossroads to end. Daphne smiled over at her and hugged her shoulder. "I'd ask you to come with me, love, but today I've got to fly. And I'm sure Elsie'll go into labor today — she's as big as a cow! And then you'd be stuck lookin' after her other three."

It didn't matter. Today was wonderful! She'd take Celeste, take fish to the albatross (would Mako have brought fish today, after what she'd said to him?), maybe even ride down to the Point to see Pauline at the lab.

"You feel better?" asked Daphne, as she pulled up outside the house. Sarah nodded, her eyes bright.

"Everything you said makes so much sense!" she said. "It's true I have trouble accepting myself . . . I keep wanting to *make* myself into something. But I still have to play the flute — "

"I never meant you had to stop," said Daphne quickly. "Don't take everything I say so much to heart, eh! Scares me! I just meant that once you accept yourself and *like* yourself, you'll find yourself doing the same with other people, too. And that'll make your music so much better — it has to!" She paused, musing.

"Mako's worth getting to know," she said quietly. "He's got to find his own way — no one can tell him; he wouldn't let them. But I don't think, eh, that he'd try to change you or expect you to be anyone but yourself. Not that you'd let him!" She grinned. "And as far as Pauline goes — she's got a few demons of her own to work out. It's good you're here; she'll have to really *look* at you. And it's better for you to see her for who she *is*, instead of turning her into some sort of ideal."

Daphne grinned apologetically to Sarah. "You see, there I go, blathering on at you. Why don't you tell me to stop?"

"I like you to talk to me," answered Sarah, suddenly shy. They looked at each other, smiling. Daphne wrapped her in a hug, and Sarah felt her throat constrict. She waved goodbye as Daphne roared off, feeling a little empty. But the wind from the gulf stirred her thick hair and the sun beat down on her face; she took the steps up the verandah two at a time. There was the package of fish, neatly wrapped with string.

He'd brought it, after all! Even after last night . . .

Celeste walked briskly, her strong head turned into the wind, ears pricked. The horse filled her with joy, the way her mane fluttered over her hands, the way the muscles in the broad shoulders bunched and rippled. The pipits were everywhere, hanging in the wind with their songs.

Sarah reached impulsively behind her and pulled the flute out from her pack. Celeste made no response to the reins being dropped on her neck, but continued steadily up the track. The wind whipped the hair back from Sarah's face, and she lifted the gleaming flute to her lips. The music came from inside; she followed no notes. She was the wind and the sea and the wild little pipit; she was the bellbird hidden in the bush; she was the ancient voice of an old, old woman. Her fingers flew over the keys.

The sound of the flute became part of her, soaring through her high into the morning sky. She *was* music! She was the albatross, spiraling into the brightness!

Mako had been out in the boat since daybreak. The sky had turned from pearly gray to pink to brilliant blue, and now the water sparkled under the wooden keel of the little boat. He navigated carefully along the shoreline, headed down toward Blind Bay. He felt at ease with the boat now, and with the maze of inlets and shoals and hidden rocks that made up the western coast of Great Kauri Island. It had not always been so. Three months ago when he had first arrived, he'd had to learn everything from Mike, swallowing his dislike of his Pakeha stepfather and boiling inside from nameless rage.

And in doing so, he'd learned to fish, learned the waters around the island, spent long hours alone with only the wind and water and the work. On clear days, if he was out far enough, he could just make out the hazy horizon that was

Auckland to the west. He would tune into Radio Hauraki, hear the familiar music and disk jockeys, and gaze homesick toward the city. Back there, on the streets of Otara and Grey Lynn and Mangere, his friends would be hanging out talking and laughing. Thinking of them filled him with almost unbearable longing and pride. They were all descendants of Maori warriors! They carried on the spirit of the true Polynesians, the fighters, the explorers of open ocean! They had only to wait . . . Frustrated and eager, Mako would lean his brown arms on the edge of the boat and stare out over the water toward home.

Kikiwa got nervous if he stayed in this mood too long. The boat would rock gently in the hidden currents that swirled through the myriad bays and coves, and the fishing lines would tremble like a dozen webs cast over a glass-black sea. Kikiwa would stir, rising slowly, and nudge him with his short black muzzle.

"Eh, Kiki!" Mako would laugh, turning back to the tasks of the boat. Bait had to be cut and sorted, lines set, crayfish traps scraped clean of slime and barnacles . . .

Today there was no time for dreaming. Blind Bay was difficult to navigate, but these rocky, shaded inlets and little islands had the best fishing. Already he had six snapper and four crayfish in the ice-filled crates in the hold below deck. If he had this luck all day, he could bring home sixty dollars worth of fish, and Mike would be pleased, maybe even give him an advance.

He worked hard for several hours, moving the boat quietly from inlet to inlet, setting the lines, making sure they did not tangle. He set several traps and tied the marker buoys to them so he could find them the next day. By noon he was in a narrow cove at the far end of Blind Bay, and the sea lay slick and still around him. When the sun was high like this, the fish rested far below and refused to bite. He had an hour or more to rest.

He stood with his back to the wheelshed against the wall. Around him the rock-edged shore, hung with puriri and totara trees, was shadowed with deep ferns over the black-green waters. Shags skimmed from the pohutukawa branches and dove under, fishing. Some days, Blind Bay filled him with depression, closing in around him. He would chafe under the work there, wishing he could fish further out in the gulf, in the open sea with the sky huge over him. There he could truly dream — dream of other worlds, other countries with strange and exciting people, places where ideas were born and lived. On the open waters of the Hauraki Gulf he could imagine himself as his ancestors must have been, filled with the same restless, driving excitement to explore, to push past the boundaries of tiny islands, to navigate by star and wind and the taste of the sea, to come to a new land, leaving behind the old stories, to build a new world . . .

But today, he enjoyed the close secret waterways of Blind Bay. He felt hidden and safe here. Today, the anger that caught him without warning time after time lay quiet and passive within him. He coiled the limp fishing lines thoughtfully. Sometimes it seemed to him his anger was *not* him, that it was a separate entity that tormented him and entered him and made him speak.

That's what happened when he was with the girl. He thought of her as "the girl," although sometimes he said her name under his breath to himself, liking the soft full sound of it. He stood now, the coiled lines dangling from his hands. Why had he screamed at her the other day? Every time they'd met, it seemed, they left in anger. Why? He hadn't meant to get angry, not at her. But those boys! They'd been taunting him; he'd had to save face, to carry on with them as if he didn't care. Stupid Pakeha boys!

He wished he was with his father. It was uncountable, how many times he'd wished that during the last year. Henare Mokutu was a big man, filled with passion and the voice to speak it. Mako's lips parted, remembering that first meeting. His father had come to find him. He had given him a name, and a past: he was Mako, and he was a descendant of Tawahi, chief of the Ngati Niwha! Then, six months later, Mokutu had left Auckland for a trip to America. In America, he said, blacks and Chicanos and Native Americans were taking their voice out of the shadow of oppression. In America, he said, people were beginning to listen. But here in New Zealand, the Pakeha still slept fitfully to the dying lullaby of a forgotten and corrupt Empire. And while they slept, Aotearoa shriveled and died under their hands.

Aotearoa belongs to the Maori! His father had cried out those words over the still crowd of listeners in an Auckland square. The face with its fierce *moko* had twisted with passion. Aotearoa must join the rest of the world, must enter the twentieth century led by the warriors of her rightful people!

Now, remembering, Mako felt the same thrill he had felt then. His father's words were powerful and disturbing. He knew how to use words, Pakeha words. Those words had become Mako's own; he shaped a dream around them. But with them had come the anger, the blinding force that consumed him and led him to lash out at people. His aunt at last had turned him away; he'd left school. But inside, he formed his silent, determined plan. With his money he would buy a boat, and with his newfound skills, he would make a living himself along the waters of the Coromandel where his father lived. And together Henare Mokutu and he would build the

ideas that would force New Zealand into the twentieth century! And he, Mako, had his own voice, his own secret with
which, someday, he would speak so that people would listen . . .

Sitting with his lunch on the warm deck, he pulled from
his pocket a thick packet of folded papers and a broken pencil.
Slowly, he unfolded the papers, turning so they would not be
blown by the wind. His mouth forming the words to himself,
he read through them. These were his, his most secret self.
Every day for months, now, he had written poems on the
cheap schoolchild paper bought at the store in Waitapu.

And every day on the boat, during the hour or so of calm,
he read them over, crossing things out, rewriting, struggling
with the spelling and punctuation and meaning. At night, in
that time he lay awake before sleep found him, words and
phrases would run through his head, so that sometimes he
had to turn on the light and mark them down.

What was he, Mako, doing writing poems! He could hardly
even read! He would never have the courage to show them
to anyone, or even to talk to someone about them. Anyway,
who could he talk to? Sometimes he thought of Russell, up
at Port William — he had all those books, eh; he would know
about these things! But Russell might dismiss them with a
snort and a wave of his hand . . . And Mako knew, somehow,
that if he could not write down these strange words, these
unquiet thoughts, he would die inside.

So he wrote alone, struggling and sweating over words,
over ideas that swam half formed and indistinct through his
mind. Reading them over today, he was as always surprised
that the voice that came through the poems was not angry or
disdainful. Instead, the words sounded strong and steady to
him, so that sometimes they did not seem to be his at all. He

wished he knew the Maori language, as his father did; he would rather write in Maori.

The poem on the top of the pile was one he'd written two days ago. He read it over now, frowning. He had rewritten it twice. It was about the girl, who was never far from his thoughts.

"Who is she!" he whispered fiercely to himself now. Kikiwa whimpered at the tone in his voice, watching him from deep eyes. "She's a kid — a Pakeha kid!"

But the words she had said to him in the bar that night in Waitapu haunted him. He had written them down on the back of the poem, so he would remember them. *"Ka tapu te tamaiti."* What did they mean? Russell would know — he was Maori, from the King country, where they still spoke Maori. But he shrank from the idea. Somehow, these words were meant only for him.

The girl had spoken them, but she had not known what they meant. He knew that. He thought of her, how she had seemed so defiant standing in the door of the busy bar. He remembered how the heavy light had fallen on her face and on her thick wavy hair. When he reached out to her, it was as much to steady himself as her. She had jumped under his touch; his fingers curled now, remembering. She really hated him! She had scorned him. It bothered him more than he cared to admit, that she scorned him.

And that bloody stupid old woman in the bush — what had she to do with him! Why he still fished for the girl he did not know. It made him so nervous that the girl saw that old witch every day. It was the old woman who had spoken those words; the girl had merely carried them to him.

Over the edge of the boat, a line twitched, then another. Mako shook the unease from him and folded his poems into the tight wad. The lines jerked taut. He had two at once, and all thoughts were buried in the action of the moment. Snapper — big ones. They brought the best prices in the posh Remuera and Queen Street restaurants. He barely finished gutting them when the lines jerked again. He ran to pull them in before they tangled the lines under the boat.

The hold in the boat was getting full. Mako peered down into the ice, a reluctant pride filling him. This was good. It was easier on his mother and little sisters, when the fishing was good. There was more money, and Mike was good-humored. He pulled in three more snapper and checked his watch. It would take him more than an hour to get back to the jetty, and he still had to get the fish up to Mike and the seaplane at Karaka Bay. He closed the hatch, coiled up the lines, and headed the boat back up Blind Bay.

At the wharf in Port William, the seaplane bobbed gently against the pilings. Mike leaned easily against a post, talking to the pilot, the glow from their cigarettes adding to the calm of early evening. Mako backed the truck down the wharf and jumped out.

"Long day," commented Mike.

"Worth it, eh," said the boy shortly. "Close to seventy, seventy-five dollars, I reckon. Snapper were biting."

Mike grunted, pleased. The restaurants would pay him well. They could advertise "Caught in the Islands" and "Gulf Specials" tomorrow night.

"Good on you, mate," said Mike quietly, putting his hand briefly on the boy's shoulder. For once, Mako did not jerk away.

"Fat check Monday, eh!" Mike grinned over at the pilot, including Mako in his glance. "Here's an advance — earned yourself a beer, eh! Don't get Russ in trouble, though — tell him you're drinking it for me!"

The men chuckled. Mako folded the twenty neatly.

"I'll push you off," he said flatly. Mike climbed in beside the pilot and Mako slammed shut the door after him. The little plane trundled off across the bay, wing and tail lights winking on. With a roar and swath of spray, it lifted off into the dusk and wheeled toward the lights of Auckland.

Mako decided he really could use a beer, so he wandered up to Russell's bar and pushed open the door. It was still early, and only one man leaned against the plywood bar. The bare bulbs and flypaper hung above the tables stirred when the door opened. Russell Johnson had come north from the King country ten years ago, a Maori who seemed to have no ties to anyone. He'd built his bar and managed to survive on this lonely end of Great Kauri Island. Everyone liked Russell; he was an easy sort, well spoken, and could tell a better story than anyone around.

Russell was polishing glasses with one eye on the television news. When he saw Mako he smiled.

"G'day, kid," he said. "Haven't seen you in a while — reckoned you'd gone back to town."

"Nah," the boy said, perching on a stool. "Wish I could, eh."

"Drinking a beer for Mike, then?" grinned Russell, drawing a draft into a glass. The boy shrugged. He was underage, but the occasional beer went unnoticed by anyone official in this remote place. He was careful not to overuse his privilege. He liked Russell, and not just because he was Maori. The man kept his own counsel, treated Mako as a friend and an equal with an ease that communicated his sincerity. No one knew what had brought Russell to Great Kauri. He lived alone in a tiny house connected to the bar by a doorway covered in a heavy blanket. Mako had been inside once; the walls of the living room were lined with books.

"Have you read them all?" he'd asked Russell, scorn mixed with a desperate curiosity. Books meant school — Pakeha school. But at Russell's they filled him with an excitement he could not fathom. He wanted to take them, handle them, and more than that — he wanted to *know what was in them*. Something stirred in him at the sight of gilt-edged leather, the titles marching across the shelves. But his face remained impassive. He would not announce his ignorance to Russell.

Tonight they watched the news together at the bar. World news . . . national . . . weather . . . a report on a political rally in Auckland. The camera panned over the crowd, then focused on the speaker. Mako recognized the campus of Auckland University. Suddenly he leaned forward.

"My father!" he cried softly. "That's my father!"

Russell put the glasses down thoughtfully, gazing at the television.

"That your daddy, Mako?" he asked. He'd heard of this man. He didn't like him. Something was off-balance with him . . . but the boy obviously worshiped him.

"A strong voice," Russell commented carefully. Mokutu's words could be heard behind the newscaster's. The man was dangerous — a self-centered energy, playing to emotions and to frustrations rather than to intelligence. A voice to stir violence.

"Everyone listens to him!" said Mako proudly, without taking his eyes from the screen. His father — in Auckland again! For how long? How could he get to see him?

"I should be there with him!" the boy cried, fervent. "I'm wasting my time here! Everything's beginning to happen, and I should be there!"

"You don't have that much hate, boy," said Russell quietly, knowing his words were poking a hornet's nest. But there was something about this kid, something worth watching — something that should not be wasted on the pointless raging of this man Mokutu.

The boy was looking at him half quizzically, half annoyed.

"I should have, then," he answered. "It's the only way, Russell! A Maori-run New Zealand."

"Naw," said the older man, his face still impassive. "You're too smart for that. Too much of value would be lost — and it's not even practical."

"You think there's a better way?" demanded the boy.

"There's plenty who think so," Russell said dryly. "The only way that'll work will be smart men and women with real vision — not ranting and raving." He jabbed his finger at the screen, knowing already that he'd gone too far. The boy was glowering at him.

"Don't get all fussed," said Russell quietly. "Man's entitled to his opinions, eh. Lot of people with different ideas. Got a good story — heard it first somewhere in Northland, then heard it again on the East Cape. Want to hear?"

Mako leaned his elbows on the bar. The anger drained reluctantly from him. Russell snapped the television off. The other customer had left the bar, and they were alone.

"Once," began Russell, "not many generations ago, there was a man who many believed was the fulfillment of an ancient prophecy. The prophecy spoke of a teacher who would come not only to lead the Maori from European oppression, but to lead the Europeans into understanding and respect toward the people they shared this island with. And in turn, this understanding would serve as an example to all the world. Not only Maori believed in this man; a great many Pakeha listened as well. But like many great teachers, the man was persecuted and outlawed until finally, in sorrow, he died.

"A long time passed, but the memory of this teacher lived strongly in the lives of the people who had heard him. Even-

tually, all the man's teachings were outlawed by the Pakeha,
along with the Maori language in which they had been taught.
It seemed that the prophecy had proved false.

"Many people were puzzled. The prophecy had indicated
that the teacher would *never* die, that he would live until
both Maori and Pakeha were brought to peace in the same
land. So they thought the prophecy had failed.

"But those people had misinterpreted the prophecy. It was
that the *message* of the teacher would never die. Although
outlawed, the teachings would still live, passed from one student to another in secret, until both Maori and Pakeha had
grown enough to be ready to listen and accept the message.

"Many generations have passed since the death of that first
teacher. But the message still lives even now, in secret, in
some one person. When that person nears death, the teachings are passed on to another person, chosen to receive the
message just as the first teacher chose someone to receive it
before he died. In this way, the power and strength of the
teacher's vision will never be lost.

"No one knows in what form the message will come, or
when the teachings can be spoken openly. Both Maori and
Pakeha must be ready to listen, to put aside hatred and violence. But when that time comes, there will be a person to
speak the message — a person who carries the true power of
the prophecy within.

"And how will this person be known? There is a sign, a
physical sign, passed with the message from each keeper to
the next, and only if this sign is seen will we know if what is
spoken is true. Around the neck, the keeper of the message
will wear a pendant of gold and greenstone, carved by that
very first teacher. There is no pendant like it anywhere on
earth. It is carved from the rarest greenstone, and woven

through by threads of pure gold, hammered from a European coin.

"The gold is the Pakeha, and the greenstone is the Maori; each was taken from the earth of Aotearoa. Somewhere, around some person's neck, this secret pendant hangs, and within the mind of that person lives the teachings that will be the salvation of Aotearoa.

"This is the story that I have heard. No one owns this story; it is spoken, and it is heard, and I share it with you."

The voice hung in the air, a living presence. Then, with an explosion, Mako reacted.

"I can't believe you listen to such rubbish!" he yelled. "Don't you know something made up by the Pakeha when you hear it? Eh! Our stories are all lost, Russell. They were stolen by the Pakeha and twisted into stupid fairy tales for their children. Prophecies . . . teachers . . . they mean nothing anymore! They only hold the Maori back."

The boy leaned toward the older man, his voice vehement.

"My mother believes in the old stories, eh! She won't go south of Arana — on her own island! Some rubbish thought up by the Pakeha to keep the Maori out of Waitapu. And there's hundreds of these stories, and hundreds who listen. It's time they listen to the truth!"

Mako's voice had become deep and resonant. Russell watched mesmerized as the boy's face became infused with the heat of a terrific intent.

"The stories, the true stories, are lost! Lost! There are only people left . . . living people. There can be no past, for the past has been twisted beyond recognition. There can only be the future! While women wait for teachers preaching love and freedom, sons and husbands lie in prisons for the insane. You have only to look to see that this is so.

"There are only the people who live *now!* The people who speak *now.* There is no room for old stories. Those stories cannot be trusted. There can only be new stories! There can only be the future!"

An eerie darkness had closed in around Russell. He could see only the boy's face, hear only the boy's voice — this boy who was not a boy. He was being held in a spell. But the black eyes blinked suddenly, shimmered, became a boy's eyes again . . .

"I want another beer," Mako said, hoarse.

Russell hesitated, but poured another lager.

"That's the last then," he said quietly. He was still the boss here; the boy was a boy. Mako wiped the froth from his mouth and left, hardly nodding a goodbye. Russell could see lines of exhaustion tightening the young face.

The man closed up the bar for the night, earlier than usual. He moved with slow deliberation, wiping the counter, straightening the stools. Once he paused, looking out into the darkness. In his eyes a light flickered for an instant, and disappeared.

Mako rolled the truck quietly up to the house, shutting off the headlights. It was late, and his mother and sisters would be asleep. He leaned his head briefly against the steering wheel, utterly drained. He rubbed his eyes impatiently.

He wasn't ready to sleep. He sprawled on the couch, watching the flickering light of the telly without turning up the sound. When the music came to him through the wall, low and plaintive, the girl's touch was clear in the notes. But as he listened, the music gained intensity, taking on a life of its own, and he felt oddly bereft, wanting to hear the girl inside the song. He wanted to see her as she played her flute. He wanted to see how her fingers moved over the slender pipe,

to see how she sat, to see if her eyes were opened or
closed . . .

The door to the flat was not locked, and he pushed it open
silently. The only light on was the one in her room, and he
could see her clearly.

He thought he had never seen anything so wonderful. He
held his breath. The music came from her and she played
within it. He watched the dark line of her brows, how they
were tight with concentration. She perched on the edge of
the bed, her hair tumbling thickly over her shoulders, her
whole body curving up to meet the flute at her lips. He, too,
was held at that point, feeling himself tremble inside.

She saw the movement and looked up. He was sure she
would be afraid, and he had already moved back to leave. But
she simply looked at him.

He knew he had invaded more than her room. The enormity
of his invasion caught him; he could only wait, watching her.
Was he an intruder, or a friend? He did not know; she would
have to tell him.

"It's OK," she said softly. "You can come in if you want."

"I wanted to see you play."

"It's OK," she said again, still looking at him calmly with
her fingers positioned on the last keys she had played. The
flute rested in her lap.

"I do not know if we are friends. I want to know," he said
to her simply. It was very simple. She would answer him,
and then he would know. He wondered why he had not
thought of this before. Still, he could not move closer to her
from the dark doorway.

"We have no say in the matter," she told him.

"What does that mean?"

"It means we are friends."

He smiled at her, happy. Sarah saw he had a perfect smile, curved at the ends like the wingtips of a bird.

"Will you play again?" he asked her.

"Do you want me to?"

He nodded, leaning against the door frame. She lifted the flute to her lips, her neck arched, her back curving up gracefully. She played for several minutes; when she looked, he was gone.

7

"THIS ISLAND HAS SECRETS!"

It was halfway through winter in the Southern Hemisphere, and Sarah pulled another sweater over her head as she rode along the track. It was late June — back home, it would be getting hot and muggy. She smiled. Celeste's hooves crunched in the cold grass at the road's edge.

It was late morning. She had fed the albatross already. The old woman had not been near the hut, but there were many days when she was not around. The albatross ate on her own now; she no longer had to have the fish mashed and shoved down her throat. Still, she was a wild animal, hissing and striking out with her beak if Sarah came too near. The sores on her neck were healing slowly.

Sarah did not know where Hattie was on the days she was not at the hut. She imagined the old woman was out fishing or gathering things along the shore; she never asked. Today, she had swept out the little pen with a rough broom, cleaned the moss, and run to the stream to fill the water bucket. The fire in the clearing was cold and white; Hattie had been gone since before sunup.

Instead of turning back toward Port William, Sarah rode up Circle Mine Road to the north. She wanted to explore the beaches at the far tip of the island. Once past the bush where Bob and Fiona lived, the terrain changed. It became high and hilly, folding around her in gullies and ridges swept with wind. The grass here was dull and sparse, and the sheep that ran through these hills were thin and skittery with ragged wool dragging the dust. There were no trees apart from an occasional stand of manuka, the wiry-trunked scrub bush the farmers used for firewood. Sarah was learning the names of birds and plants, and the guidebooks she carried in her pack had become dog-eared from use.

She had never been interested in birds or plants before — she supposed it was because she'd lived in New York all her life. But here, where life seemed so fragile and sparse, every flicker of movement and every hint of growth caught her eye. She had learned a lot about Great Kauri, and about New Zealand in general. She had learned that there had been no mammals on these islands formed from the sea — only birds. Over the last two centuries, European settlers had introduced dozens of foreign animals, all spelling disaster for the native birds and plants. The whalers of the early nineteenth century had stripped Great Kauri of the strong straight kauri tree for use as ships' masts, and the settlers had come after them with sheep and foreign grasses which sucked the nutrients from the ravaged soil. And Great Kauri Island was a tiny mirror for the rest of New Zealand.

Now, when she looked out over the hills, she saw the sharp-hooved sheep cutting into the thin topsoil, she saw the wind blowing the precious earth into dust. Now she recognized the ocher-colored caps of bare earth along the ridges as erosion. She saw the damage done by the kikuyu grass, introduced from Africa, which grew rampant and matted all over the island, suffocating native growth. Mari had told her that all the bush on Great Kauri was "second growth" — what grew back after the first massive forest cover was destroyed. Never again would the island tower with giant kauri trees hundreds of feet above the sea.

She was startled from her musings by the frightened squawk of a pukeko, and she laughed aloud when Celeste threw up her head in mock terror.

"You goose!" she giggled at the horse. "You know better than to be scared of those silly birds!" The pukeko scrambled out of the hummock grass and ran across in front of them, its white tail-patch flashing. She laughed again at the sight of the bird trying to race on long red legs and feet three times too big for its body.

The road curved near to the cliffs. It was an unfriendly landscape she was in, without a single sign of human touch — yet every hill had been stripped by humans. She thought, It must be like after a bomb drops, and everyone leaves . . . She tethered Celeste to a manuka stump and scrambled down toward the cliff edge. She could see the ocean, far more open than the bays around Port William. She leaned against the rocks, watching the waves crashing below her. A gull wheeled in, screaming. She was so alone up here! Who would know where to look for her? . . .

She shifted her position carefully, and when her head brushed the rock, she heard the hollow, booming pulse of waves coming through the stone. She worked her way to a place where the ledge was wider, and stopped again to press her ear against the rough rock. The throbbing was louder, and she pulled back, breathing hard. How creepy! she thought. But the lovely, pulsing sound of the water intrigued her, and she wondered how it could sound as if it came from *within* the rock.

The ledge widened further, and the cliff face was split in places with tiny crevices. She found a large one and wiggled the whole upper part of her body in to explore the sound.

She hung in utter darkness, and from below in the blackness a cold breath seemed to wrap itself around her. The watery thumping entered her and became part of her own pulse, became voicelike. She could almost make out words. With a gasp she jerked herself out of the bottomless crack and scrambled up the cliff to the top, lying breathless and trying to quiet her shaking. What had she heard? Her reason told her it was simply that the cliffs were hollowed in places, and that the water came in underneath. But why that fear — as if she had heard something she was not meant to hear?

She let the weak winter sun warm her in the thick grass before standing up. She was a distance from Celeste, so she could not quite see the horse behind the rise of a hill. She stood still for a moment, the last tightness diminishing. She became aware of a sound over the wind — a low, irregular bleating. Over a hill came a tightly packed mob of sheep followed by a man on a farm bike. Two dogs ran tirelessly around the small herd.

When he was close enough, the farmer waved cheerfully to her. She waved back, almost wildly, relieved to see another person. The sheep moved steadily closer, and over the wind Sarah heard the man whistle to the dogs. A long blast, and the sharp-faced animals immediately dropped to the earth. A series of short sharp whistles caused them to crawl up, closer and closer to the sheep. The herd had stopped, watching the dogs nervously. Another blast, and the dogs once again dropped. Down, crawl, down, crawl, crouch, and stare — between the man and the two dogs, the sheep were completely mesmerized and stood in a tight group without moving. Only then did the farmer zip around the edge and come to a stop in front of Sarah.

"G'day, love!" he called out, lifting his hat, exposing a weather-lined face. He was a young man, and his eyes beamed happily at Sarah.

"You're a long way from anywhere, eh!" he said, sitting back on the worn seat of his motorbike. "You'll be the American girl, then? Don't see anyone up here, most times."

Sarah smiled at him, feeling almost foolish after her fright. It was strange to be immediately recognized as "the American girl" — but on this island, all things were known.

"I thought I'd explore all the way around," she said, waving toward the north where Circle Mine Road doubled back down to the south. The farmer looked at her with frank curiosity.

"You're a cheeky one, comin' up here on your own!" He grinned. "Nothin' but wind and sheep and secrets up here, eh!" The dogs broke their crouch and darted in at the restless sheep. The man spoke sharply and they froze.

"Movin' this mob south," he said now, studying his herd. "My winter grazing's gone — the summer was that bad." He fiddled with the handles of his idling bike.

"Do you ride your bike to herd sheep?" Sarah asked curiously. "Why don't you ride a horse?"

"Horses are good for real high country, but the bike'll do for this place," he explained. "My dogs and my bike — couldn't do without 'em!" He patted the mud-encrusted machine with affection. He lit a cigarette, cupping his hand against the wind and looking at her over his fingers.

"Where've you been, then, on your explores?" he asked, tilting his head back to inhale the smoke.

"Just down to the cliffs there — " She hesitated. "Are they hollow inside? I heard the water . . . it was kind of scary . . ."

He looked at her with quiet amazement. "You climbed down over the cliffs, love? That was a daft thing to do, eh!"

He smiled at her softly. "An' they're scary; they are that."

She squinted up at him, against the sun, but his face told her nothing.

"What did you mean, there's nothing here but wind and secrets?" she asked.

The young farmer shifted on the seat, looking away from her and pursing his mouth in an embarrassed way.

"Oh, just a load of Maori rubbish, I reckon," he said. "I only meant you shouldn't be climbin' around on those cliffs, eh. Full of holes, an' all." He stared off over the empty landscape.

"It *was* scary," said Sarah steadily. "It was like I was hearing something I shouldn't have, you know? Is this Maori land, or something?"

"Maori land?" he said. "Nah — it's just common grazin' up here. Don't know who owns it, truth t'tell. I reckon it *was* all Maori land once, though. They say . . ." His voice trailed off.

"What?" she said quickly.

"Well, I heard the cliffs was used for buryin' — where they put the bones, or some such things." He laughed nervously. "Like I said, load of rubbish, most likely. This place'll get to you up here — I don't come up 'less I have to." He paused, pushing his hair back under his hat.

"It'd be a long time ago, anyway, love," he smiled, seeing her face. "The cliffs have been mined since then — fellow figured he'd get copper from 'em. Guess he made a good go of it, makin' a good livin' for himself, when all of a sudden the mines flooded an' he lost most of his men an' all his business, eh! That was more 'n a hundred years back, I reckon. Nothin' up here since but sheep!"

She could feel the wind cutting through her sweaters. She rubbed her arms, shivering.

"This island has secrets," the man was saying, nodding his

head. "Load of silly stories, eh — but this part of the island gives me the willies! I'll be like Maori, not goin' south of Arana, eh!" He laughed. "C'mon, love, hop up. I'll give you a lift to your horse. Wouldn't like to leave you here alone."

"I was alone when you saw me," Sarah pointed out, climbing on the motorbike behind him.

"I'll feel better when I see you on that horse," he answered firmly, and they bumped along the track following the sheep until she saw Celeste grazing patiently where she'd left her. The horse whickered when she saw them.

"That's a good horse," commented the farmer. "Used to be Russell's over to the bar in Port William. Know him?"

She shook her head, smiling at him and waving goodbye. When he was a quarter mile off, she scrambled on Celeste and slowly followed. She wanted to get back to the flat where she could start a fire in the grate and warm herself, play her flute, shake some of the strangeness from her . . .

The days of her summer were passing, but New York seemed very far away, the Berkshire prep school no more than a hazy dream. Great Kauri Island had entered her bloodstream, and her days were full of the wind and riding and the sea, of Daphne and Mari and the albatross, and sometimes, of Mako. He came and went in his truck, fishing most days, and when they saw each other they smiled quickly, dropping their eyes, saying only the briefest of words. But she was very aware of him.

The old woman had not spoken of him for a week. Sarah brought the fish for the bird, and on the days Hattie was there, the old woman seemed preoccupied and distracted, and spoke very little. Sarah sometimes played her flute in the little clearing, and it seemed to her the woman's face would warm a bit, a flicker of quiet entering the sea-blue eyes, but nothing was said.

One day she got back from the bush to find both Mike and Mako leaning on the railing of the verandah. She turned Celeste out in the paddock and walked slowly back. She almost went in the back door, into the kitchen to avoid them, but Mike had already seen her. He greeted her with his big voice and expansive gestures.

"Sighted a school of killer whales, off the Point!" he said, pointing toward the gulf. "Beautiful creatures — but they'll scare the fish to hell an' back, damn them!" He laughed good-naturedly. "Don't want to miss this, eh, love — I'd go with you, but I have to get the truck to Arana to the mechanic." He nodded to his stepson.

"Take the big boat — I want you to get in some practice with it, anyway. I've filled her with petrol," he said. Turning to Sarah, he said: "It'll be good fun, eh! Mari tells me you spend all day on your own — time Mako played host, eh!" He punched the boy playfully on the shoulder. Mako, his face flat, looked at the ground.

Sarah smiled at Mike uneasily. He was making Mako take her out on the boat! That would mean they'd have to be alone with each other — she didn't want that! Her shoulders slumped, and her stomach jumped inside her. She remembered the unreal night when Mako had come to watch her play the flute. They hadn't really spoken since then. There was no animosity in their avoidance; it was that neither wanted to make the next move.

They didn't speak until Mako pulled the truck to a stop beside the wharf in Port William.

"I don't mind if we don't go," she began. "I mean, we don't have to tell him."

"He'll see the petrol wasn't used," replied Mako shortly.

"Well, *you* go out," she said. "I can take a walk or something."

"Bugger it!" he snapped. "Just let's go — it's no big deal."

She bit back a reply and helped him throw off the ropes from the holdings. She jumped down into the boat and went to the prow, where she could stand without seeing him.

He's really nervous, too, she thought, staring out into Karaka Bay. She wasn't sure why either of them should be so ill at ease. The night when she had played her flute for him seemed so far away.

Mako moved the boat slowly through the few moored crafts near the wharf, and opened the throttle wider once they were out in the bay. He called down to her.

"Take these," he said. "See if you can spot them."

She took the binoculars and went back to the front. The wind slashed through her hair and cut across her skin like a whip. She squinted through the lenses, trying to keep her eyes from tearing up in the wind. All she could see was an expanse of choppy gray water and the hazy darker gray of the other gulf islands on the horizon. Killer whales — she shivered with sudden excitement. She had never seen whales.

"That all you brought to wear?" yelled Mako against the wind. She looked back at him and nodded, shrugging.

"You'll catch it," he said bluntly. He bent down, one hand still on the wheel, and rummaged in a wooden box. He held out a worn yellow slicker, but she shook her head, turning away. With a grimace of annoyance, he left the wheel and walked down to her.

"C'mon," he said. "C'mon, put it on, eh. Look — this'll be good fun. Don't worry — it'll be OK."

She pulled the slicker on over her sweaters and the wind was blocked immediately. Reluctantly she smiled at him, and he returned her smile so simply that she felt all her reserve melt. This time, she could hold his eyes for a second without feeling that her throat would close off her breathing.

"OK," she said softly. He went back to the wheelshed and she searched through the binoculars across the expanse of sea for the whales.

They were near the tip of Miner's Point, and Mako called out to her. He pointed out the drab buildings of Pauline's laboratory, and she could just make out the Land Rover parked near a doorway. No one was about. The boat continued out, leaving the protection of the bay and headed into the open gulf. Her face was burning from the cold and spray, her hair a tangled mat over the yellow slicker. She lurched against the side as she made her way back to the wheelshed; the water had become noticeably rougher.

"I need a break, eh!" she laughed, and Mako looked at her amazed, a broad grin on his face.

"Crikey!" he said. "You're turning into a regular Kiwi!" He moved back from the wheel and gestured.

"Here, you take her," he directed, reaching to pull the binoculars from around her neck. "I'll look out for a while."

The strap of the glasses had tangled fast in her hair, so that he had to touch her to get them. Their eyes glanced off each other, startled. His hand felt warm in her hair.

She jerked away. "I can't drive a boat!" she cried in a strangled voice. She pulled the binoculars roughly over her head, tearing her hair. He took them silently.

"There's nothing to it," he said. "Just keep her pointed that way." He waved his hand. "I won't be a minute."

She kept her hands clenched around the wheel, staring ahead of her. Through the wheel, she could feel the vibration of the motor. It was a pleasant sensation, and she relaxed, looking around her. Miner's Point had dropped away to a thin haze to her left, and back to her right, she could just make out the coves and headlands marching up from Karaka Bay.

At the front of the boat Mako suddenly jumped up onto a

coil of rope, jamming the binoculars to his eyes with one hand while he steadied himself against the side. He lowered them, peering, then looked again.

"There they are!" he cried. They forgot everything in their excitement. He ran back to her, pushing the glasses into her hands, and switched the motor to idle. He grabbed her hand and pulled her to the front of the boat. They tripped and stumbled in their eagerness, laughing. The wind buffeted them roughly so that it was hard to hold the glasses.

She could see them now. The water seemed alive with them. Sleek black backs and dorsal fins sliced through the grayness. She cried out softly, in wonder. There must be dozens! she thought.

"Can't we get closer?" she demanded, turning to Mako.

He grinned, but she could see the excitement in his eyes.

"Want a bit of danger?" he teased. She looked at the whales — killer whales. Were they dangerous? But Mako was laughing.

"I reckon I can bring her up a bit," he said. "They aren't dangerous — they're beauts! Look how they play, eh. I seen 'em once or twice, never this close, though."

He opened the throttle again and the boat chugged steadily forward through the choppy waves. She watched the whales, gripping the sides.

"Shut the motor! Shut the motor!" she cried. "Look! They're coming toward us!"

Mako switched the key, and they rocked in sudden silence on the water. He threw the anchor over the side and ran to join Sarah. It was very still after the drone of the motor. Only the sea gulls cried above them, and the water slapped against the wooden hull.

The whales were close enough now so they could see them clearly without the binoculars. They swam with a slow, rhythmical grace of gleaming backs and fins, the white patches behind the dorsals flashing in the light when the animals broke the surface. They could hear the sharp whoosh of air through the blowholes now.

"They're coming right over to us," Sarah breathed. They leaned as far out as they could, shoulders almost touching, hands gripping the side of the boat.

"What beauts," Mako whispered, as caught in the wonder now as she was. "Cheeky devils, eh!" He laughed softly. "Can't figure us."

And it did seem as if the whales, now surrounding the boat, were curious, puzzling them out. They were huge, some as long as the boat. They moved with such gentleness and deliberation that Sarah felt no fear. She counted fourteen of them. Sometimes one would slide by no farther away than an arm's length; instinctively, she reached out her hand. A few whales slid off, wandering under the boat, beyond them. Several hung just beyond her reach, suspended in the clear sea, rolling slightly in the currents so their gleaming white underbellies flashed up from the darkness. She could see the eyes clearly: perfect, intelligent eyes, bright with curiosity and calmness; they were watching *them*. When they lifted to breathe, the air pulled in sharply through the blowhole, Sarah felt herself pulling in her own breath.

One young whale drifted nearer, watching them with his lovely expressive eye. He hung just below them, then lifted effortlessly until his dorsal fin brushed their hands with a whisper of touch. He floated quietly and they stroked his back, feeling the aliveness of the animal, the firm coolness of the skin. He listed gently under their touch, his eye never leaving theirs. Mako's hand swept back, covered hers for the space of a breath; she did not jerk away. The whale held them both in a spell.

When he sank softly away from them, it was not a retreat or rejection, but merely a realigning of the creature with the currents that held him. He, too, moved under the boat, so close it rocked slightly with his passing. Now all the whales were moving together northward, once again rising and falling in timeless rhythm through the water.

Then, for no apparent reason, when they were a short distance off, a whale suddenly leapt free of the sea, twisting his sleek body high in the air and falling back with an explosion of spray. Then another leapt, and another, apparently for no reason other than the sheer joy of breaking free into another element.

And then Sarah and Mako were alone again on the gulf.

They did not find their voices until Mako had put the boat back in line toward Karaka Bay, and the motor was once more throbbing steadily under them. Sarah stood with him in the wheelshed.

"Every day, you go out alone — out here?" she asked. She tried to imagine him in such solitude.

He shrugged. "Nah, I don't come this far out, mostly. I fish the bays."

He shifted his weight against the wall, wanting to talk to her. It was hard to start; what would she want to talk about? But they had just shared the whales . . .

"I didn't like it at first, eh," he said slowly. "But now, every day, I can go out, just me and Kiki . . . It's . . ." He couldn't finish; it was too hard to explain.

"I'd like it," she nodded, and he saw to his surprise that she understood. "I'd sit and play my flute, and think about things."

"I think about things," he said quickly.

"What do you think about?"

He flushed. But she was looking at him, waiting.

"Oh, I don't know — home, I reckon. And my dad . . ."

She nodded, serious. It was what *she* might think about. They said nothing for a while.

"You get homesick, don't you?" she asked then. He felt a rush of something filling his throat, and turned his head away.

"At night, sometimes . . ." he said. "I can see the glow from the lights, way down on the horizon. Sometimes I just sit on the jetty, eh, looking out there . . ."

So that's why he came home so late. She'd imagined him out drinking with his friends, or roaring around in his truck. She tilted her head.

"Next year," she told him, "I will be away at school, and I'll miss New York. I can already feel it."

He caught the loneliness in her voice. What was it like, where she came from? It was so far away, he could hardly fathom such a distance. He wished she would tell him about her home.

So she told him. He loved the sound of her voice, and the way her face glowed from the wind and from thinking about her home. She told him about New York, about watching the street mimes in Washington Square, about the smell of the chestnut vendors, about running up the steps past the great stone lions into the library. She told him about the Christmas crowds at night, the curious elation she felt being part of that rushing crowd, told him about the warm stillness of evening in summer, hanging out the apartment window. She described people — hundreds, thousands of people, how they all looked so different and spoke a hundred languages, how they sat in the outdoor cafes, how they never looked at each other in winter — it was a whole new world, a huge world, and Mako drank in every word, every image.

"Sometimes," she was telling him, "I choose a part of the

city I've never been to, and go there, and pretend I'm in another country. Sometimes I can understand the languages a little . . ."

"Do you know other languages?" he asked.

"French," she said slowly. "And I can sort of read German. And of course, some Hebrew . . . and Yiddish."

"Yiddish?"

She looked at him curiously. "It's some kind of mixed-up Jewish . . . I forget what. All my relatives speak it. Do you speak Maori?"

He frowned. "Nah — they don't teach it at school." He spoke in a low, fierce tone that made her hesitate. He looked at her. "You're Jewish?"

"Technically, only half, really — Pauline isn't anything. But my dad is; we aren't religious or anything, although Uncle Johann made Daddy send me to Hebrew school for two years."

"I never met anyone who was Jewish."

She didn't know what to say to that, so she shrugged. "Well, I never met anyone who was Maori!" she shot back, finally.

He was looking at her curiously. "You don't *look* Jewish," he said.

"Oh, how am I supposed to look?" she asked sarcastically. This was getting silly. She looked at Mako, incredulous. Was it possible that Mako, the outspoken anti-Pakeha antiracist, had a few prejudices of his own? She felt annoyance flooding her.

"So?" she demanded. "What is it — I don't have a big enough nose, or what! You better not be so high and mighty about Pakehas!"

"Ah, cut it out!" he muttered. He was bewildered.

"Well, that was a really dumb thing to say!" she cried. She hadn't realized she felt so defensive herself. Was this the way Mako felt?

"I was just surprised, is all," he grumbled, shamed. What would she think of him now!

"Anyway, what difference does it make?" she said firmly. "I suppose everyone has some prejudices. The point is to get rid of them when you find them."

Mako steered the boat glumly. He'd really messed this up, he reckoned. She knew so much more than he did . . . it really wasn't any use.

She put her hand on his arm, and he jumped. She was looking at him with a half-embarrassed smile on her face.

"Look — you didn't really say anything wrong," she said. "Forget it — it's OK. Really!"

He looked at her dubiously, still bewildered. Silly Pakeha . . . He caught himself, setting his jaw and looking past her toward the approaching wharf.

"Mako . . ." His name sounded strange coming from her. "Mako. Don't back off again — *please*. We had such a good day. C'mon!" She tugged at his sleeve. "C'mon — if we can't sound dumb with each other sometimes, what kind of friends are we?"

He grunted, concentrating on steering the boat along the wharf edge. He threw the ropes up and jumped up after them, looping them around the pilings.

Only when they were in the truck did he speak. "Saw your crazy old woman the other day," he said. "She was walking down Bay Road — gave her a lift."

She looked at him sharply. "You gave her a *lift?*" she said. She was cautious, expecting an outburst.

"She told me you played your flute for her," he said.

"I think she likes it," Sarah mused. "I think the albatross listens, too; isn't that weird? She kind of holds her neck up . . ."

"She told me she knew I would be coming along the road,

and that she wanted to see me," Mako continued, as if she
had not spoken. His voice showed no emotion, and he stared
straight ahead through the windshield. Her uneasiness returned.

"Well, yeah . . . I know. She has some *thing* about you —
I don't know. She's probably a little crazy. But she's OK,
Mako — I mean, she wouldn't hurt anyone! She's probably
just lonely."

"She said she had something for me. She said she'd give it
to me at the right time, when I was ready. She told me . . ."
He paused and flushed deeply. "She told me to let
you . . . touch me. She said I needed you, I needed to hear
the music inside you. She said I could never turn away from
people, because I had everything to learn, and that *it was
important.*"

He spoke all this as if he had learned it by rote, as if Sarah
was not there. She struggled to reply. She could sense a very
real fear in him, a fear she knew she had no true understanding
of.

"She told *me* that, too . . . that I had to let you touch me,"
she said softly.

"She said I was important."

"I know — "

"What does she want, the crazy old witch!" Mako jerked
the truck violently. Sarah's mouth was dry. There was a panic
in her, and a desperate wish that she had never found the
albatross, never met the old woman.

"I'm going to tell Pauline about the albatross," she said.
"Then I won't go down there anymore. It's because of me she
can get to you. She probably — "

"No!" he exploded. "No! You have to go — " He banged
his head against the steering wheel, closing his eyes. His voice
had gone very low. "You have to go there!"

The truck swerved in the track and Sarah grabbed the
wheel, gasping. He was going to kill them both! But Mako
shook himself stubbornly.

"It's OK — I got it," he grunted. "Look, I don't know what's
going on, eh. All I want is to save my money and buy my
boat. Then I can leave this place and get on with my life. I
don't like this place, an' I don't like Mike, and I don't like —"

"You don't like me," she finished.

He turned the truck abruptly into the yard in front of the
house and stopped.

"I do like you," he mumbled.

She felt her eyes burning before she could stop it. She
hated it, when she got like this. She stared angrily into her
lap.

"Don't cry," he said helplessly. "You said there was no point
in being friends if we couldn't be . . . Look, don't worry, eh!
She's just a lonely old woman with a way about her — I told
you she had *mana*, eh. It's nothing to be scared of; it'll be all
right. You go down there — she likes you. An' you *can't* give
your mum that silly old bird! Besides, I was getting to like
fishing for it . . ."

She knew he was trying to make her feel better; she *did*
feel better. What on earth is getting into me? she said to
herself. Miss In-control-at-all-times, that's me. She sighed.

Mako's sisters poured out the door and poked at him
through the window, giggling. They climbed in on him,
swarming over his lap.

"Eh, you little nits!" he said, hugging them. He held them
all in his brown arms. She watched, feeling a curious tightening in her stomach.

Later, alone in the flat, she finished a can of beans and
flopped down on her bed, exhausted. She slipped a tape in

and closed her eyes, listening to the sweet music.

Maybe we're all under a spell, she thought. I mean, what do you *want*, Sarah Steinway! You keep saying you're going to be a famous flutist, but I don't notice you practicing much these days! And as far as Mako goes, what *is* it with you! I mean, you either like him or you don't, OK?

She flounced off the bed and went into the bathroom. In the mirror, the dark eyes glared back at her, the hair salt-tangled and tossed, the skin ruddy from the wind. She turned sideways, pulling at her sweater, trying to see her profile. Definitely chubby, she thought, bunching the sweater to hide her figure. She sighed again. What did it matter, anyway? Pauline doesn't worry about stuff like that, you can bet . . .

But Pauline was beautiful, and charming, and clever, and she never lost sight of what she wanted. She went over to her mother's closet, poking through the clothes thrown in disarray over the shelves. Look at that — a silk dress! When on earth was she going to wear that! She pulled it out slowly, and it rustled under her hands.

She struggled with it over her head. It fits terribly, she thought, surveying herself again. It was too tight over the hips, and up top — she pulled out the material where it sagged.

"Well, I guess you aren't one of those mothers who fits into her daughter's clothes," she said flippantly to an imaginary Pauline. "You'd swim."

She tugged the dress off and kicked it away from her. Why was she doing this!

"I don't like you, Sarah Steinway!" she hissed. "I don't like you at all. Not when you're like this! Daphne can say what she wants, but she doesn't see you like this."

The person she was around Daphne seemed unreal to her.

And that person was different from the one around Mako. And now, *this* one: the real Sarah, having a fit over *clothes*, for God's sake!

She threw herself down on the bed and fell asleep. She didn't hear Pauline come home, didn't hear her step quietly into her room, pick the whispery dress up off the floor thoughtfully. She didn't feel the blanket being spread over her, or the cool touch of Pauline's hand as she smoothed the hair out of her face.

8
THE PORTRAIT

Sarah played her flute alone in the clearing by the hut, and the albatross watched her attentively. She had already cleaned the little pen, and swept the clearing free of twigs and leaves broken from a heavy rainstorm the night before. It had taken her more than an hour to do this, and still Hattie did not appear. It was beginning to worry Sarah that the old woman disappeared for long periods of time. During the times she did see her, Aunt Hattie appeared tired and thinner.

Sarah lowered her flute and frowned slightly. It was true — there *was* an aura around the old woman, a certain something that made her seem *bigger*. Was that what Mako meant by *mana?* But still, Aunt Hattie was old, very old, and how on earth did she live? Sarah cocked her head, thinking. She knew nothing about Hattie . . . what she ate, if she had any family, or any money . . . What would happen if she really did get sick? Who would even know? Was she the only person who knew the woman?

Sarah felt at home in the little clearing, loving this part of her days. She usually rode Celeste back to the Crossroads by noon, some days meeting Pauline for a quick lunch in the kitchen. More often than not, however, Pauline would work right through, and Sarah spent the afternoon alone. Mari sometimes came over with tea, and if she was lucky, Daphne would stop by on her way through on her rounds.

Today, she wanted to see Hattie and resolved to sit in the clearing until she showed up. Tomorrow, she and Pauline were going into Auckland on the little seaplane, to spend a day or two in the city together. She had to tell Hattie that she would not be bringing fish for the albatross.

It was a cold gray day, damp after the rain the night before. She wished she was better at building fires; the one she had struggled to relight this morning was sputtering feebly. She sighed and picked up her flute again.

When the old woman stumped into the clearing, she gave Sarah a short look, said nothing, and went to the far side of the fire. She poked the flames once or twice, added a stick and a log, and the fire miraculously flared into heat. With a grunt, Hattie squatted near it, staring into the fire as if Sarah was not there.

Who *was* this old woman? The question had become insistent. Was it because something seemed to have changed about her? Sarah studied the old figure, took in the details of colorless rags and tattered cloth sewn into some semblance of clothing, the thick rubber boots, the ancient hat. Nothing was different.

It was as if something *inside* her had changed. It was as if the focus had changed. Something drove the old woman — Sarah was sure of it.

And what did Mako have to do with it? It occurred to her suddenly, as she sat watching Hattie, that everything that had taken place since she had come to Great Kauri had been *planned,* had some *purpose* behind it. Finding the albatross, meeting Mako, going to the cliffs the other day, hearing the stories about the Maori and the island — all seemed suddenly connected! A tremor ran through her.

"What are you thinking?" demanded Hattie. Sarah drew in her breath sharply. The sea-blue eyes pinned her helplessly; she could not look away. Sarah squared her shoulders, gathering herself.

"You know what I am thinking," she replied softly.

Hattie chuckled. "Oh, girl!" she said. "I always know where I am with you. Inside, you are brave. Oh, you are brave! Your sight is honest . . . I am lucky! I am lucky!"

She fell silent, and fixed the girl once again with eyes that held no smile. She waited.

"I want to know who you are," said Sarah steadily.

"Can you ask such a question, girl?" challenged the old woman, her voice a knife-edge of steel.

"Yes," cried Sarah. "Yes, I *can* ask you! You have something to do with my life! And Mako's . . . Yes, I can ask."

Let her deny it! Let her pretend she's just a crazy old eccentric! She's not, Sarah thought. I know it!

She felt as if she was pushing against a force that was incredibly strong. It was very real; she could feel her body tensing, yet she sat as she had been, her flute held in her lap, with the old woman staring at her from across the fire.

Sarah bit her lip with the strength it took to hold those eyes with her own. She was sweating. She would not look down. Something was trying to push her away, trying to make her forget all the questions, everything . . .

"*Who are you?*" she demanded again, setting her teeth against each word. She would know! She would not be pushed back!

The old woman suddenly slumped.

"I am only who you see," she whispered. Sarah felt herself

released. She rushed to the old woman, putting her arms around her. The old body trembled, then hardened. She shook the girl away, irritated.

"I am who you see, girl," she said again. "If you want to know me, you have only to look. You are very young. Your eyes are still milky with youth. I will not be bothered with your questions!"

The old woman looked smaller and weaker than she had ever seemed before. How thin the old body was!

"I'm sorry," Sarah whispered. "I didn't mean to . . . I mean, it's just that you are . . . you scare Mako! And I keep feeling like there's *something* going on, that I should know!" She knelt near Hattie.

"You are perfect," said Hattie strangely. "You are just who you are, and you are perfect. You will know anything you wish, because your music is true. I have heard it."

Sarah did not know what to say.

"The boy — the boy is frightened?" asked Hattie now, thoughtful.

Sarah nodded. "He thinks you want something from him. He doesn't understand why you . . ." She hesitated. "You should be honest with him, if you want something from him!"

The old woman had a strange smile on her face. "That's right, you tell me!" she said. "You are not afraid of me. The music inside you makes you strong . . . that is why." She shook her head.

"But *him* — he stands in the shadow. I cannot get to him. How can I be honest with him? He does not come. When he comes, on his own, to where I am, then I will speak."

"But he's scared of you — he'll never come!" said Sarah, impatient. Why did Hattie talk in stupid riddles? What was the sense of it! *Speak* to Mako? About *what!*

"That is what *you* do for me, girl," she said. "He will come to *you*. He trusts you. You come here. He will come to you here. Then he will be here. Then I will have him."

And the bush hung still and heavy with the words.

She almost ran into Mako as she came around the edge of the house with her pack. His eyes were shining.

"You're going to Auckland today!" he cried. He stood in front of her, so she could not move by him.

"I wish you could go, too," she said, sorry that he was so envious. She blushed.

"I mean, you could see all your friends."

"Yeah," he sighed, then brightened. "Maybe you'll go to Grey Lynn, eh! Anybody hanging out on the street, I reckon I'd know . . ." He laughed. "That's rubbish, eh! What would you be going to a place like that for? You'll go to Queen Street, go shopping, eh — you'll go to the Domain, the museum . . ."

She laughed at him, catching his enthusiasm.

"We probably won't leave the university campus," she said dryly. "Pauline's totally disorganized — she has to meet some guy there, about her assistants or something. We'll be there all day."

They looked at each other, grinning. Why couldn't it always be like this? Sarah thought.

Pauline came out with her bags and Sarah started to follow her.

"Hey," Mako called. "Want to help me clean the boat Thursday? You won't like it — it's a real dag job, eh . . . slime an' barnacles. But you want to?"

Her stomach flipflopped. She could feel the warmth of her face, and she wished Pauline was not right there.

She looked back at Mako and nodded quickly. He gave her

a little wave and went off abruptly with Kikiwa at his side.

It was hard to imagine Auckland barely an hour away. Great Kauri Island lay hidden behind the curve of the sea, and here was a great modern city with bright skyscrapers and bustling crowds. She climbed slowly off the red bus they had taken from the airport and looked around her. For a moment she could only stand and breathe deeply. The bush, Aunt Hattie, the albatross, the wind and sea and Celeste had become in the space of a few moments a far-off dream. Here, with the smell of buses and the sounds of the street — *this* she under stood! She smiled at Pauline.

They wandered up Queen Street, looking in the stores and restaurants. Even on a cool winter day, Auckland was a bright city, clean and busy. Queen Street rumbled with traffic, with cars and taxis and the bright red transit buses . . . Sarah caught her breath.

"Grey Lynn," she said, reading the destination from the sign over the driver's window. Such strange names in this city: Mangere, Grafton, Mt. Roskill, Mt. Eden, One Tree Hill . . .

"Must be a lot of hills," she commented, noticing the names. Pauline nodded.

"Auckland is built on an isthmus that is also a volcanic plain," she explained. "Most of the neighborhoods are built around extinct volcanoes. Most of the time, the actual hill is a sort of park — common land, I think. They graze animals there. We should take a bus out to One Tree Hill, or Mount Eden."

"Could we go to Grey Lynn?"

Pauline looked at Sarah with a puzzled laugh.

"Why on earth Grey Lynn?" she asked. "Its just a working-class neighborhood — no shops, sort of dingy."

Sarah stared into the window of a clothing store. She wasn't going to be able to talk to Pauline about Mako — or anything. She could see that now. Her throat worked painfully and she blinked angrily. She should have told Pauline she didn't want to go with her! Daphne had called last night, to see if she wanted to come with her on her rounds the next day. Why hadn't she said yes!

She didn't answer when Pauline suggested they walk to the university through Albert Park, instead of taking a bus. They turned off Queen Street and walked up a steep hill that soon became a little footpath lined with huge trees.

"I thought you'd be in shape by now, with all the riding you do!" laughed Pauline, when they paused to catch their breath.

"I am!" Sarah retorted. "And I'm losing weight, too."

Pauline took her hand and looked at her, laughing.

"Oh, sweetheart! What are you worrying about that for? You look fine!"

"Easy for *you* to say!" cried Sarah, pulling away. How could she expect Pauline to understand what it was like to have your mother always lovely, always elegant, always charming and bubbly?

"I looked exactly like you when I was your age," said Pauline firmly. "Except my hair was lighter — that's all." She cocked her head at her daughter, remembering the silk dress she'd found on the floor of her room the other night, remembering how it had been crumpled into a ball and thrown in the corner . . .

"You never saw any pictures of me," she said softly, almost to herself. Sarah did not answer. How could she have seen pictures of Pauline when she was a kid? Pauline hadn't been around long enough to show them to her.

They had reached the top of the path, and a small park opened in front of them with a fountain and statues and benches. In the warm sun, a few roses still bloomed on the winter bushes. People sat eating their lunch, and a woman played with a sharp-faced collie dog. The dog was a black and white streak as it chased the sea gulls in the fountain, and Sarah suddenly remembered for an instant the wind of Great Kauri, and the words of the young sheep farmer near the hollow cliffs . . .

". . . still have half an hour," Pauline was saying, and Sarah shook herself mentally back into the present. They sat on a bench facing the fountain.

"How's the flute coming?" asked Pauline. Sarah felt some of the strain drifting from her.

"It's going great," she said eagerly. "Even without lessons, I don't know — I think my playing's better. And I'm starting — " She stopped, suddenly shy.

"Starting what?"

"Well, before, I always *played* music . . . you know? I mean, I brought all my sheet music and stuff. But I've been *composing!*"

She looked up at her mother. Would she understand this?

"I've been playing music I hear in my head," she tried to explain. "Just since I've come here — "

"Do you write it down?" asked Pauline, and Sarah was startled. Pauline was really listening to her!

"I don't have any music paper — and besides, I never really thought about it. I just, you know, play mostly outside . . ." But she could not tell Pauline about the bush, and the hut, and the old woman. That was still hers, her secret.

"Then we'll stop at a music store before we leave, and get some proper paper," said Pauline firmly. Taking charge, thought Sarah. She felt something twisting inside her, a defiance, a rejection of something . . .

This is *mine!* she found she was repeating to herself. This is *me!* Sarah stared at the fountain in confusion. But she *wanted* Pauline to be interested! This was the first time she'd really shown any interest in what Sarah did. What is the matter with me! she cried silently.

"I want . . ." she began. Her mother was listening to her. "I want to *do* something really well. I want to be the best, to make a *difference!* People listen to music. I really want . . ." She hesitated again. "I want to be like you! I want to be important, to do something important in the world! You know?"

But Pauline was not answering her. There was an expression on her face Sarah could not understand. It looked . . . it looked so unhappy! But why should Pauline be unhappy?

"I just worry a lot," she struggled to continue. "I worry that I'll lose it — lose what I have, you know? Because there're so many ways you can get distracted. I mean, look at Marjory . . . Remember her?"

Pauline, startled, nodded distractedly.

"I mean, she was pretty good with the cello . . . but then she got really nuts about boys, and started going out with someone, and she just *quit!* It was really dumb!"

Sarah leaned forward on the bench.

"You just *can't* let things like that get in your way! I mean, if you *know* you are good at something — like you — you have to put it first! It's the only way . . . I learned that from you! You're the best!" Her eyes were shining.

But Pauline had made a small noise in her throat. To her horror, Sarah watched her mother look away to hide her eyes.

"Mom . . ."

"But I lost you," whispered Pauline. "I never saw you grow up. I hardly know you."

"But I'm OK! Really! Look . . ." She couldn't stand this! "You know me now . . ."

But Pauline turned toward her, and the look on her face made Sarah wince. There was nothing else she could do — she leaned over and put her arms around Pauline's neck. For a long time, so long it seemed forever, they sat. Finally Pauline straightened.

"I made my choices," she said softly, smoothing the hair back from Sarah's cheeks. "You have to make your own. You have to make your own mistakes, too. But I lost something bigger than I ever imagined, losing you and your father . . ." Her eyes looked far away past Sarah.

"I'm only 'the best' to the rest of the world." She shrugged and looked at Sarah, hesitating. "I watched you with the boy, this morning," she began. Sarah grimaced.

"It's OK to like him," continued Pauline softly. "Just don't turn away from that. People should not be harmful! I know that now — I think I could have done my work, and not lost you . . ."

She smiled now, holding Sarah's hands.

"You play music; you write it. People listen — *will* listen! And how can you speak to people, if you aren't willing to let them into your life, just as they are, wonderful and exciting and full of faults!"

The lunch crowd around the fountain had thinned, and the collie dog was lying quietly by the woman now. Sarah looked around at the roses, at the gulls squabbling in the fountain. Pauline was standing, looking at her watch.

"I've got to go, sweetie," she said. "I won't be more than forty minutes. Why don't you meet me over there, by the student center?" She pointed across the street to a little alleyway. And she walked off, her head high, her step brisk and full of charm.

Sarah wandered around the campus. A student bookstore caught her eye and she went in, trying to concentrate on the titles. Her eyes were strangely blurred; she dashed at them with the back of her hand.

She didn't know what to think. The echo of her mother's voice was in her head. She stared at a book confusedly. How could Pauline be unhappy! How was it possible she regretted everything! Sarah felt as if she were floundering suddenly, with nothing to hold to. She clutched the book angrily.

Why couldn't she have figured this out earlier! she thought. And anyway, why did she have to tell me! It doesn't make any difference now, anyway . . .

She stared down at the book, and the title came into focus. It was a collection of essays by Henry David Thoreau, including the whole of "Civil Disobedience." Impulsively, she flicked through it. She'd read many of these in school — she thought of Mako.

She thought of Mako and his impassioned manner . . . of the farmer on the road to Waitapu, with his smug, bigoted views . . . of the boys in Waitapu. She thought of Mako, sitting alone on his fishing boat out on the shining Gulf, *thinking about things* . . .

Would he hate her, if she brought him books as a gift? Would he think she was mocking him? She panicked for a moment. Maybe he couldn't really read at all — dropouts were usually illiterate, she thought. She felt a wave of shame. She could hardly think of Mako, with his burning eyes and tense energy, as a "dropout"!

Her mind made up, she searched around on the shelves, this time with a specific book in mind. There — she found it: a biography of Martin Luther King, Jr., that she'd read last year in school.

The anguish over Pauline was gone. She was excited now; she wanted to give Mako these books. Maybe it was OK, to spend some time with him . . . She stared thoughtfully at the books in her hand. Thinking about Mako didn't make her want to stop playing her flute, after all! She grinned to herself. It either made her mad, or made her want to play till her fingers couldn't keep up!

She took the books to the counter, and then made her way back to the place she was to meet Pauline.

They walked together back to Queen Street, exploring the shops, stopping for fish and chips at a corner dairy where the music blared from a radio and kids played the video machines.

They sat resting their feet at the counter. The woman behind the grill shouted something to two boys near the door in a language Sarah could not understand.

"Is that Maori?" she asked Pauline. Her mother shook her head.

"I think it's Samoan," she said. "Auckland has a huge Polynesian population — Samoans, Tongans, Cook Islanders. It's the place to find work. There's a lot of tension between the islanders and the Maoris in the city."

She looked at her watch.

"Look," she said, frowning slightly. "Why don't we get on a bus and tour around a bit? I'm too tired to go up to the museum today — we can do it tomorrow. We could go out toward Grey Lynn — I didn't mean we couldn't go. Is that where Mako's from?"

The unexpected question made Sarah blush, but she nodded. Pauline made no comment, but got up to pay the woman. They caught a bus down to the main terminal, and boarded a Grey Lynn bus.

The afternoon had turned windy and gray, and the bus was warm. They settled comfortably in their seats, watching the city roll by. Within minutes, they were out of the downtown area and in neat neighborhoods of small white houses with little fenced yards. The rooftops were all painted bright red,

and the palms, tree ferns, and citrus trees in the gardens
made it seem exotic.

The driver called out when they reached Grey Lynn. Pauline had been right — it was a nondescript little area, with a
straggly row of shops under awnings, the houses obviously
poorer and not as well kept as in some of the other places.
They decided simply to ride through it, and go back early to
the bed-and-breakfast Pauline had reserved for the night.

The bus pulled up to a stop outside a run-down corner dairy
where a number of teenagers leaned against the outside wall.
They were Pakeha kids, Sarah could see — very punk, with
tight black clothes and spiky hair. They looked bored and
tired. But as the bus began to pull away from the stop, two
Maori boys who had been standing apart from the others ran
up and pounded on the side.

Their dark faces glared angrily through the window at the
driver. They pounded again on the door, and the driver swore
and threw open the handle. The boys sauntered on, dropping
their coins with exaggerated slowness in the fare box.

They were dressed as Mako dressed, in worn jeans and T-
shirts, with dark denim jackets against the winter chill. Their
hair was as dark and unruly as his, and in their eyes gleamed
something of the same intensity. They surveyed the bus and
swung easily into seats farther back, past Sarah and Pauline.

Sarah hadn't meant to turn and look at them. They met her
glance immediately, nudging each other and grinning. She
flushed angrily and turned away.

At the main terminal, Pauline left Sarah to buy a paper
from a news kiosk. She waited, looking around her.

"G'day," said a voice behind her. She jumped, and saw the
two boys from the bus standing near her.

"Hi," she answered. They didn't seem unfriendly. She
searched for Pauline.

"Lose someone?" asked the taller boy. She nodded shortly.

"Who — your boyfriend?"

She looked at him with as much disdain as she could manage. "No, my mother," she replied shortly.

They laughed, and to her surprise she realized they were trying to be friendly.

"Too bad, eh," they teased her, and she smiled back at them.

"You're American," said the taller boy curiously. "On holiday, then?"

"I'm staying with my mother on Great Kauri Island," she explained. "She's a scientist out there."

The boys stared at her amazed. They both spoke eagerly.

"We have a mate out there, eh!" they cried. She felt a thrill, as amazed as they were.

"Mako?" she said, incredulous. They laughed with joy, barraging her with questions.

"Fishing!" they exclaimed. "Our Mako — fishing! All he knew about fish would fit in a sack with chips, eh! An' you live in his house — lucky bloke!" They added this last with a bold look in her eyes, and she blushed again. She covered up her confusion with a question of her own.

"This is really weird — how could I just happen to meet people who know Mako?" she asked. They grinned at her again.

"Auckland's not so big, eh!" they laughed. "You found us in Grey Lynn — pretty chance we'd know him, eh. We went to the same school."

Went . . . so they had dropped out, too. What did they do? Again, she remembered the farmer on the road, talking about the gangs. These were Mako's friends. She found herself liking them, despite their jostling manner and teasing. They were open and friendly. She felt confused again. These were not the sort of people she liked — had ever liked! What did she have in common with them? They just hung out on the streets, had no direction in their lives . . .

But they were talking about Mako again, and she listened, trying not to show her eagerness. These boys knew him, as she did not. She wanted to hear everything.

"He's a real good mate, eh," the taller boy was saying. "But he's different . . . a strange one. Can't always figure him, you know?"

They were looking at her, so she nodded her head.

"You ever hear him talk? He goes on about all sorts of rubbish, eh — but there you are, listening before you know it!" Both boys laughed. "I seen blokes who wouldn't sit still ten minutes at bloody school listen to *him* for an hour without a peep!"

The tall boy's face darkened suddenly, reminding her acutely of Mako when he got angry. "I miss him," said the boy simply. "He was my best mate. His mum married a Pakeha . . ." His voice was tight. "Bloody shame — "

"But he's OK!" Sarah found herself saying. "Really! I think — I mean, he's saving money, and he wants to buy his own boat . . ."

She was reluctant to go on, although both boys were watching her sharply from their deep black eyes. Pauline was coming back, paper under her arm. The boys shifted uneasily. The taller one took Sarah's hand gently and she didn't pull away. He smiled at her.

"Tell him you saw us, eh," he said softly. "We're waitin' for him. We gotta go now . . ." They melted into the crowd.

We're waitin' for him. What a funny thing to say! It didn't seem to mean they were waiting for Mako to get back from

Great Kauri, she thought. They had said *they were waiting* —
for what? But Pauline had finally reached her through the
crowd and broke into her thoughts.

"Took me forever!" she laughed. She took Sarah's arm and
steered her to one side.

"It's five o'clock, sweetie," she said. "Let's just go to the
bed-and-breakfast and put our feet up, OK? I've got to make
a few calls, anyway. We'll be right near the Domain, so we
could take a walk a little later, and tomorrow I'll show you
the museum."

Sarah realized that she was exhausted. She wanted to be
out of these crowds, somewhere where it was quiet, where
she could think. She could just sit alone in the park, while
her mother made her phone calls. Maybe there was some
bush in the park. Maybe a breeze ran through the ferns,
whispering like the voice of an old woman, smelling of damp
earth and the sea . . .

She slept deeply that night. The morning broke clear and
very cold, so the prospect of exploring the huge graystone
museum in the Domain was welcome. They walked across
the park from the bed-and-breakfast. Pauline pointed around
them.

"You see — there's the rim of the volcano," she explained.
"We just walked down it, and there's the far side. We're in
the crater now. See that little hill, with the trees? That's a
sort of bubble in the center of the crater."

It was easily seen, the wooded ridge running around the
perimeter of a huge flat area marked off for rugby games.
People walked their dogs near the little hill in the middle,
and once they passed it, Sarah could see the museum sitting
high on the far rim.

It was a great, echoing, old-fashioned museum, smelling of

dusty collections and polish. They went to the Maori hall. A canoe spanned the length of the huge room, and along the sides were buildings made of dark red wood and carved all over with intricate, spiraling patterns. They stood near a group of tourists so they could hear the guide.

"The *marae* was the center of Maori life, and still is today, especially in the rural settlements," the guide was saying, pointing to the largest of the carved buildings. "It is not only a building but a *concept* of community, with social and religious connotations." The guide ran his hand down a side beam, painted with bold patterns in white and black and red, and carved with the same spirals and loops as the center beams. Sarah studied it carefully, making out figures in the design, strange twisting figures with huge open mouths and eyes inset with shell.

". . . and the carvings all have significance, from the largest spiral to the smallest notch," the guide was continuing. "Maraes also honor the ancestors of the people, who are represented by the carvings. Entrance into a marae, even today, is by invitation, and certain protocol must be observed."

The tour group moved on, but Sarah stayed in the room, running her hand down the great sea canoe, feeling the strength of the wood tingling up through her arm. Mako's ancestors had come in canoes like this one, with only the stars and sea to guide them. How many months had this canoe ridden the waves of the open Pacific? Had they ever been afraid, those ancient navigators — had they ever lost their way in storms and night? Had they ever looked up, up into the fathomless sky to watch for sea birds sharing the elements with them on their lonely journey? And had they seen the albatross, wandering for months like themselves, with land only a dream in their hearts?

Pauline had wandered off to another exhibit, and Sarah moved from the canoe to some cases on the far wall. They were filled with small, grotesque figures carved from dark green stone. She stared at them, wanting to touch them, feel the cold smooth stone in her hand. The little figures were in a curled-up position with huge heads, great eyes, and open mouths.

"TIKI" was the heading on the sign under the case: "Tikis were used as protection against curses. A tiki represents a fetus, embodying a good spirit to ward off curses from the bad spirits."

She stepped quickly back, almost bumping into a standing case that held massive clubs carved of the same green stone. She stared at them also: war clubs so heavy they could crush a human skull with one blow . . .

She moved quickly from the exhibit cases and found herself in a narrow hall hung with paintings of Maori warriors and chiefs. She gazed at them, marveling at the lavish feather cloaks and patterned grass skirts. The faces of the men were covered with the same intricate patterns as the carvings on the buildings, tattooed in blue on their dark skin. She thought she had never seen anything so fierce. She read the dates and names, sounding them out as she moved slowly down the hall.

"Te Rauparahia, Hone Hika, Murupaenga, Tawahi — "

She stopped, staring up at the painting above her. She said the name over under her breath. "Tawahi . . ."

How did she know this name? Had Mako said it, or the old woman? The name came to her from a distance, like the sound of the sea deep within a cave. She shook her head. She couldn't remember. But she knew it . . . *Tawahi*.

This had something to do with Mako! She stood frozen, gazing at the portrait. This man, this terrible, awesome warrior: this was Mako's ancestor. The face stared back at her, covered with the fearsome design. The eyes were Mako's eyes, but they held something more. In addition to the gleam of pride and aggression, the painter had captured the old chief's vision of a culture disintegrating around him. In the raised club was not only threat, but despair at the dying of his land, his way of life. And he faced this with shoulders squared and a face set in determination and sorrow.

Tawahi. Perhaps Mako *had* told her, the day he talked to her about his father in Waitapu . . . She could not remember. But this man was his many-times great-grandfather. She stepped back, glancing around the hallway. She was alone.

"Your grandson is alive, and he remembers you," she whispered to the portrait. The hall was very still. Her words hung there long after she had spoken, long after she had walked away.

9
THE GIFTS

The sun was just hanging on the pinnacle of the Needles when Daphne clattered up to the yard in her old pickup. Sarah ran out to meet her.

"I've only got a half hour, love," laughed the nurse. "But you could come along with me today, if you wanted."

Sarah hadn't been to the bush hut for three days, because she and Pauline had arrived back from Auckland later than they had expected the day before. She was worried about the albatross and anxious about Hattie. She wanted to get there and back today in time to meet Mako down at the boat.

"I think I'd like to explore around in the woods a little," she said cautiously. "Would you just drop me off a little past Port William?"

Should she tell Daphne about the old woman? What if she really were sick — would they take her out of the bush, send her to an old person's home in the city? She shuddered.

Daphne was studying her pensively, and Sarah dropped her eyes. She was upset that she could not tell Daphne. She wasn't like other people. She would understand that the old woman could not be forced from her home . . .

"You all right, love?" asked Daphne now, and Sarah mumbled a reply. She was relieved when Pauline came down the steps to greet them with her usual high energy.

"I wish everyone were as cheery as you in the morning!" Daphne said, smiling.

Pauline threw her bag in the Land Rover and gave Sarah a quick wave. "You're going to be down with Mako at the boat, aren't you — so I won't come home for lunch," she said.

She'd remembered! Sarah waved as her mother drove off.

"Something's bothering you," Daphne said, after several moments of silence. Sarah hesitated, then nodded. She looked searchingly at the big woman.

"Can't you trust me, love?" said Daphne softly.

"I trust you . . ." Sarah said. "I just . . . I don't know if I can explain everything."

"Just tell me the main bits." Daphne smiled. "I don't have to know all the details."

"It's sort of a secret — I'm afraid of what might happen, if I tell you," she whispered. Daphne looked straight into her eyes.

"I won't do anything to betray you, or anyone, if you ask me not to," she said.

As she and Daphne drove up Circle Mine Road, Sarah told her about finding the albatross and meeting the old woman. She left out all reference to Mako, but otherwise she gave a straightforward account. The bird had been injured . . . The old woman had offered to help . . . She had wanted to do this *herself*, without Pauline's help (this Daphne was sure to understand) . . . and now the old woman seemed ill and tired, and Sarah was worried for her.

"Maybe you could just come down and meet her," she finished. "I think maybe all she needs is vitamins, or something like that."

Daphne frowned, and was silent a moment.

"I might not be able to tell much, down there," she said at last. "If she would come to Auckland, for tests — "

"No!" cried Sarah. She clutched Daphne's arm. "She can't! I mean, she *can't* leave the bush! She's — " She stopped.

Daphne pulled the truck over and braked.

"I've never even heard of her," she said now, puzzled. "I thought I knew or had heard of everyone on this island. What's her last name? Does she have family?"

Sarah slumped in her seat. This had been a bad idea! Now what was she going to do? Daphne would ask around . . . Hattie would be forced to leave the little hut . . .

But Daphne put her hand on Sarah's. "I said you could trust me, love," she said. "I won't go back on it."

Her big eyes gazed into Sarah's, and the girl felt a surge of love. Daphne was a nurse, trained to help people. It was asking her a great deal, to promise to do nothing to help someone. She struggled to explain.

"It's just that . . . Hattie isn't *ordinary*," she said slowly. "She's got a *reason* for being where she is. I never asked her where she came from. I just know it's really important that she doesn't get bothered, or moved out." She stopped and took a deep breath.

"Mako and I met her together," she said in a rush, watching Daphne's face. "And . . . it's like she *wants* something from Mako — well, I don't know!" She shook her head miserably. This was impossible to explain! But Daphne held her hand again, saying nothing, waiting.

"He's scared of her. He won't go near her. But she wants to talk to him, to tell him something. It's really important." She realized that *she* believed this now. It *was* important. "And my albatross — she is almost better! And I really don't

want Pauline getting her and tagging her and all that stuff,
you know! I just want to see her fly."

Daphne squeezed her hand. "Look, love — I told you you
didn't have to worry, eh! I've seen a lot of amazing things in
my nursing — more than can be explained by medicine or
science. I may not be able to explain it, but I can accept it."

The woman held Sarah at arm's length, smiling. "It doesn't
really matter that I know what your old friend is doing. I'll
just go meet her, eh; I can ask her if she wants my help.
Later, when you understand, and if you want to, you can tell
me more. OK?"

Sarah nodded. Daphne started the truck and within a few
minutes, Sarah had directed her to the path through the bush.

They pushed through the ferns. It was cold — colder than
a few days ago. And although the sun was out, inside the bush
it was very dark and very still. No breeze stirred the ferns.
Sarah took a few steps down the path, Daphne behind her,
and then stopped, tilting her head.

Her body felt oddly heavy. Her arms hung leaden at her
sides. She stood still. She didn't understand. She took a few
more steps down the path.

A flock of kakas exploded above them in the trees, shattering
the forest stillness like a barrage of bullets with their black
bodies and their screams. Sarah cried out. They were gone
in an instant.

She was aware of Daphne's silence behind her, but she did
not turn to look at her. She took another step, turning her
head first one way, then another, listening. What was happening? What was she listening for?

The sound was so low she only felt it. She stood absolutely
still, no longer aware of Daphne. The dog rose in front of her
from the shadow of the ferns. For a long minute the dog stared

into the eyes of the girl. Finally, she spoke his name.

"Kikiwa."

The dog half crouched, several feet from her. The rumbling growl deepened; the fur on his back and neck stiffened. She could see the perfect white of his teeth curving against the black lips. He faced her with feet planted. When she took a step toward him, his whole body tensed in readiness.

Daphne stopped her with the lightest touch of her hand on Sarah's arm.

"Don't," she whispered. "Let him be."

But she could not. She stared down at the dog, the great black dog who never left Mako's side, who greeted her with calm dignity when they met.

"Kikiwa," she said again. But the dog shifted deeper into his crouch. The strong claws scored deep into the earth, the lips pulled back farther from the teeth.

Once again, Daphne's touch stopped her. The dog did not move. The bush hung like a suffocating cloth over them.

"It's not you!" whispered Daphne. "It's me — he doesn't want *me* down there! He's protecting something — can't you see? Come back, come back."

Step by step, they moved back from the dog. The animal sank slowly into the dark ferns, still watching. The deep growling subsided. Within a few more steps, they could no longer see him. They moved carefully out into the bright sun.

"But why is he here?" Sarah cried. Her whole body trembled. "He's always with Mako!" She forced the trembling to stop. Daphne too looked shaken.

"I don't know," said the nurse slowly. "But I do know it wasn't you he was warning; it was me. I could feel it." She did not take her eyes off Sarah's face.

"You'll go back there," she said now, a statement. Sarah

stared at her mutely. They both knew it. She *had* to go back in the bush, alone.

"I'll be safe," she said. She had to go back. Daphne had to trust her. She looked at the older woman, knowing how much she was asking.

"I'll be back in the surgery by noon," said Daphne softly, throwing her bag in the window of the truck. "When you get back, you call me."

They looked at each other for a long minute. Everything in Sarah urged her to get in the truck with her, to drive off, to leave the bush behind, to forget . . .

"I know you'd come with me, if I asked you," Daphne said now. "I *should* ask you . . ." She paused, smiling wanly. "But I believe you; I believe you are safe. And your old woman . . ." She stopped again and shrugged her shoulders.

"If you don't call me by one, I'll get the whole island out looking for you, old woman or not." She said it lightly, but Sarah could tell she was completely serious. She swallowed.

"I'll be back," she whispered. Daphne drove off, and Sarah turned back into the bush.

Gone entirely was the heavy stillness. Once again the path stretched light and cool in front of her, once more the earth smelled fresh and alive. The ferns swayed as they always had, and the kakas played above her. Kikiwa was gone, and she soon came to the bridge above the stream. Here she paused.

She knew she had a choice — a choice to go on or to turn back and forget. If she stepped onto the little bridge, she would pass a point from which there would be no looking back.

She stepped onto the swaying, woven track of the bridge. She pushed her way through the ferns, stepped into the clearing, and came to the hut.

Kikiwa lay across the doorway. He stood and greeted her calmly.

"Kikiwa," she said. "I am going inside."

The dog moved aside and lay down, head on his paws.

At first she thought the old woman was dead. With a low cry, she knelt by the rumpled form lying on the blankets. But the old face was warm to her touch, and the eyes flew open and fixed her immediately with their sea-blue light.

"Where have you been, girl?" she grumbled, sitting up. Sarah almost laughed in relief.

"I figured you would know," she said fliply.

"I'm not a mind reader, girl," retorted Hattie. "I had to waste a whole day fishing for your bird! You think I have nothing better to do? It wore me out."

The old woman shrugged the blankets off and shook herself like a dog. She stumped to the grate and poked at the ashes, grunting. Sarah stood watching her.

"Something happened," she said finally. Hattie shoved a stick into the thin flame and lit her pipe with it, sucking at it deeply. She looked at Sarah from under her brows.

"What is it, girl; what is it?"

Was it possible the old woman did not know? Was it possible Sarah had dreamed the whole thing, that she was imagining things? She saw Kikiwa lying as before, outside the doorway in the clearing. She took a deep breath.

Hattie followed her gaze, moved to the doorway and looked out. She took the pipe from her mouth and nodded, seeing the dog.

"Something has happened." She repeated Sarah's words. She looked pleased. "I see. The dog is here. Yes. That is good." She nodded again.

"He almost attacked us on the path!" cried Sarah, suddenly indignant. The old woman was playing at riddles again!

"You were bringing someone down here?" Hattie demanded, turning sharply. Sarah looked away. Hattie reached for her, took her face in one hand, forced her to look up.

"You were bringing someone here! Someone who was dangerous to me!"

"Daphne's not dangerous to you, for God's sake!" cried Sarah, jerking her head away. "Crikey!" she yelled. "I was just worried about you, that's all! Daphne's my friend — she's a nurse! I mean, look at this place!" She pointed into the room. "You don't eat right, you sleep in a dump, and you looked sick the other day . . ." Her voice trailed off. Hattie had dropped her hand, and an unexpected look crossed the lined face.

"You were worried about me?" she asked, in a voice gone very soft.

"I just thought . . . I mean, she could have just given you some vitamins, or something . . ." Suddenly she stamped her foot.

"What's wrong with that!" she burst out. "You're crazy, you know that? Everything down here is nuts! Got it? Nuts!" Her eyes burned with tears. "I don't know why Kikiwa is here, but he's Mako's dog, and I'm taking him back right now where he belongs, and then I'm going to help Mako clean his boat, and then . . ."

Aunt Hattie was ignoring her, rearranging the sticks in the grate. Sarah stomped over to her, fuming.

"And don't pretend you can't read minds!" she yelled. "You know very well why I couldn't get here yesterday, and you know why Kikiwa is here! You know *very well!* And if you aren't going to tell me, I don't care! You hear that? And you can just leave Mako alone, too!"

Without warning, the old woman turned and took Sarah's face in both hands.

"I don't know everything," she said softly. "I know some things, but I don't always look carefully at what is in front of me. I am an old woman; my sight is failing. I did not know you cared for me."

"Then why do you think I keep coming down here?"

"There are other reasons . . ." The old woman dropped her hands and stared into the fire. "All those I know — but I did not know this one, and it touches me here." She poked at her chest. She glanced back at the girl.

"Do not worry about the dog," she said. "A dog is just a dog. Who knows why a dog does things? He protects what is his to protect; that is all. Do not worry about him. He will go back with you."

She smiled, an old cracked smile, and the blue eyes were as warm as a summer sea.

"Go on, girl!" she said, pushing at Sarah. "I will feed the bird. You will come tomorrow. Soon we must let the albatross go free. She is very sad. She looks up and sees only trees — no sky. Her heart is begging to fly. Every day she tries her wings now."

Still Sarah hesitated. Hattie pushed her again.

"Go on!" she urged. "The boy is waiting for you. You are both so young — go on! You have days together ahead of you; don't waste them."

Her face burning, Sarah turned and ran up the path. Kikiwa bounded happily ahead of her, a big joyful animal.

A farmer passing by gave her a lift back to the Crossroads. No one was in the flat next door, but she went in anyway, looking anxiously at the clock over the stove. It was after noon. She cranked the phone and got the exchange in Arana.

"Waitapu 86" she said, and the phone hummed busily. Daphne's voice sounded far away.

"I'm back," said Sarah.

Daphne laughed at the other end. "Well, that's a relief, love! I can't believe I let you go."

"I'm OK — I told you I was safe." She didn't know what else to say. Daphne chuckled again.

"OK, love; I'm glad. You going to help Mako? Don't spend all your time scraping barnacles!"

Sarah blushed and stuttered goodbye. She walked the road down to the jetty with Kikiwa ranging near her, sniffing things. Mako was waiting for her, leaning against the tailgate of his truck. When he saw them, his face lit.

"Eh, I was hoping you'd not forget!" he said. He looked at the dog in disgust, fondling his ears. "I left him in the truck when I went out this morning. Sometimes there's no room in the boat." He snorted. "Fine mate he is — can't even wait a few hours for me!"

He mistook Sarah's look.

"I don't mind if he goes with you, eh!" he said. "I wasn't worried — figured he'd gone back to the house or something."

He gave her gloves and a scraper and they set to work on the hull of the boat, which had been winched up on blocks near the jetty. On the still-wet wood, clusters of barnacles clung, and slime covered the paint.

She was glad of the hard work. She was afraid to speak for a while, afraid of her voice betraying her. How could she tell him about what had happened? Any mention of the old woman put him in that strange mood, made him angry.

Mako grinned at her from the corner of his eyes.

"You've got green slime in your hair!" he said. She dropped her scraper and groaned in disgust.

"That's what I get for not having it cut in Auckland!" she

cried, shaking her head to get the seaweed out. "It always gets in my face, anyway, when I'm playing the flute."

"Oh!" he exclaimed softly. "Don't cut it! It's beautiful." He almost put out his hand.

"It's a pain," she said shortly. She grabbed her tool off the ground and began scraping again. He watched her, head cocked.

"Why don't you take a break, eh?" he said. "Too bloody hard to do all at once."

They sat on the tailgate of the truck, swinging their legs. After a minute, she reached for her pack and took out the two books she had gotten for him in Auckland.

"I got you something," she said. He turned the books over in his hands intently, not looking at her. She was overcome with regret. He wouldn't like it; she should never have bought them.

"But I don't have anything to give you," he said softly.

"Why would you have to give me anything?" she muttered. "I just thought you might like them, is all. You don't have to take them, if you don't want."

He looked out over the bay, fingering the books. He opened his mouth once, but shut it without speaking. Sarah picked at the rusting paint on the tailgate.

"I do want them," he said. He took a deep breath. "But I can't — "

"You can't what?"

"I can't read them." He said it simply, and looked firmly into her eyes. Now that he'd told her, he shrugged. She stared back at him.

"I don't believe that," she said. "You just never wanted to read Pakeha stuff."

"I can't read well enough to read these," Mako said. He looked at the covers, his lips forming the words of the titles.

He wanted desperately to read these books. The girl squinted at him in the sunlight.

"Then I'll help you."

"It won't do any good," he told her, trying to appear nonchalant. "I'm just not smart, eh. A few teachers tried . . ."

"They didn't care as much as I do."

He held the books tightly. She was sitting too far away, or he would have turned then, to hold her against him. It was all he wanted to do. Instead, he slid off the tailgate.

"OK," he said. "You teach me. I want to read these books you have given me. Thank you."

They returned to the boat. It was hard work, the angle awkward. They worked side by side, getting in each other's way. They did not look at each other, but often they would bump an arm, brush a shoulder, move away as if bitten.

Sarah set her teeth and scraped furiously. This is ridiculous! she thought. What's wrong with me! Her stomach was a knot inside her. Every inch of her was aware of the boy working silently next to her. She wanted to do *something;* she didn't know what she wanted.

She flung off the gloves. "I'm tired," she said. "I'm going over there." She walked stiffly toward the rocks at the far end of the little cove.

He caught up with her after a few yards. She didn't turn around. He grabbed her arm.

"Here," he said. "Here! I do have something for you. Take it."

He was holding out a tightly folded wad of paper. He shoved it into her hand and turned abruptly back to the boat. She watched him until he began to scrape again.

She settled herself on a rock in the sun. She unfolded the papers and squinted down at them. She smoothed the pages carefully on her knees.

It took half an hour to read through them, to decipher the rough handwriting, the crossed-out words, the misspellings. But she was caught in them immediately. The passion and energy of Mako's poems spun off the grimy pages. She drank in the words. She was aware of nothing around her but the sound and power of those words.

When she had read them all, she sat holding the papers, shaken. Mako's voice filled her. It was Mako, but a Mako she had only sensed. She imagined him sitting on the deck of the boat, alone . . . for she knew, suddenly, that the boat was where these poems had been written.

She knew exactly what she wanted, now. It did not surprise her to find that he was standing silently behind her on the rocks. She folded the papers carefully and handed them to him. He put them in his pocket, not hurrying, not taking his eyes from her.

It took no movement at all, to hold him. She could feel his heart pounding against her. He was holding her, too, and his big hands were very still. She could feel his breath in her hair.

They could not move, as much from fright as from wonder. It took a long time for her body to relax against his, a long time before his breath slowed. His hands moved up her back tentatively, until they were buried in her hair. He tilted her head back so he could see her.

"I am scared," he whispered. She pushed her face into his neck.

"I am scared of *you*," he said. She was trembling. "I don't know what you think of me. I don't know who I am, with you." He wished she would not tremble.

"You come from so far away — " he said, but now she would not let him speak. She moved her face against his; he found her mouth with his own. She was clumsy and unsure; he wrapped himself around her. He could not believe how precious she was to him.

The wind came off the bay and cut through their clothes. She pulled back from him gently, smiling up at him. She touched his face with her fingers.

"You're freezing," she said. She took his hand and they walked back along the packed sand to the truck. He buttoned his jacket, and the bulge of the folded papers showed. She touched the pocket where they were.

"You gave me everything, with them," she said softly. He flushed. They stood apart.

He wanted to pull her against him, feel her along his body, feel how warm her skin was under his hands. But she was making him look at her; she was holding herself back.

"What will happen?" he asked. His whole life hung in her eyes. He wanted to stay helpless like this forever.

"I told you before it's out of our hands," she answered.

He gazed at her. "How beautiful you are — "

To his dismay, her face flushed angrily. "I'm not!" she snapped. "Don't say that!"

He was bewildered and hurt. What had he said wrong? That she was beautiful? But she was. He reached to touch her, and she turned away.

"You don't have to say that," she muttered. He trapped her against the tailgate, holding her tightly so she could not turn away.

"You *are* beautiful," he said, stubborn. "You are perfect." The touch of her against him made him kiss her. He turned and sat up on the tailgate, still holding her. He pulled her up into his lap, burying his face against her.

She struggled after a moment. "I'll crush you," she said.

He held her out from him, looking at her in wonder. That was it! She thought she was fat; she did not think she was beautiful. He grinned at her, and she scowled.

"What are you laughing at?" she said crossly. He would not let her go.

"I'm laughing at you, eh!" he said. "Don't you know you're beautiful? You're beautiful just the way you are."

She winced every time he said it. He still grinned at her. Girls were so daft, always worrying about their weight . . .

"Is that all you care about — how I look?" she snapped at him.

"You're the one who brought it up, eh," he pointed out. It did not bother him, that she was spitting at him like an angry little rock lizard. He held her, feeling the muscles of her back. He only wanted to sit like this forever, touching her. He put his mouth close to her ear and talked to her.

"I care about everything you are," he said. "I care about how you talk and how you play your flute, and how you look at things, and how beautiful you are. I love you."

He slipped his hands under her shirt and ran them along the strong muscles of her back. For a moment she was still tense, trying to pull away. Then she relaxed, looked up at him.

"I love you, too," she said. It was very simple. She smiled. "I'm scared, too," she said, more quietly. "I didn't mean to be so dumb. I never felt like this before."

She was being held so tightly she couldn't breathe. Too much was happening; she couldn't keep up with him.

"I don't know what to do," she whispered, suddenly nervous. She felt as if she were drowning in him. His mouth was too hard. "I hope you know what you're doing, because *I* don't!" She tried to laugh.

He pulled away. She looked at him, astonished.

"*Don't* you know?" She wasn't sure, exactly, what there was to *know*. But hadn't he had girlfriends? Most of the girls she knew had boyfriends, by tenth grade. She hadn't.

"No," he mumbled, looking away.

She loved him, then, very much. She slid off his lap and laughed softly, making him look at her. She cocked her head.

"We'll just have to wing it, then," she said. She made him laugh with her. It was all right, then.

The afternoon had dimmed to early evening, and it was colder than they could stand. They were filled with a nervous, elated energy so that they dropped the tools and buckets as they collected them to put in the truck, stumbled over pebbles. Even holding each other, feeling their hearts pounding into each other, did not help.

Mako wanted her with him; he did not want her out of his sight. He did not quite believe that she was with him. What would she do? Did she want to come over and watch the telly with him? But everyone would be there . . . He thought about Russell's but discarded it immediately. He didn't know how old she was — fifteen? sixteen? Russell would have his neck if he took her in there.

He drove helplessly toward the Crossroads in silence, finally pulling the truck off to the side of the road. It had become dark now; a morepork called from the trees above them. The lights from the house twinkled some distance away. He sighed.

She giggled in the darkness.

"We're a great pair!" she said, smiling at him. He grinned reluctantly back. "We don't even know what to do with each other, now." She looked at him quizzically. "Didn't you have a girlfriend, in Auckland?" She couldn't believe that he hadn't.

He was torn, wanting her to think he had, not wanting to admit otherwise. She drew her finger over the frown on his forehead.

"I liked a girl once," he said now, his voice low. "Her name was Te Aniwa. She was older than me. She wasn't like you; she had been angry and hurting for a long time before I knew her. She wasn't free, like you; she wanted to *belong* to someone . . ." He paused.

"I come from a different place than you," he continued. "In my city, things are hard for the Maori. The families are broken; there is no *marae* for most of them. Te Aniwa was unhappy; I wanted to help her. But I could not. There is nothing to do. She was pregnant, and the man beat her. But that man is not with her now; he is very sick, in a mental hospital. Many Maori men are in this hospital. It is what happens, when people have no place."

She was as caught in the voice as she had been in his poems. It was the same voice, the same lilting intensity of rhythm. He had never spoken to her in this way.

"The Pakeha will tell you about the gangs in the city, how terrible it has become. But it is only that they are seeing the anger of a people whose place has been taken from them; they are recognizing this anger for the first time, and they are afraid.

"The city swallows up the Maori. There is no family. Te Aniwa's baby died as soon as it was born. There was no one to help her bury it; they took it away, in hospital. Then she went away. There is a big hole, and she disappeared into it . . .

"There is a hole, and the Maori are being swallowed. The Pakeha says: The government gives everything to them, and look at them! Lazy! Drinking all the time! But they do not think about what they say. They cannot see the humiliation that *being given* things creates! For why must the Maori *be given* anything by the Pakeha? They *had* everything; they had Aotearoa! When it was taken, the heart was taken from a whole people.

"But the Pakeha are falling into a hole of their own. They, too, are humiliated. They can hardly support themselves on the land they stole. The Maori makes them angry, angry. Deep inside, the Pakeha is afraid, because Aotearoa is dying, dying, dying."

His voice had become trancelike. The girl heard him, and heard the stillness around them. It was very dark. The morepork was silent; the crickets still. She held her own breath quiet in her throat. There was only the voice of the boy.

"Aotearoa dies. The trees have been cut, and the rain no longer comes down over Aotearoa. The earth dries. The sheep tear the grasses. They cut the earth with their hooves. The wind comes. The grass shrivels. The earth blows away. The Pakeha tears and tears at the land. He is very afraid now. He tries everything. He pours chemicals on the land. He moves his sheep from here to there. He plants pine trees; pine trees poison earth. He plants fruit trees; fruit spoils easily, and costs much to ship. The world does not want his sheep; no one wants his butter.

"The Maori has been waiting a long time. Someday the Pakeha will have to go. But as he waits, the Maori loses things, one by one. He loses his language. He loses his stories. He loses his mind. He sees the television; he reads the papers. There is a world beyond him, beyond Aotearoa. But the canoes are rotted away, and the navigators are dead. He does not know how to go. He cannot turn back. He cannot move forward. He breaks things in rage. He breaks things in despair. No one knows what to do —

"Te Aniwa died six months ago," Mako said, cutting himself off in midsentence. "She overdosed on drugs." He shrugged. "I did not know her very well."

Nothing was stirring outside the truck. There was a cool touch on his face; he reached up, felt her hands. He sat back, let her caress him. She touched him. He breathed deeply, looked at her.

"You sure you want to know me?" he said. What had he been saying? He shook his head softly; he couldn't remember. But he had been talking very long, for a very long time . . .

The girl nestled closer to him on the seat. He lowered his face into her hair; it was cool, like her hands. It smelled of the sea and the wind.

"It is out of our hands," she said. He wondered, Why does she keep telling me that? It disturbed him. He found the pulse of her neck with his mouth, lay quietly against her.

"I want to know you, Mako," she said now. "I am afraid now. I'm going back soon. It hurts already."

He felt the ache of that, too. They would know each other for the shortest of times. A whole world lay between them, after that.

"I will stay with you as long as I can," he whispered. He tasted the salt on her skin, not knowing if it was from the sea or from tears. He found her mouth again and she held him strongly. They were cold, and very hungry. Mike would be coming in, from the big boat in Karaka Bay. Mari would be cooking. They looked over at the lights of the house. Inside, it would be warm, and the little children would be playing. They wanted this very much. Mako drove up to the yard and they stumbled down from the truck. Kikiwa slipped silently under the verandah. They went in, to Mari.

10
THE MAP

Sarah had not gone to the bush for two days. She did not want to see the old woman, have her boring holes in her with those eyes that saw everything. She would know . . . she would know! She spent one day on the boat with Mako, and another wandering around the coves near the jetty.

But this morning she could not avoid it any longer. She held the wrapped fish in her hand. The albatross would be hungry; she was not sure if Hattie had caught fish for it. She thought of the bird, waiting captive in the pen, straining her graceful wings, staring up through the lacing canopy of bush. The injury on her neck was almost healed, the feathers beginning to hide the scar.

She rode Celeste slowly up the track, tethered her, and walked down the path. She hesitated before pushing through the ferns. She couldn't bear it if Hattie probed or jeered . . . She couldn't stand it! She set her mouth and made her way into the clearing.

The old woman looked up sharply. For a moment she searched Sarah's face, and then a slow smile spread over hers.

"I did not think I could miss anyone so much, girl," she

said. "My ears miss the sound of your flute, and my eyes miss your smile."

Taken aback, Sarah gulped, dropping her pack near the pen. She inspected the albatross carefully through the wire, so she would not have to look at Hattie. The woman got up stiffly, putting aside her work of fashioning a shelf out of a fish crate. She came to stand behind Sarah.

"She is not doing so well," said Hattie. "It will be a close thing, to free her after she is healed but before she dies of sorrow."

And it was true. The albatross sat listless on her nest of moss. Her beak was partially open, as if panting. Her eyes blinked, staying shut for several seconds. She watched Sarah without the snap and hiss of the weeks before.

"Has . . . has she eaten?" Sarah whispered. She could not believe the albatross might die, not after all this! She knelt in the dirt and peered through the wire.

"Maybe we should let her go now! She might have more of a chance."

The old woman shook her head thoughtfully.

"Now it is too cold to be without feathers. Her wing is not strong enough; it droops . . . you see?"

The wing on the side of the neck where the net had cut most deeply hung just slightly out from her body. Sarah nodded miserably. Now she knew it had been wrong, wrong to try to help this magnificent animal herself when there were people more qualified. If she had taken the bird to Pauline, it would live.

"Do not lose your courage, girl," said Hattie softly, behind her. "Your heart is with this bird. You will know when the time to free her comes. She will live. You came today because you love her, although you are afraid of me . . . " She smiled almost sadly.

Sarah turned and looked at the old woman, saw the tired old face, the worn skin, the labyrinth of lines around the amazing eyes. Hattie cared for her. She was ashamed that she had been afraid, afraid Hattie would tease her about Mako.

"I don't know why I've been afraid," she said. The woman touched her cheek lightly with one gnarled finger.

"You are afraid because you are so young, and it is a big thing, these feelings you have discovered. You do not know where to go with them, and the boy does not know either."

She felt her throat grow tight. She wanted to throw her arms around Hattie, like Daphne would, or Pauline . . . but her arms hung at her sides.

"Play your new songs for me, girl," commanded the old woman, her voice returning to its normal gruffness. Sarah grinned happily. Hattie seemed fine — not sick at all. She was stomping around the clearing with her old energy. She worked vigorously on her crate, swearing under her breath occasionally, while Sarah played.

The music was growing inside her faster than she could write it down. She had begun to make notes on the paper bought in Auckland. But she never forgot any of the melodies. She could play them over and over, as if the songs were part of her blood and breathing. They were strange melodies, full of the trilling of pipit and bellbird, full of the rustling of ferns in the wind, full of the crash of waves, and now . . . full of love. She played them for no one but Hattie.

Today, after half an hour, she put the flute down to rest. Hattie looked up from her task.

"You see, girl," she said, some of the old smugness creeping into her voice. "Did I not tell you? Did I not tell you how the music would come, if you let yourself be touched?"

She came over and squatted next to the girl.

"You love him very much," said the old woman. Sarah

averted her eyes. She was not ready to talk about Mako, about what she felt. Hattie chuckled, poking at her.

"You still put up walls for me, girl!" she said. "I am too old to climb over them. You must talk to me."

"Don't you think some things should be private?" snapped Sarah. Hattie was back in her usual mood. It was too much to expect, that she would continue to be gentle and soft as she had been that morning.

"Anyway," she muttered, shoving her flute back into her pack, "You know everything anyway, so what does it matter if I talk or not?"

Hattie guffawed loudly, settling back on her heels.

"You only imagine I know things," she said, with a strange glint in her eyes. "I do not know everything. It is good to hear about love. I am very alone here."

The words were so simple, spoken without pain. But Sarah was filled suddenly with the enormity of the words: *I am very alone . . .* In little more than a month, she would be gone from Great Kauri Island. The old woman would be alone. She herself was going to a strange new school, where she knew no one. She would be alone. And Mako . . . what of Mako? She could hardly bear to think of him alone here, after she had left. Who would he talk to? Who would read his poems? Who would touch him?

Tears filled her eyes. She looked helplessly at Hattie. The old woman gazed back at her calmly. She reached in the pocket of her baggy coat and produced a rag, holding it out to Sarah. The girl took the grimy torn cloth. She dried her face. The rag smelled of seaweed and smoke and tobacco.

"Soon the bird will be free. She will hold all of us in her flight," said Hattie. "Soon. You will see — no one is alone."

They were comforting words. They were telling her something — something she could not yet understand. A peace

entered Sarah; she could feel it warming her, relaxing her.
She watched the old woman, but no flicker in those eyes
betrayed what she was thinking. In a moment, Hattie stood,
grunting, brushing off her clothes.

"You go now, girl," she said bluntly. "I have work. I will
feed your bird. Come tomorrow, if you can tear yourself
away . . ."

Sarah opened her mouth to retort, but to her amazement,
the old woman *winked* at her. So there was nothing she could
do but grin.

It had turned very cold now; it was deep winter. In the
morning, when there was a heavy frost, it almost looked to
Sarah like snow. It took all her imagination to know that this
was her summer holiday; that it *was* a holiday had lost all
meaning. It was as if she had been on this island forever.
There was no passage of time — there was only being with
people and being alone. There was no middle ground. To be
alone meant to be on the beaches or on the windswept plateaus
where no human beings touched her — as if there was no
other but herself in the universe. But to be *with* someone,
here, was an experience that touched her more deeply than
she had ever imagined possible. To ride with Daphne in the
old truck, sharing her boisterous energy and joy; to have a
quiet hour with Mari while the little girls napped in the afternoon; to lose herself in the depths of the bush with Hattie —
even the too short times with Pauline — all this was the mea-
sure of her existence. And to be with Mako was to feel *alive*
as an animal must be — instinctual, alert, vibrant, intelligent,
perfect.

He was difficult. He was unpredictable and moody. Loving
her did not prevent his sudden rages, his glowering sulks, his
defensive opinions. There were times when it seemed the
whole untracted universe lay between them, and it was a

wonder to Sarah that they could even understand each other's words.

And she pulled back, too, when she felt herself whirling around in emotions she had no control over. Some days, she could not tolerate him, actually feeling a repugnance toward him that scared her. Why couldn't he just let her love him? Why was there always a challenge? She would become haughty with him, then, and he would lose all expression and become a wall to her, a wall she could not even touch.

She turned Celeste out in the paddock, and found Mako waiting for her on the verandah. There was no one around the house, so he pulled her quickly against him, as if he were hungry.

"Fishing's bad today," he muttered into her hair. She pushed at him playfully.

"That's a thin excuse, Mako," she snorted. "It's a perfectly good day. But maybe fish don't bite on Tuesdays — "

He pushed her onto the steps to wrestle her, and the paperback edition of Thoreau tumbled out of his pocket onto the ground. She picked it up slowly. It was dog-eared and thick from spray, and the pages were marked in pencil. She leafed through it while he watched her.

"I didn't know you were reading this," she said at last. He shrugged.

"You gave it to me," he said. He took it from her and studied it a moment, then gave it back. The pages were scribbled on, some of the passages lined or circled, some with question marks by them. He hesitated, then spoke.

"This man was American — he lived a long time ago?"
She nodded.

"He talks about freedom," he said. "It is hard for me to read, but it is useful."

Useful? She tried reading some of his notes, but could not make out the smudged pencil very well. "Civil Disobedience," in particular, was marked heavily.

"You have books," he pointed out. "Are they stories? Why did you bring them?"

"There're some stories, but some are poems . . . I thought I might get bored . . ." She grinned at him, and he reached for her. He was much bolder than she was, touching her, but she was never embarrassed with him. This amazed her.

She was curious about him. She wanted to know everything — what it was like where he came from, what he thought about, what he wanted to do after he'd bought his boat, how he felt when she touched him . . .

"Are we going to sleep together?" she asked him. She threw a stick for Kikiwa, who bounded off the verandah to catch it.

"Do you want to?" he asked, cautious.

She noticed distractedly how their sneakers were equally dirty and torn. It was strange, how quietly she was sitting with him, when inside she was a turmoil of restless excitement.

"I don't know," she answered him. She looked at him out of the corner of her eye.

"Well, if you don't know, I don't know, eh," Mako muttered. He took a deep breath.

"I like this," he said. He was holding her gently. She nodded. "I reckon we could . . . we could just leave it, for now. If you want."

She nodded, relieved. It was easier to do that.

Mako jumped up. "I thought you were going to teach me to read!" he demanded. "Teach me from those books you have."

They sat on her bed. She was very aware of him next to

her — of the bed, and the small room where they were hidden. She felt a little shock of fright. She didn't really know him! It was incredible, how little she knew him.

"Read to me," he commanded gruffly. She frowned at his tone, but when she saw his face, she thought, He's scared, too! So she pulled a book off the bureau and opened it. It was a collection of poems by Dylan Thomas.

She read a short one. He said nothing, and she could not tell what he was thinking. She was determined that he should love the poems as she did. She stopped when she knew he wasn't listening.

"You're not listening," she said, annoyed. He wanted her to teach him! He was going to have to make a little effort.

He sprawled across the foot of the bed, sighing.

"It's rubbish," he said shortly. She slammed the book shut. "What does it have to do with anything, eh!" he cried, rolling over to look at her. "It's the same kind of Pakeha rubbish we had to do in school."

"Dylan Thomas was Welsh," she said in disgust. "He was a great poet."

"He was a great *Pakeha* poet," sneered Mako. He was baiting her. "You're wasting your time with me. I told you! I don't know what that stuff means!" He jabbed his finger at it.

She held her breath a moment, then let it out in a huff. She wanted to hit him. He was being his horrid arrogant self. But something in his words pricked at her. She looked at him; he had his arm thrown over his eyes as he lay on his back. He was afraid! He was afraid he was stupid!

"It's not supposed to mean anything," she said softly. "I don't know what it means. I just listen to it — you know? The way the words sound, like a song, like a song-picture . . . Listen . . ."

She searched for the one she loved most, "Fern Hill," where the words pulsed and grew, sinking to a drone, rising to an emphatic chant. When she was done she said nothing, but let him lie there with his eyes hidden. Finally he looked at her.

"You play your flute like that," he said. She flushed. It was what she wanted.

"You listened!" she said softly.

He stared at the ceiling. " 'Oh as I was young and easy in the mercy of his means,/Time held me green and dying/ Though I sang in my chains like the sea.' "

She felt the strong brown fingers close around her hand. She didn't know why it should make her want to cry, that he said those lines. It was the voice. It was the same voice with which he had told her about Te Aniwa and the shriveling grasses and the losing of a place. It was Mako, and yet it was not Mako . . . It was bigger than the boy, the energy that was held in that voice.

"It is better to just listen," mused the boy now. "Otherwise it doesn't make any bloody sense, eh."

He let her read to him for half an hour, but when he became bored, he got rude. He thought her books silly. He shoved them all onto the floor and fell on top of her in the bed.

"If you want to learn to read better, you have to concentrate," she said primly. "And stop saying everything's rubbish."

He lay along her and ran his hand down her side.

"Stop telling me how to be," he said softly, his mouth near her own. "I don't tell you how to be."

She was silent. It was very warm in the bed. His hips pushed into her and she wanted to move with him. His hands explored over her skin; they were hard and rough from the salt and fish lines. She buried her face against him and felt herself melting into a place where it was warm and dim and unbearably exciting . . .

"If Pauline comes home we'll be in big trouble," she whispered.

His face was only inches from hers. "Would she mind?"

She raised her eyebrows at him. "What do you think?"

They looked at each other and laughed. They struggled up and sat on the edge of the bed, hardly daring to touch.

"We better not come in here again," she said.

He grinned. "I don't mind — "

She punched him. The spell was broken.

"I *want* you to help me read," he said seriously. "It is important. We'll go to Russell's, eh. He has loads of books all over the place."

They decided to walk, and catch a ride back with Mike from the wharf. She pulled another sweater on over her clothes. Kikiwa trotted ahead. The road ran through the low swampy land, and everywhere was the same bleached dun color. The island cattle hunted in the raupo and hummocks for grazing. Kikiwa ignored their nervous bellows.

"See how dry it is," said Mako. She remembered him telling of the trees being cut, and rain not coming, and the earth drying up and blowing away.

They walked a good distance in silence, only their hands touching. It's funny, she thought, how many things I can't talk to him about.

She never mentioned Aunt Hattie or anything about her time in the bush. It was if she moved between two different worlds — but she knew the old woman and Mako and she were all tied to one another. When would they come together? She knew something would happen, sometime . . . she could feel something coiled and waiting. She felt it in the old woman's silences after she mentioned the boy, she felt it in Mako's voice the day he'd spoken of Aotearoa.

He said suddenly: "You really like Daphne, don't you? You talk to her a lot."

"She's amazing!" Sarah replied. "I never had a friend like her."

"Aren't I your best friend?"

She looked at him in astonishment. He gazed back at her with such young eyes. How could this boy be the same as the boy who spoke with a voice older than the sea, as powerful as the wind?

"You are my friend. You are my . . . love," she said softly. She stopped walking and they sat in the hummock grass at the road edge, spinning pebbles out over the cattle grid.

"You're smarter than me, eh," he said. She snorted.

"For God's sake! That's a dumb thing to say!"

"I just mean . . . You can really *talk* to Daphne, eh. You tell her everything."

"I don't tell her everything." She thought about the old woman. What she didn't tell her, she knew already. Even to Daphne, she did not talk about Hattie.

"Look at your mum," he was saying now, deliberately pressing himself into despondency. "She's got degrees in everything, I reckon. And your dad . . . You will, too, eh. You'll go to your snooty school an' forget all about me."

"Oh, Mako!" She laughed, blowing the dust off her hands into his face. "What's happened to you? You used to think you were the greatest!"

How could he think he was stupid? With a start, she remembered her own despising attitude toward him. Was it possible she had once thought him too ignorant to bother with, a real punk, a dropout? But she hadn't really *seen* him then; she'd been too busy passing judgments.

She realized that during the last two weeks, everything had changed. She hadn't worried about her weight; she hadn't driven herself to practice the flute, determined to push herself to the top. The time she had spent with Pauline had been relaxed. She remembered something Hattie had said a long time ago: Was it possible that she *liked herself* better?

She looked at Mako with a worried frown.

"I know you think you're dumb because you left school, and it seems like I know all this stuff about books and everything," she said slowly. "But I don't think smartness has anything to do with that. It's more how . . . how you *look* at things, you know? It's more how you see things for what they are, and how you connect things together in your mind. I used to think . . ."

"What?"

She shook her head a moment. But she wanted to tell him, because it was important how she had learned from it.

"I guess I was kind of snotty, really," she said, not looking at him. "I used to think you were a real punk. I used to think . . . you were a smart-ass kid, a loser. And I thought I was fat and unfriendly and sort of dull . . . and that my mother had everything I wanted to have." She grinned. "I thought everything wrong."

"I *am* a smart-ass kid," he said lightly. She put her hand on his knee and looked into his eyes.

"You are . . . something . . . You are special. You are not like anyone else. You are important." And the words did not seem to come from her, but from an old voice, a voice she knew. He did not answer.

They walked down the track into Port William. Russell was sweeping the front step on the bar when they came up.

"G'day," he said, putting his broom aside. She liked him immediately. She liked his quiet intelligent eyes, and the way he shook her hand. She was glad this man was Mako's friend.

And Russell liked the girl. He'd seen them walking a few minutes before they'd reached him, saw their hands touching, their bodies moving together. When he took them into his flat, and saw her go immediately to the books with the boy, a curious excitement swept over him. He put the kettle on the burner, watching them.

She's getting him to read! he thought. He held himself quietly in the background, letting them come to him in their own time. They needed him; they needed the books. He watched the boy unobserved. He hadn't seen him since the evening he'd told the story of the teacher. Had he grown? No — what was it? Something was coming together; something in the boy was beginning to *focus*. He seemed the same, and yet a little larger, a little stronger.

He saw how the girl was leading him. The boy would appear at times bored or snappy, but ultimately he was listening to her. He looked at the things she was showing him in the books. It was good that this was happening! It was important! Russell's eyes flickered briefly, and he settled into a chair, pretending to read the paper while the tea steeped.

Finally they came and sat down with him, drinking the tea gratefully in the chilly flat. Mako finished the plate of cookies.

"You think biscuits grow on trees, mate?" grumbled Russell, tearing open another package.

He washed up the dishes patiently. They still had not approached him with what they wanted. But the boy had so much pride. And he had a temper. Russell was not to know that the boy needed help reading — *wanted* it. The girl was orchestrating the slow careful exploration around the flat; the boy followed.

She took a book down, leafed through it. It was a fairly new collection of New Zealand poetry, with a good number of

Maori poets. She frowned slightly. Mako could not call *this* rubbish. And he would have to help *her* with some of it — that would be good.

"How did you get all these books here?" she asked now.

Russell dried the cups one by one and put them away. He smiled his broad, slow smile. She liked his face; it was open and wise.

"I had 'em mailed in," he chuckled. "They all came into the post office in Arana at once. The islanders thought I was daft, eh. I went down in the car to pick them up, and Mrs. MacNeil — you know? — she said: 'Those are all *books?* But if you have that many books, how many *clothes* do you have!' They just couldn't figure it."

He turned the teapot upside down on a towel and pointed to the book in her hand.

"I got that last trip to Auckland," he said in an offhand manner. "You might want to look at it, eh. Don't think you'd find it in America, I reckon!"

So she was able to take it without having to ask. And Mako's secret was safe. (Russell felt sure that it all *was* a secret: that Mako could not read well, that he *wanted* to read at all, that the girl was helping him — it was just between the two kids.)

She was still looking around the flat. She would not have expected this sort of thing, here on the island. Daphne's place was a homy mixture of magazines and light reading and bright pictures on the walls. But Russell — he *studied* things. The books were an impressive combination of classics, literature, science, religion. And the pictures on his walls! She examined them closely. A contemporary print here, a nineteenth-century watercolor there, an old photograph, a map . . . She caught her breath.

It was an old map of Great Kauri Island!

"That is a treasure," he said softly, coming up behind her.

Mako hung in the background. Russell traced the outline of the island.

"It's more than a hundred and fifty years old," he said. "See — the mines are marked! And look how the kauri forest is marked here . . . and here."

She studied the map in wonder. The kauri forest covered almost two thirds of the island. Only the far southern portion was low bushland. But there, in the east, a long beach and a great curving headland . . . It was bare. No forest had grown there. She pointed to it.

"What's that?" she asked. "Why is there no forest just on this bit? See — there's forest all around it, but none there."

Russell moved away from her; she turned. In the dim light of the flat, it seemed to her that his open, kind face had gone flat and blank. It shook her slightly.

"Oh, I don't know . . ." he said. But now Mako had come up to look at the map. He ran his finger down the curve of the great beach, and then out into the vast Pacific.

"You've never been over to the ocean side," he said to Sarah. "It's different than the bay side. It's just the ocean out there . . . all the way to Peru!" He peered at the old map.

"I think that's Goat Hill," he said, moving his finger over the dip of land at the far end of the beach. "Heard there's good surfin' there, but no one hardly goes there . . . There's an undertow or something."

"Maybe we could go there," she said. "I'd like to see that beach, and the Pacific. I'd like to see Goat Hill."

She was aware she was disturbing Russell. She wanted to be perverse. She was sick of riddles and secrets and *not knowing* things!

"Don't go to Goat Hill," said Russell flatly. "It's not a good place; it's dangerous. The cliff breaks off into the ocean."

"We won't climb too close to the edge, then," she said

stubbornly. Mako was watching them both now. It felt to him as if they were pushing against each other.

"Go here," Russell said, pointing to a headland closer to Arana. "It has a beautiful beach, with a rock in the center, with caves in it."

But she was not going to give in. She was fascinated by the great wild beach with the massive headland at one end, where no kauri forest had ever grown.

"Why is it called Goat Hill?" she asked. Russell hesitated, looking at the girl. She had such an intense, serious face . . . a strong face.

"That is just a Pakeha name," he said softly. He moved up behind her, to the map.

"That is a place you should not go," he said again. "It is a sacred place. It is where the canoe navigators went to die."

The girl was waiting for him to continue, but Mako was slumping back into the shadow. The boy did not like these stories; he would fly into a rage.

"It is a place where the sky is very big. At night, the stars are not hidden by the great trees. So the navigators go there when they are ready to die. They walk down the little valley and climb the hill, which is broken off straight down into the ocean. They sit on the edge, staring into the night. They know all the stars, all the paths. When they have mapped out a path for themselves, when they know the way, then they die."

He hadn't wanted to tell her this story, because he knew it would put the boy in a fury. He did not know why Sarah had become so fascinated by looking at a place on a map. Why had it caught her eye? Simply because it was bare of forest?

"Eh, Sarah!" cried Mako. "Don't listen to his rubbish!" He swung the kitchen chair around and it crashed over.

"You and your stories, mate!" growled Mako. "Didn't I say they were just fairy tales, eh! Is that what comes of readin' all these books?" He swung his arm around the room in disgust. "Fill your head up with all sorts of bloody crap!" He took Sarah's arm.

"We can go to Goat Hill," he said aggressively. "I told you: I go where I want! No story's going to stop me. I'll take you there, eh!" He slammed out of the room.

Sarah stood in the center of the room, still clutching the book of poems. She looked at Russell with uncertainty. This was her fault. She knew it. All her questions . . .

"Don't worry, love," said Russell softly. "He always gets like this. He just doesn't know where he's going, yet. He's still living on anger and his daddy's dreams . . . It's good that he knows you. You're very brave . . . and very stubborn!" He grinned.

She thanked him for the book. He was the second person who had told her she was brave. She didn't feel brave at all. As she went out the door, she gave him a little wave and he nodded at her.

She looked past him to the old map; he saw where her eyes went.

"Be careful," he said.

11
GOAT HILL

The storm hit late that evening. Within an hour, it had blown down the few power lines connecting Port William's makeshift electricity supply, and the house at the Crossroads went dark.

It was nothing like the persistent, rain-heavy storm that had kept Sarah housebound when she'd first arrived on Great Kauri. This storm was different. It came unexpectedly, slashing the island with streaks of lightning and hurricane winds. The rain battered the house with a fury that sent Sarah running down the dark hall into Mari's kitchen. Surely the house would be torn from its base!

"Your mum'll be all right, love," said Mari gently. She and Mike lit the kerosene lamps that Mako had brought in from the shed outside. He stood dripping and laughed at the look on Sarah's face.

"I love it, eh!" he cried, and the lamplight settled deep into his eyes. Even Kikiwa had been allowed into the kitchen on this night.

"This kind of storm blows out to sea by morning," said Mike. "But it'll be too rough to take the boats out, eh." He smiled at Sarah. "They have cots and food and stoves down at the

Point — your mum's stayed there before. They'll be OK."

They loaded her with blankets and put her on the couch for the night. She thought she might even be able to sleep, with the family around her. It was very dark. The little girls never stirred. Mike and Mari shut the door to their room.

She knew he would come, then. They touched blindly. The couch was narrow. Mako did not get under the blankets, but tucked them around her and lay along her, holding her. "I love storms," he whispered, kissing her. She could taste the rain on his skin. His mouth was warm and full. She fell asleep before he crept back to his own bed.

And in the morning, he came out and stood looking down at her on the couch. The wind still battered the house, but through the window a strange, clear sunlight came in against the dark sky.

"Today we can go to the ocean," he said, his eyes burning with excitement. "I will take you!"

She knew where he would take her. She could see the great sweep of beach in her mind's eye, the line of the map curving up to form the massive headland. She could hear Russell's words in her ears: 'Be careful!'

She ran down the hall and dashed off a note for Pauline. She stuffed her pack full of sweaters and a blanket, grabbing some food from the kitchen. Mako was already waiting for her by the truck, Kikiwa in the back.

"This is the best kind of day to see the real ocean!" he cried. Sarah laughed with him. The storm and the wild day made them giddy. Mako spun the truck out of the yard and down the track toward Port William.

A little farm track cut east from Port William out through the hills. On either side of them, the mountains rose black and broken with mist. The Needles seemed to glower like guards planted at the gates of the storm. The track at times was no more than a shadow in the white grass. They went by a tiny farm set up in the hills, passed through two rusty gates, and then there was nothing — nothing but the bare dun-colored hills and the sky raging with clouds.

The island was at its most narrow point here, and within fifteen minutes the track melted into dunes and disappeared. They left the truck where they stopped, and walked down toward the Pacific.

The dunes were wide, but with gullies and pockets of scrubby bushes. It wasn't until they had scrambled up the last steep dune that Sarah could look out over the whole beach. Her eyes followed the white curve of sand. Against the blinding elements of sea and sand, a black hill rose to meet the black of the sky. So powerfully did the hill break against the horizon, so violent was its effect on her sight, that she gasped aloud. Mako, too, stood awed, his hand buried deep in Kikiwa's fur. For a timeless moment they stood poised on the ridge, looking over at Goat Hill.

But the wild wind and whirling gulls screaming over them were more than they could resist. They raced down the dune, tumbling and rolling against each other, the dog barking in excitement. What a day this was! The air still snapped with electricity, the wind still carried the last taste of the storm. They screamed with laughter and energy in the cold sand, tumbling toward each other until they clung together more insistently than ever before. They could hardly breathe. The dog barked again, and they broke apart, breathing hard. They stared at each other, wide-eyed.

There had never been such a day, such a wind. The beach stretched away on either side of them, and the Pacific smashed against the sand and covered them in spray.

"Why is the hill black?" Sarah asked, when they at last

walked quietly on the packed sand. Their hearts still beat at them, with the running and laughing and wind.

"The farmers do it," he answered. They both stopped now, and stared over at the dark headland. "They burn off the tough winter grass so it's easier for the new grass in spring."

They wandered slowly. The sand was littered with great strands of kelp and clumps of bright green weed; under their feet were a dozen kinds of shells. She gathered them as she went. Mako grinned at her.

"You'll need another pack just to carry them!" he said. She bent and arranged some in a pattern on the sand. She showed him one that was broken, so that the delicate, spiraling insides were exposed. His brown finger traced the soft pink.

"You are like this shell," he said softly, pressing against her. "I have never touched anything so perfect." He ran the shell lightly over her lips.

A mist came in over the dunes; the light dimmed. The wind turned heavy and sluggish, stunted by the mass of hill ahead of them that blocked it. They walked steadily now, with purpose. They no longer explored the beach around them, or danced away from the waves. They no longer spoke or touched.

It was not easy to get onto the hill. A muddy stream drained from the lowland into the sea, and there were wire fences to climb. The beach ended in a fall of rocks, slippery with rain and spray. Still, they pushed doggedly on, Mako ahead. Once she slipped and banged her knee. She made no noise but the boy turned instantly, reaching for her.

They came to a low saddle that connected the hill to a narrow valley hidden on the far side. The wind died. No gulls or terns wheeled above them. They stood looking up at the blackness of the hill.

The blood throbbed in Sarah's head; she could not catch her breath. Her chest ached. Mako's back was toward her so she could not see him. She looked around. The mist swirled in threads of cold through the grasses.

How was it she was so tired? Her body was a dead weight. She could hardly stand. She wanted to reach out to Mako, to touch him, but already he had moved away. Her constricted throat could make no sound. But they were going to climb the hill! There — Mako had already begun. She struggled to follow him.

Why wouldn't he wait for her? Why didn't he turn to look at her? She whimpered; her body was falling asleep even as she moved. She could not believe how tired she was, as if she had never slept. Must have been the wind, she thought fuzzily . . . must have been all the running . . .

And, suddenly, there was the black dog Kikiwa. She sank helplessly into the tall grasses that fell away down the saddle into the valley. The dog moved his body between her and the hill, so that he seemed in his blackness to be a part of it. He shielded her from the wind. She could no longer see Mako.

She could no longer think of him. She could no longer think at all, nor did she care. She wanted to sleep; she *would* sleep. Around her was nothing — only silence, and the little valley below her. Nothing was alive here. There were no sea birds. No insects stirred in the grass under her cheek. Nothing existed.

She fell asleep. It was deeper than sleep. It was nothingness. She was not there at all; she was gone.

And when she woke, it was if she had never slept. She sat up immediately. The dog lay alert near her. She looked at him calmly. The wind touched her face, smelling of the sea. A beetle skittered over her sneaker and was gone. Above her, a sea bird wheeled in the bright sky, bigger than any bird she had ever seen, more brilliant and more perfect than anything on earth.

It skimmed over her and rose on the wind until it hung just off the peak of the black hill. And there, below it, the navigator walked. He was a tiny figure, so far away, with the sun behind him; he was coming toward her. But why was he coming back? Why did he not stay up there, waiting for night? . . . The dog stood up.

She squinted in the light. Her mind snapped into focus and she jumped up. That was Mako, coming down off the black hill! Why had she not gone with him? She looked down into the little valley — an ordinary little valley, where a few roan cows foraged and tiny yellow finches flittered through the scrub.

She frowned. Something pricked at her mind; something disturbed her. What was it? She struggled to remember . . . She'd fallen asleep! Yes! That was it — but why? She shaded her eyes with her hand and watched Mako slowly descending the black hill. How much time had passed? It must be late afternoon! she thought wildly. But we were here in the morning . . .

Kikiwa stood between her and the approaching boy. Suddenly irritated, she stepped around him. She wanted to run to Mako, to touch him. But the dog shifted quietly, once more blocking her way. Again, she stepped past him. But by now the boy had almost reached them, so she waited.

He came right to her. He ran his hand from the top of her head down her arm to her hand, briefly touching her fingers. She felt as if he were *checking* her somehow, to see if she were all right. But she did not like the little faraway smile, or the faraway focus of his eyes. It was as if he was not really there.

He led her back over the rocks onto the beach. It was late

in the day. A pair of oyster catchers scurried away from them. Finally, she could not stand it any longer. She took his hand, trying to get him to run with her as they had before, trying to shake him out from the strange mood he was in. She wanted to open her arms and race down the sand; she wanted the clean wind to wash through her, wash away the hill . . .

He came with her without protest. When she stopped running, out of breath, she was startled to notice that his breathing was normal, as if he had never run.

"Mako!" she cried softly, frightened now. Suddenly she was terribly frightened. "Mako!"

He focused his eyes and looked at her.

"Don't worry," he said. She stared at him.

"I want to go back," she pleaded. "I want to go to the truck."

He nodded. She took his hand. It hung in hers, not responding. Where was he! What had happened, up on that hill! She felt another whimper tugging at her throat. She pulled him along with her.

They struggled up the steep dunes, sliding and falling in the fine sand. She went ahead. They had almost reached the top when she stumbled and lost her balance, rolling down against him so that they both slid back to the bottom.

She giggled a little hysterically, spitting sand from her mouth. Mako lay under her, curled tightly where he had fallen. She looked into his face and saw he was trying to smile for her, but it was a desperate try. She wrapped her arms and legs around him and held him.

"Oh, Mako, what is it!" she whispered. His body was so hard under hers. "What happened up there? Please . . . please . . ." She was begging him. She wanted him back. She wanted Mako, not this hard, faraway person who had come to her off the black hill.

"I cannot tell you. You would not understand. It is not

possible to tell you," he answered her at last. The dull tone
of his voice shocked her. She shook him.

"I would!" she cried. "I would understand! It frightens me
not to know!"

His whole body was resisting her, his eyes unrecognizable.
A tremor passed through her, a flimsy web of trembling, with
a thought scuttling off like a spider just departing. She grabbed
at it violently, forcing her mind to be steady. She breathed
deeply. Aunt Hattie! Aunt Hattie! She stared deep into Mako's
eyes, willing him to look at her. She *would* know! He *would*
tell her!

He turned his head away desperately.

"I cannot . . ." he whispered weakly. They lay for a long
time. The dog watched them without moving.

"You can," she said. "You went up the hill. You did not
wait for me, and I fell asleep. I was *put* to sleep. I was not
meant to go with you, Mako! I was *put* to sleep!"

She brushed the sand from his face. She had said the words
as she thought them, and she knew she was right. It took all
her willpower to hold off the fear. Aunt Hattie! Aunt Hattie!
She shook her head angrily. She had everything to do with
this!

So she said the old woman's name aloud. It was the only
thing left for her to say.

Mako's body arched under her. He pushed her violently
off. His wide mouth was parted, and his teeth showed strong
and white like an animal's . . . like the teeth of the black dog.

"Why do you say her name!" he demanded. "What has she
got to do with this!"

When she didn't answer, he pulled himself up and covered
her roughly with his body. He was crushing her. She couldn't
breathe.

"What goes on down there!" he cried. "What does that old

witch say to you?" He shook her violently.

She flung a handful of sand into his eyes. He reared back, and with a sob, she jerked free onto her knees. She refused to run from him. Her stomach was clenched in pain. Her teeth ground together. She stumbled to her feet and looked down at him.

He had curled into a tight ball, as if to shield himself.

"Mako," she said. "Mako. Get up. Get up."

He immediately uncurled himself and stood. She would not let him turn his head away, and she did not drop her eyes. She did not trust him, so she made him look at her. He reached out his hand, but she stepped back.

"Please come sit next to me," he said at last, turning and kneeling on the sand. His eyes were dull, but in his voice was a dignity that reached through to her. Because of the dignity, she joined him.

"I am afraid of her; I am afraid of the old woman," he said. "I am afraid, because there are things happening to me I do not understand. There are stories . . . I am frightened. So I hurt you."

Some feeling was returning to her tense body. She could listen to him. He was not excusing himself. She was fiercely glad that he did not apologize. It would have made her ill.

"I hate you right now," she said.

"I know," he said simply. He could see the pain in her eyes, and it cut into him. He was helpless.

She did not trust him. She wanted to poke at him, to see what he would do. She turned away deliberately, to hurt him, and waited.

He began to talk then. He told her about the black hill. "I climbed a long way up the hill," he said. "It was a very steep hill, and it was hard. When I looked back, you were gone and Kikiwa was gone. But I still went on up the hill. I did not think about anything, or care. I just wanted to get to the top.

"It was horrible up there. I was scared. The hill is broken in half, and drops hundreds of feet into the ocean. I thought the wind would blow me off. I had to lie on my belly, eh, because of the wind. I started to crawl away, because I wanted to go back . . ."

His voice trailed off. He was sitting next to her now, and she reached up to touch his face. His skin was cool and moist from the mist, and the muscles along his jaw jumped under her fingers. He looked out over the water.

"I wanted to go back," he repeated, determined. "But I heard a voice tell me to stay, and not be afraid."

Now he looked at her, almost defiant. But she nodded. She believed him. He pulled his breath in jaggedly and went on.

"So I lay there for a very long time, waiting. I was supposed to wait. I waited for the voice to talk to me. It was a nice voice. I liked it; I wanted to hear it again.

"But then I started thinking I was crazy, eh. I was cold. I sat up, and the wind hit me. I was afraid again. I thought I must be crazy.

"And then the voice came again and told me not to go yet. It said: 'Wait.' I was getting mad. I didn't like it up on that hill. I wanted to go down. I was afraid that — "

"That what?"

"I think . . . that you were frightened." He nodded. "I thought, What if you were hurt? I wanted to get down, to find you. I hated it up there.

"Then a lot of voices came at me, all jabbering at me. They kept saying things to me, but I couldn't understand them. I was very afraid, because they were getting inside me, all those voices . . .

"So then I got bloody mad, eh! I said, 'Speak up! Speak up!' They were all whispering away, but they didn't like me saying that. They went right away then, eh. That shut them up. So it was very quiet again, and I had to rest.

"And after a while, the other one came. At first I thought it was the wind, but then I knew it was her voice . . . the one I liked. She said: 'It is a good thing, that you did not listen to the others. Listen to me.' So I listened, because I could understand her . . ."

"It was a her?"

"Yes," he nodded slowly. "Yes, I am sure, eh. Then it said to listen only to her voice, not to the others. I thought that was OK. Then she said to go down the hill, and not to worry about you. It said you were *being watched* over . . ."

They were locked in each other's eyes, now.

"So the voice said I was to listen carefully, for the next time it spoke. She said, 'I will come again, so listen for me. You will hear me. Then I will talk to you.' She told me to be sure to pay no attention if the others came, whispering and jabbering in my head.

"So I got up and went back down the hill. At first, I was all right. But when I saw you waiting for me, I began to get afraid again, eh. I knew I was crazy. It was all crazy! I am so scared," he said. "I don't want to be crazy!"

She reached out a hand to him.

"And then," he continued, more softly now, "I could see that you knew something had happened. I knew you were going to make me tell you, eh. But I was so scared, and I knew you would see that I was crazy. I thought, If I could just have some time by myself, I'd be OK. But you kept pulling at me. And then you said *her* name . . ."

He paused.

"I never wanted to meet her! But you took me there . . . and she talks about me! I know she does. I know she wants something from me, I don't know what. And you keep going there to see her. She talks to you. I want to know what she says." He ground his teeth.

The sand was so cold. It was chilling them through their clothes. Sarah wanted to ask him something.

"You know, in Waitapu, when you were talking about your dad — did you ever tell me about Tawahi?" she asked. He hid his face against her shoulder, and shook his head.

"You never said his name?" she persisted. He drew back and looked at her, then shook his head again. He was too exhausted to be startled.

"I started to, eh," he said softly. "But remember those two blokes walking by? . . . And then I never did."

She looked away a moment, frowning.

"Well, somehow — I know." She hesitated. "I was in the museum, in Auckland. There was a big hall, with a huge canoe, and buildings . . ."

He nodded.

"And there were paintings, of Maori men. They were chiefs. I read all the names. I saw Tawahi. I knew he was your great-great-great-grandfather. There was no one around. So I told him about you; I told him you remembered him."

He realized he had been wanting to cry for a long time. It was no longer possible to hold back. He could not even hide his face from her. He cried and cried, and all the scariness and hurting washed out. It was a most wonderful relief.

"I love you. I love you," he said.

12
THE ANGER

Hattie had been sitting by the fire most of the day. She had not moved, and by now the fire was just embers. She was cold. In the pen, the albatross stirred. The old woman got stiffly to her feet.

She peered in at the bird. The injury was completely healed, and the feathers on the neck and wing were almost grown in. But the bird was listless. She no longer hopped the length of her pen or flexed her beautiful wings, as she had a short time ago. And she had stopped eating well.

Hattie gathered a pile of manuka sticks and shoved them into the embers. The fire caught at once, flickering on the dark canopy of ferns. She took her broom and swept the earth of the clearing, pausing every once in a while to listen.

But the girl did not come. She had not come for two days — since before the storm. The old woman cleared her throat. It bewildered her, how much she had come to look for the girl. She loved the bright flurry of her steps down the path, the quick whoosh of the ferns as the girl parted them to come into the clearing. She was so very, very alive! And the songs she played on her flute — that was life itself!

Hattie jabbed the old broom at the earth. She had not counted on the girl: she was the unknown factor. The boy, of course, she had always known would come. It was part of the prophecy, that she would find *someone* . . . But it had been such a long wait — a whole lifetime! And still, he had not yet come. He had to come to *her;* she could not drag him in. But he loved the girl. He would come for the girl . . .

The old woman was tired. For many weeks she had been tired. The waiting was almost more than she could bear. She just wanted to *let go*. Would the boy never come? Where was the girl?

She looked again at the albatross. The bird was dying — she was powerless to change that. It had to be set free. But everything — *everything* — had to happen at the right time, at the same time. But the girl would be gone soon, and if the bird died . . . the boy would be lost! Lost! He would never come on his own.

The old woman felt the cold weight of panic inside her. It was a sensation she was not used to. She paced the clearing. She was hungry, but she could not concentrate on finding food. It was more important that she *think*. *Think!*

Something had happened to the boy and girl the day after the storm. The old woman had been filled with a tremendous force of energy that day. It had grown and grown inside her. The storm was blowing itself out over the Pacific, and the bush was roaring above her. All that day she had walked, the blood rushing through her like the waterfalls of the stream. Her muscles and bones felt young and strong.

And then, as if a drain had opened, it had all rushed out of her. All the energy, all the anticipation — gone. She had been left as she was now, tired and waiting. Once more she squatted at the fire, pipe between her teeth. She waited. She waited.

*

Sarah looked up in surprise. It was midafternoon — Pauline never came back from the lab before six. Maybe she wasn't feeling well. She put down her flute and met her mother at the door. Pauline didn't look sick; she looked excited.

"You're home early," Sarah said brightly. She felt an unexpected stillness pass through her, a premonition. She shook herself, frowning. Pauline probably had just discovered a rare two-headed bird or something, she thought sourly. I just hope she doesn't have some *plan* for us this afternoon!

She was waiting for Mako. He had taken the little boat out for the first time since the storm, and wasn't planning on fishing far from the shoreline. He'd promised to come back early so they could take some crayfish traps down to Arana to be mended, but here was Pauline, looking as if she had some bright idea for her this afternoon. She smiled at her mother dubiously. Pauline's cheeks were flushed, and her step was quick and happy as she went into the kitchen.

"I had to come and tell you, sweetie!" she cried, throwing her bags on the floor. "This just came in the mail!"

She held out a thick envelope for Sarah to see. She took it, frowning. It had a New Zealand postmark, and the return address read: Tairoa Head Reserve, Otago, Dunedin. She looked up at her mother.

"Tairoa Head — that's where they protect the albatross, isn't it?" she asked slowly. Pauline laughed and took the envelope, pulling out a letter.

"They want me to come!" she said. "They've invited me for six months to study the breeding colony at Tairoa Head! Remember I told you what an honor that was? I can't believe it!"

Sarah grinned, relief flooding her. She was glad for Pauline, and glad she was not going to be asked to drag along on some errand or other. She twisted her mouth ruefully. Pauline was always trying to kill two birds with one stone — spend time with her while doing some other task. The metaphor made her giggle.

"That's great, Pauline!" she said, giving her an awkward hug around the shoulders. "I remember you said you'd love to go there — that's super!"

Why did she always have such mixed feelings with Pauline? Come on, Sarah Steinway — it's not as if you *wanted* to do anything with her this afternoon, for God's sake! But . . . somehow . . . she should have guessed it would be about Pauline's work.

She lit the gas under the kettle and made some cheese sandwiches for them both. Pauline sat reading over the letter.

"I'll have to work fast, to finish up here," she was saying, almost to herself.

The kettle screeched and Sarah jumped. Again, she felt a stillness, a chill . . . "Why?" she asked.

Pauline laughed, the worried little frown gone. "Oh, it's nothing — I can do it. They'd like me there in two weeks." She tapped the letter on the table. "When does your ticket say you're going, sweetie?"

The cold stillness engulfed Sarah. She felt a roaring in her ears. She sat carefully at the table, saying nothing.

"I don't think we'd have any trouble getting it changed," said Pauline. "Tairoa Head is pretty strict . . . I just don't think you could come. And I wouldn't feel right leaving you here alone . . ."

The roaring was threatening to deafen her. Her throat was so tight she could hardly breathe. Go back to New York — *early?* In two *weeks?*

"If they'd just given me more notice — but no matter. I'll just have to work nights to write up the data here, and show

Peter . . ." Pauline's voice trailed off, lost in her plans.

"You want me to change my ticket . . . and leave early?" whispered Sarah. She gathered herself inside, willing herself not to cry out. She sat very still. Two weeks — but she had more than a month left! More than a month — and Mako! Oh, Mako! . . .

"Oh, sweetie — I know!" said Pauline, distracted. She patted Sarah's hand briefly. "I know you've got new friends here, but really, sweetheart, you know I can't just go off and leave you here! Mari and Mike don't have time. Anyway, don't you think it would be a good idea to leave some time at the other end to get ready for school? I mean, you must have some shopping . . ."

Sarah couldn't believe this was happening. She was utterly powerless. Everything — her whole life! — was being shattered, and there was nothing she could do about it. And Mako — Mako! The pain of it cut through her so she almost doubled up. They hadn't had enough time — there was no time!

"Look," Pauline was saying. She heard the voice through a haze. "We could go to Auckland again, just the two of us, OK? Before you go? We'll have a real fling!"

And she watched her mother sitting across from her, saw the puzzled, pretty little frown, the slight irritation . . . Her daughter was just a bit inconvenient now, now when she had this chance of a lifetime. The stillness inside Sarah had begun to focus, to form into a fist. *Pauline did not care!* She saw nothing but her ambitions. She did not see Sarah, did not see the things that were important to her — her flute, the island, Mako . . .

What did she think this was with Mako — a silly child's crush? Something she could lightly leave, to replace with a shopping spree in New York? Did Pauline have any idea what had happened to her during the last month and a half? Did she know how the music had grown in Sarah, how her fingers could fly over the keys — did she know how it was, to ride at a gallop along the beach with the wind hurling spray in her face? Did she know how it was to lie with Mako in the hollow of a dune, feel his hands on her, listen to his curious, compelling voice?

She knew none of that! She knew nothing of Sarah's life at all! The stillness had become such an anger as she had never before felt. Pauline knew nothing of anyone, because it was easier simply to *leave*. When things got in the way, she left! She put them out of her way, like she had ten years ago . . . like she was doing now!

"I won't let you mess my life up again," she said, measuring each word. A startled expression crossed her mother's face.

"What do you mean?"

"You know what I mean, Pauline," said Sarah. She could hardly believe her voice, low with hatred. Yes, hatred! She hated Pauline! Maybe she had always hated her. Hated her for being so charming with everyone, for being beautiful, for her bright promises that she never kept . . . She hated Pauline for leaving them, her and her father. She remembered that summer, ten years ago. You can remember a lot from when you are six, she thought.

Everyone loves Pauline, she thought bitterly. Even Daddy, years later, still loves Pauline! And how she used to wait for the letters, the bright, bubbly letters filled with adventure and promises! Pauline had flaunted her newfound freedom in their faces! What right did she have to send those letters!

"I'm not going anywhere!" she said now, staring into her mother's eyes. "I have five weeks left, and I'm staying! *Alone* — what do you mean, alone? You've always left me alone! You can't start playing mother now!"

Pauline seemed to rock back from the shock of Sarah's words. Her hand was frozen around the teacup. Sarah was standing now, leaning toward her.

"You can't just shove me away because it's simpler that way! You can't get away with it anymore, you hear? Everyone else might let you, because you're successful and charming and wonderful, but *I won't!*" She shouted the last words. The room was buzzing around her. She grabbed on to the back of the chair.

"I almost *died* when you left! Did you know that? Remember that summer — you just left. *You left me.* I got sick with something. Daddy didn't tell you. He couldn't even find you!"

She slammed her tea mug into the sink, to keep back the sob that was choking her.

"I really wanted to come here and be with you," she whispered. "I really felt OK, you know? I thought I was all grown up, that I could really understand why you left. And I was OK, and Daddy — he was OK too. I thought I could really get to know you, and you'd like me . . ."

She couldn't hold back the sob this time. She bit her lip. She had to finish this.

"I wanted to *be* like you! I really admired you — how you worked really hard, and were the best . . ."

Pauline opened her mouth to speak, but Sarah ran over her with her words.

"Well, I don't want to be like you! I can see a lot more clearly now! I *like* being who I am! And I'm still going to be the best. I'm good — I'm really good! I'll play the flute — but I'm not going to be *nothing* inside, like you!" She knew she was really hurting Pauline, now. "I *will* love people. I love someone now! And I'm not going to just leave him, because it's easier for you!"

Pauline was standing now. Sarah backed away. She couldn't

stand the look on that face. Her heart twisted inside her. She wanted to open her mouth and howl. Why didn't her mother *say* something? Why didn't she fight back!

"Why did you leave me?" Sarah whispered. "Why did you leave?"

Her mother held her hands out, turning them palm up, a helpless gesture. All Sarah wanted was to touch her, to hold her, to be held . . . but she could not move. Her face was stone.

"I have five more weeks here. I love Mako . . . I love him! I have that much time with him. I'll probably never see him again. I'll never see Daphne again . . . or anything." She was crying now; she didn't care. "You aren't going to shove me aside, just because it's more convenient for you! I don't care what you do, but I'm staying! I'm staying! You'll have to drag me kicking and screaming all the way to Auckland and push me on the plane, 'cause that's the only way you'll get me there! And that's not very *convenient,* is it!"

She threw the chair away from her and spun out the back door. She noticed vaguely that it was quite late — the sun was low over the hills. She didn't know where she was going, but there was only one place she *could* go — she threw a bridle on Celeste and cantered out of the yard onto the road. If she didn't come back tonight, they'd never know where to look; even Daphne would never remember the exact spot in all those miles of bush. Only Mako knew the little path . . . Mako . . .

She knew the path by heart. She tethered Celeste hastily inside the bush, so she couldn't be seen from the road. Soon it would be dark. She ran across the little bridge.

The old woman was standing waiting for her when she pushed through the ferns.

"Long before your footsteps, I heard your sorrow and

anger," she said softly, leading the girl to the fire. It was a big fire, and warm; she sat by it gratefully. The old woman stumped into the hut and came out with an old jacket much like the one she had on. She draped it over Sarah's shoulders. The girl pulled it around her, burying her face in the strong, familiar smell. Hattie squatted beside her.

"First, girl," she said firmly, "you will not leave the island until it is right for you and everything that touches you. Do you understand what I am saying? You will know when it is right."

The ferns moved gently around her in the dusk. The fire was warming her. She swayed, relaxing.

"Second," continued Hattie, "you will mend the hurt you gave your mother." She held up her hand to silence Sarah's protest. "You must do this. The emptiness your mother lives with comes from all the hurts she caused and never healed. You must do this, or you will be as empty as she is. You do not have the strength to live with such emptiness. It is lucky you do not. Your music would be swallowed forever."

Sarah stared into the flames, feeling the heat on her face. But everything she'd said to her mother was *true!* She wasn't going to take it back! The old woman's eyes pierced into her.

"And third," said Hattie, as if taking care of necessary business, "you must tell me what happened to you and the boy, the day after the storm."

Sarah swallowed, hugging the jacket around her. She could not tell the old woman about the black hill. That was Mako's secret. She could not betray him. She peeked at the old face from under the corner of the coat. How did she *know?* She shivered.

"You are fearing me again, girl!" said Hattie softly. "I thought you were long past that."

She struggled to withstand the eyes. But under the fierceness was something else . . . hurt! Sarah swallowed again. Hattie was hurt that she feared her!

"We went up a hill," she said dully. "He heard voices."

The bush had grown very dark. She had never been here at night. It was so still. The old woman was waiting.

"I fell asleep, in the grass. And then Mako . . . he tried to get me to tell him about you. He's scared. He doesn't know what's going on. He thinks you talk about him . . . want something . . . and you do!"

She jerked the coat over her back and stared stonily into the flames. She refused to look at Hattie. Why couldn't she just leave her alone! Leave Mako alone! Why couldn't *everyone* just leave them alone!

The old woman gazed into her fire. The corner of her mouth curved into a tiny smile. She breathed deeply several times. Just slightly, her body rocked, as if nodding.

"I'm not going to harm him, girl," she said at last. "Do you trust me?"

It was an unexpected question, and it shook her. Did she trust the old woman? Could you trust someone who spoke in riddles, who badgered secrets from you, who knew what you were thinking and what happened to you?

"I trust you," said Sarah. That was the second time, she thought — the second time I've told someone I trusted them. She did not think she had ever said it to anyone before.

Hattie nodded her head.

"I knew that, girl," she chuckled. "If I did not know that, I would not have let you come."

Sarah sighed, standing up and stretching.

"You know," she said, "All Mako wants to do is buy his boat and go off and be with his dad. And all I want is to love him. And play my flute," she added quickly, grinning. She couldn't stay annoyed or uneasy over Hattie for long.

The old woman chuckled again.

"He can do all those things," she said. "And you can too. There's just more . . ."

But she would not finish. They peeked in at the albatross. The bird's eyes blinked slowly back at them. The vitality seemed to be draining from her. Sarah looked anxiously over at Hattie.

"Will she make it?" she whispered. "Will she fly?"

Hattie sucked deeply on her pipe.

"Soon," she answered. "Soon."

And it did not seem to Sarah that she spoke only of the albatross.

Mako took the boat farther down the island than he had intended. He checked his watch and frowned; he didn't want to be too late to meet Sarah and go to Arana. But the fish were running south along the shoreline. The storm had put Mike out of operation for several days, and money was tight. So Mako followed the fish.

He skirted the tip of Little Penguin Island and cut across the southern outlet of Blind Bay. He stopped to drop lines there, but the fish had moved again. Exasperated, he hauled up the hooks and opened the throttle on the boat. It was noon now, and the weak winter sun hung limp above him. The fish would not bite now. He decided to move further south.

For more than an hour, he leaned against the wall in the wheelshed with the motor throbbing under him and the sun warm on his back. He lost track of time. Kikiwa lay asleep in the shadow of the shed; even the sea birds, usually his constant company, wheeled away. He propped his elbow against the wheel and took out the book on Martin Luther King.

His reading was less labored. He could read without moving his lips, and he didn't get caught in a sudden jam-up of words and lose his temper as he used to. He read aloud to Sarah now, where once she had read for him. He loved reading to her, loved the way she would become still and rapt, watching him. And he loved the way his voice came from him when he read — especially the poetry. Then it would almost soar, taking on its own life: just the words and the voice.

He read aloud now, as he moved the boat steadily down toward Waitapu Bay.

" 'I have a dream!' " he said, his eyes burning. " 'I have a dream!' "

He drank in the words, drank in the sense of the man. There was something here to learn from! His eyes shone. He wished he knew more — more background about America, about the blacks in America, about the *world*. New Zealand was so small, so isolated. But there were no inner cities like those in America, where the problems could be hidden, ignored by the majority of the country. There were no vast deserts to stick a whole race of people, out of sight — in New Zealand, everyone lived caught on a tiny bit of earth set in the broad ocean.

He caught his breath, looking out at the water. Maybe the isolation was an advantage! Maybe here, because everyone *had* to live together, *had* to look at one another every day, maybe the big changes would finally come about. Maybe New Zealand could be an example to the *world!*

But how? How? He shoved the book deep into his pocket. The boat was chugging down the great headland protecting Waitapu Bay from the north. He had to concentrate on the steering now.

He set the boat and let down the lines. He inspected his hooks and bait, shading his eyes to look over the water. The fish should be here.

The water flashed around him. He leaned tensely against

the side. Again the water boiled with a million diamonds of light. He grabbed the binoculars. Fish! A huge school of snapper! But something was disturbing them.

The school of snapper turned the water to froth. Suddenly, a huge body broke the water just to the left of him. He swung his binoculars, waiting, his lips parted. Again, the animal plunged half out of the sea, and this time Mako saw the gleaming blue-gray skin, the violent slash of tail — shark! He watched, hardly daring to breathe.

It was *his* shark — the mako shark! It was a shark like this that his great-great-great-grandfather, Tawahi, chief of the Ngati Niwha, had battled and slain. It was from such a shark that the tooth Mako wore in his ear had come. He let out his breath in a shout.

The shark was a loner, playing with his food, driving the snapper into a frenzy. Once or twice, half his body reared clear of the water, so Mako could see the gill-slits, the tiny eyes, the rows of teeth . . .

He hadn't known sharks to leap and dive like this. How beautiful he was! The sun varnished the sleek body, played along the rippling muscles. Mako dashed along the boat, pulling in his lines. The snapper seethed around him, frantic. The lines would get tangled beyond recovery. Now, like a sheepdog, the shark was herding them under the boat.

Taut with excitement, Mako rushed to the wheelshed and threw the boat into full throttle. The shark leapt ahead, slicing through the sun-backed water like a gleaming blade of steel. The snapper turned and jackknifed, thousands upon thousands of them, leaping clear to escape the predator among them. Mako followed instinctively, his eyes glued to the magnificent animal in front of him. How perfect he was! The water sheared off the notched fin; the shark rolled in the water and dove. Row upon row of teeth flashed and disappeared into the sea. The man who would fight such an animal to the death was a chief of men indeed!

With a violent lurch that threw him against the wall of the wheelshed, the boat ground to a stop. Mako cried out, stumbling out onto the deck. He had run into a sand bar that sloped twenty feet out from shore. He shaded his eyes. The shark had led him to the northern end of Waitapu Bay, where the Arana River let out into mud flats and mangrove swamps.

He pulled off his boots and jumped over the side, landing in the sand. The water came to midthigh. He checked the rudder and the hull of the boat — nothing was damaged. He'd run headfirst into the soft sand. He shaded his eyes again and looked around.

The shark and the snapper were gone. The water lay silty and sluggish here, the stink of mud and mangroves filling his nose. He studied the waterline and realized with relief that it was dead low tide. With luck, in an hour or two, the incoming tide would lift the little boat clear of the sand bar.

He climbed back into the boat and sat on the tilted deck, rubbing the arm that had crashed into the wall. Not much to do now but wait, he thought. He sighed; he would miss the time with Sarah. He wished she were with him — they could have good fun, exploring the mangroves.

He reached into the hold for the metal-tipped stick he used for spearing flatfish, and took the bucket hanging on a nail by the hatch. May as well use the time, he reckoned — get a few flatfish. He heaved a heavy rope over the side and jumped into the cold water.

A log protruded from the sand at the edge of the bank, and he slogged toward it with the rope, which was attached to the boat at the other end. He yanked on the log; it didn't move.

He looped the rope around the log, testing the knots. If the tide came up faster than expected, the boat would not float away.

The water was quite cold, and he knew he could tolerate only half an hour of hunting flatfish waist-deep in the sea. He moved away from the main river channel to where the water was relatively shallow and clear. Almost immediately, a spurt of sand and a quick movement at his feet caught his eye. He darted the spear down and impaled the flounder. He grinned.

Mako hunted for twenty minutes, moving along the shoreline and filling his bucket with flounder. He climbed out on the bank after a while to warm himself. He squinted his eyes at the boat. Was it his imagination, or had it just lurched to one side? The tide was swelling the little estuary visibly now, so he grabbed the bucket and made his way back down the sand bar to the boat.

He left the bucket and spear and pulled himself along the rope to the stump. The water had risen a foot higher on the bank, so the log was now half submerged.

The rope was wet and swollen, and he could not undo his loops. Swearing, he found his knife and sawed at the thick hemp. Mike would have his neck — the rope was expensive.

The water was swirling around his knees by now, and he hung on to the log with one hand while he worked at the rope. He could feel the heavy texture of the bark, grooved and notched under his fingers. He picked at the mud-filled crevices absently as he struggled with the rope. His finger traced a groove as it spiraled down and around . . .

He stopped and looked at the log, then rubbed the wood roughly. His breath caught. He took the knife and scraped at the slime and mud, then sloshed water over it with his hands. The current was tugging at him; he anchored his leg around the rope and dug frantically with his fingers at the log.

His whole body hummed with a strange excitement. He scrubbed at the wood, racing the rising waters, panting. Soon the tide would come, the river would shift, the sand and mud would cover it as they had for more than a century . . .

He ran his hands down the sternpost of an ancient war canoe. Under his fingers the intricate carvings vibrated with life. The post curved upward into the sun as it must have done so long ago, when it swept proudly over the sea by the power of many paddles. His fingers traced slowly over the spirals and loops.

He didn't know he was almost numb with the cold. He was caught in the lovely mystery of the thing. Whose canoe had this been? How had it come to be buried in the mouth of the Arana River? He traced and retraced the pattern . . . Why was it so familiar? A curve here, a series of notches, another curve . . . Now he knew!

It was the same design he'd seen drawn in blue lines on his father's face, the first time he had heard him speak! The pattern of this carving matched exactly the moko on Henare Mokutu's face! He would never forget that day, with his father crying out his words in a vehement chant, his face wild and fearsome and wonderful. Later, he had explained the moko to his son, explained that it could only be worn by the directly descended sons of Tawahi . . . and he, Mako, was the first son of this new generation!

Under the slime and encrusted deposits on this ancient sternpost, the design was unmistakably the same. What could it mean? Through the cold of the sea, another chill eddied closer to his heart. He shivered, clenching his teeth to keep them from chattering. Grimacing with cold, he dried his hands as best he could on his upper jacket, and pulled from the pocket a pencil and a scrap of the paper he used for his poems.

His whole body trembled now, and it was difficult to hold

the pencil firmly. He pressed it against the wood, carefully tracing the dominant design of the pattern. He had to be sure; he had to record it. Painfully, he covered the paper with the design until it became entirely soaked and threatened to disintegrate. He folded it carefully and put it back in his pocket.

The boat was floating free. He pulled it slightly toward him, slashed at the rope, and raced through the water to climb aboard. He brought the boat slowly out of danger. There, he idled the motor and looked back at the sternpost. Only a foot or so showed. The sun hung heavily at the edge of the sea. For an instant, the golden light struck the sternpost and it glowed as if from an inner flame. The flame burst and died, the tide washed over the ancient carving, and it disappeared into the sea.

Mako took the boat back up the island. The trees and hills turned black and still, and the sea lay flat around him. He was terribly cold, and he was afraid. He wished desperately for Sarah. She could calm him; no one else made him feel peaceful inside. His arms ached, thinking of her. He wanted to be lying alongside her in the warm hill grasses, watching how she moved, watching how she spoke.

He felt he lived with a shadow, and she was the warmth that cut through the shadow. Never had he felt the shadow so clearly as that day on the black hill, lying on his belly in the terrifying wind, with that relentless voice filling him . . . And there, back there in the mouth of the Arana River, with his hands touching the sternpost of an ancient canoe, he had felt that shadow again. And Sarah had not been with him.

He trembled in his wet clothes. He wrapped the rain slicker around his body to cut out the wind, and felt a little better. By the time he rounded the tip of Little Penguin Island, it was dark, and he could see the lights at the Point twinkling dimly. In the dark, he hauled the ice-filled crate from the hold and heaved it into the truck. He had missed the plane; the fish would have to be stored until tomorrow in Russell's refrigerator. He was shaking with exhaustion and the strange, shadowy excitement. The folded paper in his jacket pocket seemed to burn into his skin.

As he drove past the Crossroads toward Port William, he looked over longingly at the lit windows. If he worked fast, he could be back in half an hour. He looked again, frowning, slamming the truck into reverse. What was Bill MacNeil's ute doing in the yard? He was the island's only resident policeman. He knew Mike, but they weren't mates. What was he doing here? And there was Pauline's Land Rover, too — and she rarely got back this early.

He took the steps up the verandah two at a time and threw open the door.

"Mum?" he called. "Mum — you all right?"

But Mari was there, with the little girls and Mike. Pauline sat on the couch and Bill MacNeil leaned in the doorway. They all looked startled when he came in.

"Have you seen Sarah?" asked Mike.

Sarah! Something had happened to Sarah! He stood taut with apprehension.

"I just got in, eh," he said, swallowing. "What happened? Where is she?"

"She ran out five hours ago . . . and it's dark now, and the horse . . ." Pauline's voice cracked. He ran to the kitchen window and peered out; Celeste stood in the paddock.

"She came in an hour ago, trailin' her reins," said Mike.

Sarah! The blood rushed to his face. Had she been thrown? But Celeste wouldn't throw her, not now, now that she knew her. He looked at Pauline, her face drawn and fearful. Sarah had *run out?* Something must have upset her!

"Why was she upset?" he demanded.

There was a small silence. Pauline shifted on the couch. He stared at her. What had happened?

"We had a fight . . ." said the woman, her voice small. Haltingly, she told Mako about the letter from Tairoa Head, and how it meant Sarah would have to leave a few weeks early, and how she had flown into a rage and run from the house . . .

He knew he was staring at her; she dropped her eyes under his. His face had gone dark with shock and pain. Sarah leave early! But there was so little time as it was . . . He could not bear it! He *would* not bear it!

"She can't leave!" he cried, his fists clenched. "She still has another month. She can't leave!"

Pauline shrugged helplessly. "Do you know where she is?" she asked, her voice still small.

He stared at the woman who was Sarah's mother. Selfish! he screamed at her silently. Selfish!

"She won't leave!" he said to her darkly. "You can't mess up her life this time. You can't."

He ran from the room and down the steps. Kikiwa stood like a guardian in the back of the truck. He put the truck into gear and spun out onto the road.

He knew where she was. He knew without any question. They would never find her. He pounded the steering wheel in anguish. How could he live here — anywhere — without her! They never spoke of when she would leave, although it was always with them. But they still had this month! And he would not let it be taken! He wrestled the truck over the cattle grid.

It was a very dark night — no moon, no stars. But he knew exactly where to stop, knew exactly where to part the ferns, how to put his feet on the path. He ran without faltering down through the bush, and Kikiwa glided silently ahead of him.

He thought only of her. He did not wonder why he had found the path so easily, how he could follow it as if in daylight. It did not concern him that the old woman would be there . . . He thought only of Sarah, whom he loved.

"You can't go!" he cried softly as he ran. "I need you!" She had pulled him from his silence and his rages; she had pulled him into the world. She had shown him that he could speak and learn and grow. When she touched him, his body and his mind leapt in response.

He slipped once on the swaying bridge. At once, Kikiwa pushed against him so he could regain his balance. He followed the dog through the dark wall of ferns into the clearing.

The fire threw shadows high into the infinite canopy above them. The girl jumped immediately to her feet when she saw him, and with a little cry threw herself against him. Her face was streaked with tears.

They held each other in the soft bush darkness, just outside the glow of the fire. They did not speak. He bent his head against her, moving his lips in her hair. She stood strongly; he could feel the strength in her. She was with him. It would be all right.

They stood together a long time. Kikiwa lay watchful beside them. The old woman said nothing. She sat back, content. He was here. The girl had brought him here at last. She breathed deeply, trying to still herself. The wait was over, but now she struggled with a strange longing, a desire to stop it all from happening. How much easier it would be to forget, to just let go . . . to sink softly into sleep, to sleep as she had been waiting to sleep a long, long time . . .

In the light of the flames, something flickered and fluttered toward the earth. She reached out and grabbed it. It was a piece of damp, wrinkled paper, fallen from the pocket of the jacket the boy had just wrapped around the girl. Hattie looked at it, her eyes once more bright shards against the darkness.

"Where did this come from?" she demanded.

The boy spun around, holding the girl in one arm. For a moment, their eyes gleamed at each other over the firelight. The boy stepped forward. Hattie shifted warily.

It was his tracing of the pattern on the sternpost. Now *she* had it, had it in her hands — it was impossibly dangerous to him for her to hold that paper. He took another step toward her, letting go of the girl.

"That is mine," he said softly. "Give it to me." He wanted that paper back. He could not let her have it. He tensed his body.

"Give it to me!" he screamed, lunging for her.

"Mako!"

The girl gasped his name, grabbing his sleeve. For a moment the three were frozen, the only movement the flame flickering over their bodies. Then Hattie deliberately smoothed the paper in her hands, tilting it to catch the light, and studied it.

The boy slumped in defeat. Every fiber in his body urged him to run, to get away . . . but he knew it was too late. Somehow, now that she held that scrap of paper with its crude design, it was too late. He did not know any more than that. He could only stand waiting while the old woman moved her finger slowly over the lines, intent and soundless. Sarah moved up behind him, her hand reaching for his. She, too, watched the old woman.

At the far edge of the firelight, the albatross raised herself and beat her wings against the pen. The boy's hand in Sarah's jerked convulsively. Kikiwa rose, bristling.

Calmly, the woman stood and faced them. She folded the paper carefully and handed it to Mako. He forced himself to meet her eyes, and it took all the strength he had. He feared this woman more than anything in the world.

"You are afraid of me," she said.

"Yes," he answered. She stepped toward him. He willed himself to stand still. She touched him. He let her touch him. He felt the dry old fingers trace over his face. He let himself be captured in her eyes. There was no one else. There was only the old woman.

"I have something to tell you. I will tell you now," she said. She took both his hands.

"I have been waiting, and now you have come. You have found the canoe of Tawahi, boy. You have touched it, and there is no going back. There is a story, and a curse . . . but there is no reason for fear. I have something to tell you . . ."

The voice went on and on, filling the bush, filling him. There was nothing else but the voice. It was not old. It was not that of a woman. It was not human. It was the voice from the black hill.

13
THE CURSE OF TAWAHI

The voice went on and on. It felt to Sarah that she was alone
in the bush — the voice was not a human voice. She was held
by the fire as if the flickering webs of flame had bound her
tight and immovable. She could not think. Her body could
feel nothing. She could only sit and listen.

". . . so the Pakeha Edward Whitsun moved to this island
with all his men," the voice was saying. "In the north, the
island was rich with deposits of copper in the cliffs and with
silver in the mountains. The trees grew tall and perfect here,
and the Pakeha used them for their sailing ships. Then the
sheep men came, and the miners. And not just here, but all
over Aotearoa, the land was being chopped and cleared and
used by the Pakeha.

"This island was the home of the Ngati Moana, a peaceful
people who made their living fishing and gathering pipis. They
had their kumera pits high in the hills where it was cool and
dry. But the Pakeha came and forced the Ngati Moana farther
and farther south, until they lived only on the swampy lands
below the river. The kumera pits were gone. When the fishing
was scarce there was nothing to eat.

"And then they began to notice more terrible things. The

hill-that-touched-the-stars, the hill where the navigators went to die, was fenced and run with sheep. And the caves which were more sacred than any other place, the caves in the cliffs under the shadow of the pointed mountains, were being blasted and mined by the Pakeha Edward Whitsun.

"The Ngati Moana were deeply upset. Deep into the night, for many nights, the elders discussed what could be done. They were not a fighting people. They thought they should talk with the Pakeha. But the Pakeha had noticed the Ngati Moana conferring among themselves. They were afraid they were preparing for war. Edward Whitsun was a most powerful Pakeha, and he stood to lose the most. He decided to wipe out the Ngati Moana. But he had to do this in a way which would not disturb his leaders in England. He had to make it seem that the Pakeha had nothing at all to do with it.

"Across the water from this island lies the peninsula that was the home of the great warrior people, the Ngati Niwha. The greatest man among them was their chief, Tawahi. Tawahi commanded many powerful tohungas, and these keepers-of-knowledge were not only feared and respected by his own people, but by many others as well. When Tawahi saw the sailing ships of the Pakeha approaching his shore, he took his tohungas and walked out to meet them. Tawahi was not afraid of the Pakeha.

"Long into the night, Tawahi and Edward Whitsun talked. A written note was passed between the two. At last, Tawahi commanded his warriors to prepare for war. All that next day, they bound their greenstone clubs and polished their greenstone axes. And to a few of the best warriors, the Pakeha gave guns. They readied the great war canoes and when night fell again, the warriors of Tawahi slipped out across the waters of the channel toward the island. The sailing ships moved silently away across the gulf, as if they had never been.

"The three great canoes cut through the dangerous currents of the channel and into the bay at the mouth of the Arana River. Night was still upon them as they hid the canoes in the mangroves and made their way down toward the settlement of the Ngati Moana.

"They attacked just as the dawn turned the sky to red. They attacked on the beaches, and the sea ran red with blood. They stormed the pa, and the houses ran red with blood. They killed the elders and the tohungas of the Ngati Moana. They killed the women and the men and the children. They burned the houses and the gardens. They killed every last person of the Ngati Moana.

"And when the pa lay burning and broken around them, and when the last dying cries of the Ngati Moana stilled, a terrible storm rose out of the Pacific and swept across the beaches and hills that still ran red with blood. The fury of the wind was awesome, and the waves crashed in over the land. The warriors of Tawahi were afraid. They had to retreat before the storm.

"They ran back to their hidden canoes. But only two canoes lay as they had left them. The third canoe, the great war canoe of Tawahi himself, lay broken and mired in the black mud of the river. The men were very frightened. All around them the sky was black with storm and with the choking smoke from the burning village. The warriors turned to Tawahi.

" 'Why have we done this thing?' they asked him. 'Why have we massacred a peaceful people of our own race?'

"And Tawahi turned the note given to him by Edward Whitsun over and over in his hand. He read the English words. The note promised him money and guns, and more than that: It promised that the lands of Tawahi would remain untouched by the Pakeha. But the warriors were still afraid. The canoe lay broken before them by the storm. This was a very bad thing. They paddled slowly home in the two remaining canoes.

"Many weeks passed. One day, Edward Whitsun received a letter from Tawahi.

" 'Where are the money and guns you promised us in exchange for the killing of the Ngati Moana?' said the letter. 'You have broken your word. My warriors mistrust me. They sicken with strange maladies. And already the Pakeha have begun to cut the forest of my people.'

"But Tawahi received no reply from the Pakeha. A great fear began to grow in him. He had killed a peaceful people — people who were cousins to his own wife. He knew the storm had come to break his canoe, and the fear grew and grew.

"But Tawahi was a great chief. He was clever and resourceful. He had the most powerful tohungas in Aotearoa. Tawahi was angry. The Pakeha had tricked him. They had lured him with promises to do their dirty work. It was he, Tawahi, whose canoe lay broken in the mud. It was he, Tawahi, whose men sickened and were afraid. And the Pakeha remained untouched.

"So the tohungas of Tawahi devised a curse against Edward Whitsun and all who followed him — the elements of the earth which they had stolen from the Maori should turn against them in the same way the storm had turned against the Ngati Niwha. The curse was very strong. Within a week, the copper mines had flooded, killing dozens of men. Edward Whitsun himself barely escaped. The silver mines cut deep into the mountains collapsed. The grasses all over the island began to wither.

"But Tawahi himself had no idea how far-reaching and powerful his curse would be. For many years later, Edward Whitsun, more rich and influential than ever, became prime minister of New Zealand. Now, *all* the Pakeha on Aotearoa followed this man. And so the curse grew to fall on them.

"Aotearoa lies under the curse of Tawahi still. No tohunga since that time has been powerful enough to remove it. All Maori people can see the effect of this curse; only the Pakeha remain largely blind. The blindness is part of the power of the curse. The Pakeha see what they want to see. But the earth under their feet and the sea around their shores have indeed turned against them.

"And the Maori wait. They wait. Aotearoa waits and suffers. The Pakeha farms the earth, but his grasses will not grow. He imports grasses from across the ocean, and this grass sucks the goodness from the soil. He cuts the trees. The wind blows the earth away, and the rain stops coming. He moves his cattle and sheep endlessly from grazing to grazing. The children of the Pakeha move away — the brightest among them go to Europe or America, where they have a chance to make a life for themselves. The world no longer buys the lamb and butter the Pakeha try to sell.

"This is the curse of Tawahi. But they who curse from fear and anger discover they must remain angry and afraid, to keep the curse alive. So the Maori, too, wanders angry and aimless on Pakeha streets. The Maori, too, lies under the agony of a land that is dying.

"*Aotearoa must not die!* The world has grown very small; people can no longer hide behind a range of mountains or a vast ocean. What happens in one place affects the world. All people watch. Aotearoa must not die! The curse must be lifted and Maori and Pakeha must live in peace on her land. The world can learn from them.

"I am telling you something that is true; it can be done. Many, many years ago a prophecy was spoken and a great teacher came — "

The albatross rose in her pen and beat her wings violently against the wire. Sarah cried out, throwing her hands over her eyes. For a moment she did not move, then slowly she dropped her hands.

Nothing stirred. The bush around her was dark and still. The fire had died to embers. Mako and the old woman sat facing each other without a sound.

Sarah struggled to her knees, stiff with cold. She was overcome by a wave of nausea. She moaned, and crawled closer to Mako.

But he did not see her. He was staring deep into the eyes of the old woman. A little smile curved the corners of his mouth, a calm, sweet smile that she had never seen before. And Hattie held him softly with her eyes. In the glow of the embers, the pale smoke curled around him and bound him to the old woman. And Sarah knew she was alone. The boy and the woman had passed into a realm where she could not follow.

She called his name. Desperately she tried to rouse him. She beat on his back. She shook his shoulders with both hands. But his body was strong and his eyes never left the old woman. It was as if Sarah did not exist. She screamed at them, but she was screaming at the bodies of two people who had long since left.

She was suffocating in her terror. She could not reach them! Where was he? Where had he been taken? She sank to her knees with a moaning cry.

And then Kikiwa slipped from the shadows and came to her. He pressed his great warm body against her. He touched her with his cool, moist nose. His tail lifted slowly in greeting. He was vibrantly, completely *alive*.

"Kikiwa," she breathed. She held him with both arms. He

braced his feet and stood solid. She buried her face deep into the animal fur.

Kikiwa had been sent to her. She knew this suddenly, as suddenly as the strange peace that entered her. He had been sent to calm her and warm her. Somewhere, somehow, *they* knew that she was here alone, frantic and terrified.

"Oh, Kikiwa," she said again, and already her voice was stronger. She stood up. She had to get help. Hattie had told her she would not harm Mako. She was torn in her trust.

She looked back from the edge of the clearing at the old woman sitting with the boy. What was passing between them? She hesitated.

"Mako! Mako!" she called again, but he did not move. Kikiwa watched her from the fireside. He would not come with her; he was guarding *them*. She took in her breath raggedly. She could not go on alone. She needed help. She had to find Daphne. Daphne would come with her, without question, without fuss.

Celeste was gone. She found the broken reins still tied to the tree. She swallowed, looking out at the dark road back to Port William. She squared her shoulders. She would have to walk.

She had no idea what time it was, but she knew it had only taken her an hour or so to walk back to the town. To her surprise, the lights were still on in Russell's bar, so it was not yet eleven. Composing herself, she walked up the steps and pushed open the door.

There was only one other man there, a farmer who leaned on the bar talking to Russell. He looked startled when she came in, but Russell's face remained impassive. She looked straight at him, ignoring the other man. Russell moved quietly down to the other end of the bar.

Something has happened! he thought. He looked at the

girl's face, dirty from smoke and streaked with tears. He let
the girl find her own words. She was searching his face for
something — something she could trust.

"Can you call Daphne for me?" she whispered at last.
"Please, Russell? It's . . . it's important. I can't tell you . . ."

He took her hands between both of his. His hands were
large and warm, brown like Mako's. She stared down at them.
She could trust Russell. He would do what she asked.

The farmer came over to them. "You want the nurse, love?
Anything wrong?" he asked, shoving his hat back from his
sun-brown forehead. "I reckon she's down to Arana tonight,
eh. Heard Mrs. Morris has trouble with her newborn."

She stared at him, open-mouthed. Russell still held her
hands. She felt a stab of fear. This farmer would stick his nose
in now, get Mike or the police or something . . . She raised
her eyes to Russell, mute.

"Thanks, mate," he said, nodding to the farmer. "I reckon
it's just a personal thing, eh." He smiled at Sarah. "I'll just
close up early and take her down to find Daphne."

The farmer looked doubtful. "She don't look in such good
shape, Russ," he said slowly. "She's just a kid! I think her
mum should know . . ."

"Right, mate," said Russell smoothly. "I'll drop her off at
the Crossroads and then go find the nurse. Morrises don't
have a phone, eh."

He steered her firmly from the bar, leaving the farmer
inside with his beer and the door unlocked. He put Sarah in
the pickup and turned onto the road.

He didn't speak until they had passed by the lights of the
Crossroads and headed up into the hills toward Arana.

"*Are* you all right?" he asked quietly. She nodded. Russell
had *lied* for her. She squeezed her hands together. They were
still warm from his holding them.

"I can't tell you anything, Russell," she whispered. "I just . . . I just want Daphne. I can't . . . Mako . . ."

So it was the boy. He had known it the minute she'd walked in the door, he realized. His hands tightened on the steering wheel. He had to remain calm for the girl. She seemed so small and frightened on the seat next to him. But she was very strong. He could feel it.

What was happening? Would he ever know? Something important was taking place right now . . . and that was all he knew. He would simply play his part, as it came to him.

They just missed Daphne leaving the Morris farm. She was headed back to Waitapu. Russell slammed the accelerator of his ute and the pickup bounced over the road. Within minutes, the taillights of Daphne's truck could be seen rounding a bend ahead of them. Russell leaned on the horn.

The old truck ahead of them slewed to a stop and Russell pulled up beside her. Daphne asked no questions when she saw Sarah, but reached up and pulled her down beside her.

"She's all right, love," said Russell softly to the nurse. He held Sarah's hand briefly and turned to go. Then he stopped, turned, and looked back, searching the girl's eyes.

She looked back at him. He had the kindest face she had ever seen. He hadn't asked her a single question. She smiled at him, and he smiled back.

14
AUNT HATTIE WAITS

Daphne was a nurse, but she had not spent much of her career in hospitals. On Great Kauri Island she was called on for more than nursing. Daphne had learned there was more to this job than healing the body. The human mind had more mystery and strength and healing powers than she would ever understand.

So she let the girl beside her gather back her strength in her own way. She took the truck back over the hills toward the north. And when Sarah finally spoke to her, she listened quietly, leaving her own questions for later.

"I didn't know what else to do, Daphne," she said. "I could only think . . . of you. Of finding you. I don't know what kind of help I need. And I don't know how to begin telling you . . ." She shook her head, panic rising in her again. How could she possibly explain to Daphne — when she herself didn't know what she was explaining?

But somehow the story came easily, slipping from her tongue as if it had been waiting to be spoken. She told Daphne about Aunt Hattie, about how she seemed at times a tired old woman living as an eccentric in the bush, and at times a person of extraordinary powers, who commanded thoughts and time and a great black dog.

"Remember . . . how Kikiwa was, in the bush?" she said. The nurse nodded slightly. Could she ever forget?

She told Daphne of Hattie's intense interest in Mako, and how Mako was afraid of her.

"When he first met her, he dropped his eyes, Daphne! It wasn't like him — I knew that even then, when I didn't know him at all. He sort of turned his head away . . . "

"He would do that with someone he sensed commanded enormous respect and fear," said Daphne softly. "He is Maori, and young, even if he is angry and proud."

The story did not take very long to tell. It came from her so simply, so directly, she wondered how it had been that she could not explain it before. She told Daphne of the portrait of Tawahi and of the black hill.

"And all the time," she finished, "every time I went down to take fish to the albatross, Hattie would talk to me. When I was there, it seemed *normal* really — you know? But later, I would get scared . . . It's like she wants Mako for something. Something that is really important, really *big*. She was waiting for him . . . I think she's been waiting a long time. It's like she's *chosen* him — but it's even more than that. It's like he already *was* chosen, and she just recognized him. And she told me that I would bring him to her . . . and I did . . ." She choked suddenly on her voice, tears close to the surface again.

She thought of Mako, all alone with the old woman in the dark bush. It was very cold out, and his clothes had been damp. He could freeze . . . and she thought of him, listening to the terrible story of Tawahi, the ancestor he held as an ideal in his heart. All his dreams were born of meeting his father, the man with the blue-lined face who preached the expulsion of Pakeha from New Zealand . . . and his father was directly descended from Tawahi!

But Tawahi was as corrupt and greedy as the Pakeha he dealt with. His blood ran in Mako's veins. And somehow, as if it was meant to be, Mako had found the sternpost of the broken canoe, the canoe of Tawahi flung by the storm into the muck of the Arana River. And somehow, as if it was meant to be, he had come at last to the clearing in the bush, to the old woman — because he had come to find Sarah.

"He must have heard . . ." she whispered now. Daphne had pulled her tight against her as she drove.

"Heard what, love?" she asked.

"Pauline wants me to go home early . . . She got some grant, and I was so mad. And Mako must have heard, and known where to look for me, and that's why he came down to the bush."

"Whatever is happening, it's not your fault, Sarah," said Daphne. "I don't pretend to understand your story. But I do know that there are undercurrents in human existence that go far deeper than the accidents of race or country or time. Perhaps we are all caught in these currents whether we know it or not. We Westerners have lost sight of more senses than we now use. We see only the surface of things with our eyes. We hear only the smallest range of sounds. Our smell is almost gone. Our touch — we still can touch." She smiled sadly, it seemed to Sarah.

"I am only a nurse, love," she said. "But I work with people who are hurting and afraid, and when they are, they let down barriers . . . I see more than I will ever understand. You have broken through the surface into another level you do not understand. Mako, too, sensed this . . . and fought. But I do not think he needs to be frightened . . ."

Her voice trailed off. She took a deep breath.

"It may be that those undercurrents, those powers we do not understand deep inside the human mind, are the very forces that push us to survive and to grow . . . It may be that *that* is where true healing comes from."

They had driven past the Crossroads and the last lights of Port William lay behind them. Sarah sat quietly. Her mind had calmed and her thinking had almost returned to normal.

Is this really you, Sarah Steinway? she asked herself. A little over two months ago, she'd been organizing the annual spring concert at school, and in another six weeks she'd be walking to class through golden maple leaves. And what was this? A dream in between? What was the island, the graceful albatross, the tiny old woman, the boy with wild hair and burning eyes? A dream? She smiled. They were no dream. They were part of her.

Daphne had a powerful flashlight, but to Sarah every root, every dip and pebbly part, was as familiar to her as her own bedroom. A little morepork hooted above them; it was a friendly, sleepy sound.

The clearing was empty. The ashes from the fire lay white and cold. Daphne moved the flashlight around the bush — nothing. Just the breeze, the crickets, and far off, the sound of waves lapping the sand.

The light moved around the perimeter. When it got to the pen, Daphne held it steady. With a small cry, Sarah flung herself on her knees.

"She's dead!"she cried. "Oh Daphne — she's dead!"

The albatross lay with wings outflung in the open doorway of her pen. Her neck twisted limply over the dirt, and her eyes were closed. Sarah pulled the limp animal into her arms, rocking in anguish.

"She told me she wouldn't die! She said so! Oh," she

moaned, "it's my fault! She was getting sicker; I knew I should
have taken her to Pauline. But I didn't. I wanted her all to
myself, because I hate Pauline . . . I hate her! And now she's
dead . . ."

Her voice had slipped into a low keening — born, Daphne
knew, of fear and exhaustion as much as sorrow. Quickly she
knelt by the girl, took the bird from her. Who knows what
had happened in this place? Whatever it was, there was no
one here now but a girl close to the edge of hysteria and
exhaustion. Whatever it was would have to wait. The girl had
to be helped.

Daphne's fingers were deep in the still white feathers of
the albatross, and she felt something flutter under her touch.
She pressed deeper to the skin, exploring the neck. Where
was the pulse of a bird? There — at the throat: a fluttering.
The bird was alive!

Even as she discovered the pulse, the bird stirred, hissed
weakly. The great wings trembled, the eyes opened. Sarah
reached out for her.

"Look!" she said softly. She sat up straight, and the light
returned to her eyes.

"We have to take her with us, Daphne. She has to be set
free . . . tonight! And I have to find Mako . . ."

"I'm taking you back to the Crossroads," said Daphne
firmly. "I let you go once before when I shouldn't have, eh.
I'm not going to do it again!"

They struggled to wrap the albatross in blankets from Hattie's hut so she would be easier to carry. Sarah's mind raced.
She knew Daphne would not let her go this time. She looked
at her friend, and loved her. Without a word, she embraced
her. Daphne held her strongly.

"I'll go back with you," Sarah said finally, softly. Her mind was very clear now. "But then I *will* go find Mako. He's out there somewhere, and he's hurting and scared, and I'm going to find him. You know I have to."

They took turns carrying the huge bird up the path. They made a crude nest of ferns torn from the edge of the bush for the back of the truck, and placed the albatross on them. The bird made no move, but it seemed to Sarah that at the sight of the open sky above her, she grew suddenly stronger.

The lights at the Crossroads were still on, although it must have been after midnight. As soon as she got out of the truck, Sarah saw Russell's ute parked in the yard near the policeman's truck. She swallowed. He had gone to Pauline after all!

They were all sitting around Mari's table when she came in with Daphne behind her. Pauline jumped up, almost knocking the chair over. But after her first move, she hesitated.

"Sarah . . ." she said. The girl stood in the doorway, a confusion of responses jumbling in her. She wanted to run to her mother, bury her face against her, forget the long evening behind her . . . and yet, it was because of Pauline . . .

The old voice came to her from a long distance off. 'You must mend the hurt you gave your mother.' She reached out her hands, and her mother took them instantly.

"I didn't know what to do . . ." Pauline said, her voice cracking.

"I'm OK, Pauline. It's OK," Sarah said. Still holding her hands, she turned to see the others. Russell sat near the policeman, talking in a low voice. But when Sarah glanced at him, he put a brief hand on the other man's shoulder and stood up.

Daphne poured herself a cup of coffee from the pot on the stove. "It's after midnight," she said. "What's going on?" She sat next to Mari, and Mike talked to her in a quiet voice.

Russell cleared his throat. The girl would not meet his eyes.

He wished he could speak to her without the others around.

"Mako came by the bar an hour or so ago," he said reluctantly. "I'd just been out a minute . . ." His eyes slid over Sarah, and she looked away. "He was smashing the place to bits. It seemed to make him worse, when he saw me. Kept screaming at me about my stories . . . that it was all my fault."

Sarah had to look at him now. He was speaking only to her.

"He said I'd filled his head up with rubbish, eh," Russell continued softly. "He kept yelling, 'What am I supposed to do now? What am I supposed to do with it all!' And then he yelled that he was going to kill his father. He said his father had lied to him and betrayed him, that everything was lies, and that he'd kill him . . . and he'd kill the old woman . . ."

His voice had dropped so low no one else could hear him. Sarah moved close to him without knowing it.

"I *had* to call Bill," said Russell now. His eyes held hers firmly. "I had to call him — the boy was going to hurt himself, eh. But he spun out in his truck before I could do anything."

Mako was in trouble with the police. Her head pounded numbly. She had to find him. She pleaded silently with Russell through her eyes.

"We aren't going to press charges," said Bill MacNeil, coming over to them. "We try and settle things ourselves, here on the island. But we have to find him before he does something we *can't* keep to ourselves, eh, love. He needs help."

They wanted her to tell them where he was. She studied her hands.

Mako does not need help, she thought. He needs the truth. He needs to mesh the past with the present, and find a voice for the future. He needs to know who he is and where he belongs. He is like me. He can't be his father, any more than I can be Pauline. He must be *who he is*. He must speak with his own voice.

And the story? . . . the curses? He could no longer ignore the old stories. He could no longer ignore his place within them. He had chosen to step past Arana, down to where the sea had run red with blood. He had touched the sternpost of a broken canoe in the bay at Waitapu — *sacred water* . . . He could no longer see Tawahi as a proud dream . . . Tawahi was a man, like other men, and he had lived with shame.

In her mind, she could hear the old voice droning on and on in the firelight. She, too, had been meant to hear the story of Tawahi and the massacre at Waitapu, but after that . . . She shivered, remembering the awful silence of the bush, the *aloneness*. The old woman had lured Mako to a place only she and he could see — and then she had let him go. Sarah could feel his rage.

She looked up at Russell, moving slightly so they could speak alone.

"I know where he is," she said softly. "But I have to go to him alone. I'm the only one who knows . . ."

Russell's eyes never left her face. This was Mako's friend, she thought, and he was also Maori. He knows there is something . . . He doesn't ask any questions . . .

"I only know this," she said. "I can only tell you this: '*Ka tapu te tamaiti. Me mataaratia. Kua kite mai ahua i te ariki paerangi.*' "

The words came from a great distance. She could repeat them without faltering. Russell's face never moved. But she could feel the shock hit him. She could feel him closing her off, closing off his mind. Why? Why was he turning from her? Was it because she was Pakeha? She put her hand on his arm.

And then she felt the change. It was as if he had suddenly changed his mind, made a decision. He was no longer shutting her out.

" '*The boy is* tapu,' " he whispered. " '*Look after him. I have found the next young chief who comes from afar.'"*

He had both her hands in his again, as he had at the bar. He was excited; it sparkled in his dark eyes, flushed his face.

"Is that what it means?" she asked. He smiled.

"Roughly translated," he answered. This time the sudden light in his eye was of quiet understanding. He turned back to the others, who were talking around the table.

"Sarah and Daphne can find him," he said. "Look, Bill, eh — let her go. He'll listen to her. He'll only fight, if you go. She'll be all right."

Pauline half stood to go to Sarah. Russell put his hand on her shoulder. "You should get some sleep," he said gently. "Daphne's with her. It's better this way."

"I'll be OK, Mom," said Sarah. She hadn't used that word in a long time; they were both surprised. She hugged her mother, feeling the narrow little shoulders, smelling the sweetness of her hair.

Daphne went to start the truck. Russell went out on the verandah with Sarah. In the back of the truck he saw the glowing white albatross. The bird had her neck up, beak half open, staring at the sky. Russell looked at her quizzically, head cocked. Sarah smiled.

"She'll fly free, tonight," she said. Russell knew nothing of the bird. But he smiled back at her, content to accept what he did not quite understand.

Then, as she took the last step off the verandah, he said softly, "Look after him." And he knew she would.

Sarah directed Daphne down the road to the little jetty where Mako's fishing boat was kept. The night was clear, and the stars filled the sky with light.

"Am I going to leave you alone, then, love?" Daphne asked.

Once more, Sarah had to ask more of Daphne than she had a right to. She trusted Daphne. But did Daphne trust *her?*

"A lot has happened to me since I've been here," she said now. She wanted to answer Daphne, *completely*. "I used to always have to be in control. I mean, I didn't really want to get close to anyone, you know? Maybe because I knew it *hurt*, to love someone and then you couldn't depend on them . . . I just wanted to depend on myself. I just wanted to be the best on the flute, to be famous. I still do!"

She stared out into the sky. How incredibly perfect the stars were! And how close — as if you could walk among them along a path . . .

"I wanted everything to be predictable, you know?" she continued. "That way, I could just sort of wrap myself up inside . . . And then I got here. I don't really know what happened. First you, really, I guess . . . then Aunt Hattie. And Mako. And I don't know — somehow I learned that touching someone doesn't mean depending on them. It means trusting, and *being bigger* — a bigger person, inside. And loving someone is sort of . . . I think, first you have to love yourself."

She put her hand on Daphne's arm.

"I don't know what's going to happen tonight," she said. "I don't have any control over it. But I love Mako. And I trust him . . . he trusts *me*. I know you're worried he'll hurt me. But if I don't *take this chance* for him — for *me* — then what does all this stuff I've learned really mean? Oh, I don't know if I'm making any sense . . ."

"You make perfect sense, love," said Daphne, smiling. "It will only be good, what happens tonight."

The truck rolled down onto the beach by the jetty. Everything seemed very still, very dark. The boat bobbed gently in the water. But when the headlights of the truck were switched off, Sarah could see a small red glow of light on the deck. She walked toward it.

"You've been a long time, girl," said the cranky voice of Aunt Hattie. The old woman stood, taking the clay pipe from her mouth. She eyed Daphne.

"You leave this girl with me," she commanded. "She will be safe. You are a good friend, but you cannot come with her." She stumped across the little deck.

"You have brought the bird — that is good," she said. "Ah, look at the white one's head! She can smell the sky. She can taste the sea! She is impatient — see how she struggles! She is strong now. This is the right time, girl."

Daphne helped Sarah lift the heavy bird, still wrapped in the blankets, over the side of the boat. They walked back to the truck together.

"Maybe he won't show up," said Daphne. Sarah smiled.

"Hattie's here," she answered. They looked at each other for a long moment. Daphne put her hand on the door of the truck.

"Well then, love, I'll leave you here." Her voice had an edge to it that cut Sarah's heart. She wished she did not have to ask Daphne to do this. She did not know how long her friend would have to wait, worrying. She stood mute.

Daphne backed the truck up onto the road. Sarah watched until the taillights disappeared around the curve.

She went down to the boat. Aunt Hattie was sitting once again, pulling contentedly on her pipe. She watched Sarah climb in.

It was a peaceful night. A morepork hooted once, and another answered. A pukeko squawked from the marshes nearby. The crickets filled the night with sweetness.

Aunt Hattie took her pipe from her mouth.

"Good," she said. "You are not afraid. That is good. Be prepared. Soon the angry one will come."

She settled her tiny old body against the wooden planks,

leaning against a crate. The albatross lay serene and alert beside her.

"It is exactly the right time," sighed the old woman happily. "Tonight, the albatross flies free. Tonight, each of us will choose our path." She gestured into the stars. "I am very happy tonight, girl."

15
THE ALBATROSS FLIES FREE

Mako arrived and the night exploded. He braked the truck on the loose stones, and it skidded violently around toward the beach. Kikiwa slammed against the tailgate and yelped. The boy jumped out and ran around to the back, humping a full gas can up onto his shoulder. Only when he approached the boat did he see the old woman and Sarah.

"What are you doing here?" he snarled. He yanked the cap off the gasoline and began to pour it into the fuel tank. Hattie looked calmly off into the night, ignoring him.

Sarah put out her hands to him involuntarily. Her heart jumped inside her. He was so alive, so vital! It really was Mako! The strange spellbound boy sitting by the fire in the clearing was gone.

"I came to find you," she said. He pushed her aside roughly and ran down to check the oil gauge. The cloying smell of gasoline hung in the air.

"And every-bloody-one else will follow, eh," Mako said. Kikiwa slunk to the front of the boat.

"I came alone."

"What about the old witch?" he snapped.

"She was here when I got here," said Sarah quietly. She drew in her breath slowly. The butt-end of his rage had bruised her already.

Mako leapt up onto the little wharf and began to unfasten the ropes. She felt a twinge of apprehension. He was really going to take the boat out. She would have to go with him, if she was to have any chance of talking to him. He wouldn't *really* take the tiny boat across the channel to the Coromandel, would he? He wasn't actually going to try to kill Henare Mokutu? Sarah glanced quickly at Hattie, but the old woman looked almost smug and sat unperturbed in the shadows near the wheelshed.

"Mako!" Sarah said, forcing her voice to be strong. "You have to come back with me! You're not in trouble — really! Russell won't press charges. But you have to — "

"Do you think I give a bloody *fart* about Russell?" He threw a rope that narrowly missed her head. "Who the hell do you think you are, little Pakeha do-gooder? Stop trying to save me!" he sneered. She climbed out on the wharf after him.

"Henare-bloody-Mokutu lied to me. I'm going to kill him," he flung back at her over his shoulder.

It was not his coarseness, but the deadly quiet of his voice that shocked her. This was no temperamental outburst. This was true rage. He was serious. He was going to take the boat across the channel and kill his father.

"I don't care what you think I am," she tried once more, desperate. "You can't do this! As soon as you leave the island, you're in someone else's district. They won't care. They'll just take you in."

He ignored her. Then, with stunning suddenness, he swung down into the boat, yanked open the throttle, and jerked the wheel.

"You're crazy!" she screamed. The boat was pulling away

from the wharf. Sarah jumped. Her ankle crunched under her. She gasped, the pain a white flash in her eyes.

"You're stupider than I thought!" she screamed. She clutched the side of the boat. "You're a stupid ass! Who cares what you do? You're just wallowing in self-pity, aren't you! You just love it when you're mad! Poor little Maori kid — the whole world's against him! Pity pity pity!" she screeched. She thrust her body toward him.

"Well, *no one cares!* Do you hear? No one cares about your stupid tantrums!"

She pulled herself over to the wheelshed. "You didn't smash up Russell's 'cause you were mad," she sneered. "You did it because you're *selfish!* Nobody else has it as tough as you, right? So make them suffer — 'specially the ones that love you!"

The boat lurched on a swell and she fell against her twisted ankle. The pain made her sick. She heaved dryly and whimpered. The boy turned without thinking at the sound, grabbed her as she stumbled.

The pain on her face passed over his own. A spasm went through him. He crushed her against him, saying her name over and over.

"I'm only going to hurt you," he cried, his face buried in her hair. "I keep hurting you. You have to let me go. I don't know how to be with anyone. Just forget me."

"You don't get to have it that way, Mako," she said through clenched teeth. His body was hard against her. "Stop whining! I can't forget you, even if I wanted to. Besides, I'm on this stupid boat with you and I can't go anywhere until you decide to go back." She pushed herself away and glared at him.

"I don't know what you think you're going to do," she said, more quietly now. "You think you're going to kill your father . . . That'll just land you in jail for the rest of your life.

Well, it's your decision. Personally, I think it's dumb. You have more important things to do."

"I don't know what I am supposed to do," he said sullenly. He looked across the Hauraki Gulf toward Auckland. Along the curve of the horizon he could not find the faintest glow of lights.

"I really don't, you know," he said now. He shrugged. "What do you think there is for me, back there? The most I might hope for is a job in construction, or maybe the slaughterhouse, eh. That where you want to think of me?"

"Don't put this on *me,* Mako!"

He slumped against the wheel. The boat had slipped past the dark hills of Little Penguin Island, and was heading out into the open gulf.

"There's nothin' back there," he said dully. "The gangs — ha! They're like a family, eh. They all feed on each other's anger. Someday I'll just smash up the wrong place. They'll put me in the psycho ward. They put a lot of us there. More of us in than out, I reckon."

He straightened, some of the fury leaping back into his eyes.

"You think I feel sorry for myself, eh! You an' your books and music and fairy tales! What has that to do with me — with what's out there?" He swept his arm along the horizon. "It isn't real! Being with you isn't real! Don't you understand?"

He growled at her, a scornful growl.

"No, eh! How could *you* understand! You with your posh school and music lessons . . . you *live* in a fairy tale!"

She refused to be hurt. She would not let him hurt her. She could feel herself shutting down, shutting herself in, until she was just a small little knot looking out through her eyes.

"Is that what you think, Mako?" she said. "A bit of money, a nice school . . . and no one has any questions anymore? You have a corner on the market? I have everything — so I don't get to have questions?"

She put her hands on his face, forcing him to look at her.

"I never pretended to know what it's like for you, and you know it," she said. "But don't you dare try to tell me how easy my life is . . . that it's some kind of fairy tale! You know what's back there for *me*, if I choose it? All the competition . . . all the ambitions . . . like what Pauline chose? I don't fit anywhere either, Mako."

She let her hands smooth the hardness of his mouth.

"If I shared my books with you, and my music . . . I wasn't taunting you. Is that what you think? I shared them because I love you. I used to think . . . there was only one way to be. Nothing else was acceptable. But I learned something from you, Mako. People can be totally different, going in a whole different direction. But if they are accepted for who they are, allowed to speak in their own voice, then all their beauty shows."

She had curled herself into the curve of his arm. She could feel his heart slowing, and some warmth crept from him into her body.

"My father speaks in his own voice, and he lied," Mako said. He wouldn't meet her eyes. "All that bloody rot about Tawahi, eh . . . the greatest fighting chief — crap! How can I have a dream that's coming from lies?"

Her eyes shone. She pulled away from his body and stared up into his face. He could not help but look back at her.

"That's it, Mako!" she cried. "That's *it!* You can't! It has to be from the truth, or it won't work. Don't you see? That's what I meant by *choosing*. You can choose to be yourself, choose your own voice, choose to learn and understand from the past — or you can choose to blame others, shut people out with anger and hurt."

Sarah looked out over the water. She thought of Pauline, waiting for her back at the Crossroads.

"My mother chose things that I tried to build my own dreams on," she said softly. "But it wouldn't have worked. We are different people. We have different ways of going. Remember how Russell told us about the navigators — how they each had to map out their own paths? No one could show them how to go."

She watched the struggle passing over Mako's face. The muscles along his jawline jumped.

"You can still love your father," she whispered. "But you have to go your own way. He didn't betray you — he has his own path. He has chosen from the past what he wishes to see, and maybe he just doesn't see very clearly, you know? You can see clearly, Mako! I know you can! You don't have to accept his life of anger — but you can still love him."

She searched for the right words.

"Our past is part of us," she said. "We can accept that and still choose our own voice, choose what is strong and beautiful from that past."

His face was still. His heartbeat was as steady and strong as the throbbing of the motor in the little boat.

" 'Time held me green and dying / Though I sang in my chains like the sea.' "

He spoke the lines in the voice she had come to recognize, the voice that had told her of the shriveled grasses and the girl who had died . . . It was the voice people would listen to.

And she knew that, because his voice had touched her, her music would be more wonderful because of it. And she also knew that when Mako spoke, his voice would carry within it the memory of her own songs.

"You love me," he said now, in wonder.

"I love you," she replied simply.

They forgot everything but each other. There was nothing but their bodies against each other, their eyes, and the insistent, throbbing pulse of the motor. They did not know where they were going; they only knew each other.

The soft darkness of the gulf surrounded them with secret currents and the rhythm of waves. They stood wrapped within each other, each caught in the passion of the other. They wanted only to please each other. Sarah slipped her hands under the heavy jacket, under the thick warm shirt to where his skin lay smooth and strong over his ribs, over the muscles of his back. His hands were full of her. They could not stand close enough.

His mouth was insistent. She shifted slightly, and the movement sent a tremor through him. She was pulling at him, easing him to the floor, to where they could lie in a small, secret space. There was nothing but this feeling of each other's body and of their own, more demanding than they could understand, more wonderful than they could believe.

The boat rolled. The albatross threw back her head and cried a wild, haunting scream at the sky. From the shadows, the old woman stirred.

"It is time!" she said. "The bird is ready to fly. It is time!"

The voice replaced one spell with another. Mako took the wheel, easing back on the throttle, nosing the boat once more into the waves. He did not know where they were. He stared around him at the vast space. Off to one side, the sky hinted at the first pearl-pink wash of dawn.

Hattie stood. Her whole body seemed to Sarah to quiver with electricity, so she could almost see sparks like stars against the water.

"Put down your anchor, boy," the old woman directed. Mako moved without hesitation, slinging the heavy sea-anchor over the side.

Hattie knelt now by the blanketed albatross. Swiftly, she undid the wrapping. The feathers glowed in the starlight. The bird sat utterly still under the old hands. Her jet-black eyes sparkled under the white brows. Hattie ran her hand down the wings.

"I will follow you," she whispered. "When you fly to the stars, I will follow."

She turned abruptly to Mako and Sarah.

"Help me with her," she said. She leaned over the boat and dipped her hands in the black water. She cupped the water and lifted it, and a million green-white diamonds of light scattered over the feathers of the bird.

Sarah lifted the albatross in her arms. The bird seemed to weigh nothing, as if already filled with the freedom of flight. Mako held his arms under hers and they lowered the albatross over the side. Hattie watched.

Sarah let go. The albatross sat lightly on the silken water. Slowly, slowly, the girl drew back. Now no hands touched the bird.

Gracefully, the albatross dipped her head. She tasted the water. Her wings fluttered against her body. She lifted her head back, back until it pointed to the stars. Her beak opened slightly.

And then, with a tremendous surge, the albatross opened her wings. A wave carried her up, up . . . and she slipped down the other side. Then another, and again she was up, and the great wings found the rhythm of the waves. Beat, beat . . . she arched her strong neck. Beat, beat . . . the wings pulsing like the heartbeat of the ocean's current. Beat, beat . . . and the heavy body began to lift, the feet folded in, the long narrow wings pulsing faster and faster until she broke free of the surface with a trail of jewel-green drops.

And then she was part of the sky, rising higher and higher

until her wings became perfect and still and she curved silently up into the stars.

Hattie fell heavily to the deck of the boat.

They moved together, Mako catching her under the arms, Sarah cradling her head. For a moment they were too shocked to know what to do. The old woman's eyes were open. She gazed first at one, then the other.

"Thank you, girl," she said. Sarah leaned so close her hair brushed the old face.

"You brought me the albatross and you brought me your music. You brought me the boy. He is everything. Thank you." The old woman trembled in Sarah's arms. Carefully, Mako lowered her so that she leaned half against him. The battered hat had fallen off, revealing hair whiter than the feathers of the albatross. Still looking at Sarah, Hattie smiled.

"You have grown, girl," she said. "You will play your flute for many, many people, and they will feel more alive for hearing you." She reached out one hand. Slowly, the old fingers moved over her face. They felt like the light brush of the ferns along the bush trail.

"Now leave me, girl," said Hattie, dropping her hand. Sarah moved back. From his post at the prow, Kikiwa glided to stand against Sarah, pushing her gently farther into the wheelshed. Mako was left with the old woman.

And once again Sarah knew she was alone. This time, she felt no fear. She was very tired. She curled up on the floor of the shed.

And once again, Mako was led away by the old woman he held in his arms. Her white hair shimmered in the starlight, falling over his arm. The old hands found his own. He held them.

"Take care of what has been given to you," whispered Hattie. "Let your voice grow, and be true. It is time for the voices of all people to grow, for nations to grow. Take care of what I have passed to you. *It is important.*"

She weighed no more than a memory. He held her for a long time. The burning sea-blue eyes closed. She was dead.

Sarah stirred. Kikiwa stretched his massive body.

"Mako?" Sarah called. He looked up. The ancient hands slipped from him, leaving in his hand something small and warm and hard. He looked down at the tiny pendant.

It lay cupped in his palm with the supple thong draped over his wrist. It was still warm from being around the old woman's neck. It was hardly more than an inch in length. It winked and gleamed softly in the rising dawn. The stone was of the deepest, clearest greenstone, and a thread of gold laced around it. He touched it with his finger, and it seemed alive, as if it had a heart beating within it. Without thought, he slipped the leather thong over his head and the pendant settled warmly against his bare skin.

". . . There is a sign . . . and only if this sign is seen will we know if what is spoken is true. Around the neck, the keeper of the message will wear a pendant of greenstone and gold . . ."

Unbidden, the words came to Mako. The little pendant burned against his chest. He put his hand up to tear it off, and then hesitated.

Mako arranged the blankets gently around the body of the old woman. Sarah folded one and knelt, placing it under the old head. "Do you know where we are?" she whispered, looking around them at the sea.

"I know where we are," said Mako. He stood and made his way to the wheelshed. Sarah picked up Hattie's old hat, feeling tears starting in her eyes. She rubbed her cheek against the rough, greasy material, smelling the wood smoke, the tobacco . . . Never again would those eyes pierce her from across the fire, never again would the old voice snap at her as she came through the ferns. She sat for several minutes, and then went to join Mako.

"Look," he said softly, pointing to the sky. She settled next to him and looked out into the dawn. Above them, sliding off on the edge of night to where the last stars still shone, the albatross flew. Sarah caught her breath. The dawn light turned the feathers to soft fire; the bird had her beak open to taste the wind.

"You see! You see!" whispered Sarah in triumph. "She is where she is meant to be! See how perfect she is!"

Mako felt his heart beating against the tiny pendant. It lay around his neck as if it had always been there. *It was where it was meant to be.* And he chose to keep it.

The albatross belonged to the air and to the open oceans. But she had been touched by the dappled light of the bush, by the rich dark earth, by the wind through the ferns. Would she carry the memory of that time forever in her flight, and would her flight be more beautiful because of it? Mako reached for Sarah's hand.

He belonged to one world, she to another. But their voices would be brighter, for having known each other. He could choose his voice. And that voice had a place where it was meant to be. He carried inside him everything the old woman had told him, everything that had been told to her. Perhaps, in his lifetime, it would be his voice that would finally speak aloud. Perhaps, in his lifetime, people would be ready to listen.

The little fishing boat rose and fell in the waves. Mako bit his lip. They had drifted far to the south of Great Kauri, and the boat was being drawn into the treacherous currents of the channel. He turned it carefully, trying not to get her broadside of the waves. He began to feel anxious.

He checked the gas gauge; it was hovering on low. If the current didn't sweep them too far out, there would just be enough to limp into Waitapu Bay.

"Will we make it?" Sarah asked, coming to stand by him.

Mako turned the wheel another degree.

"We'll make it, eh!" he grinned at her. She threw back her head to catch the new sun full in her face. Her thick hair whipped out behind her. They laughed. The day was so bright. Great Kauri Island lay before them, a jewel on a sea of light.

They spoke very little. The boat moved steadily through the sea, and it was as if time disappeared. The memory of the long night filled them. So when the scattering of bobbing boats in Waitapu Bay caught their eyes, they felt a faint surprise. There was a world out there, a world full of people and words and everyday things. People would be waiting for them both. They stood very close.

They spoke just before Mako pulled the boat up to the wharf.

"She has no family, Mako," said Sarah. "There was only us. I can't believe she's gone . . ."

"She's not really gone," he told her. His voice was full and deep. She was caught in that voice. She touched his face, ran her hand down his chest. For a flicker of a second, her fingers brushed against something small and hard. His eyes pierced into her.

"No . . ." she said quietly. "She's not . . ."

The boat bumped against the wharf.

EPILOGUE

Early winter had shaken the last golden leaves from the maples and scattered them on the surface of the gray water. The day was cold with the wind, and the lake water had roughened into white-capped wavelets that slapped against the stones of the little jetty. A girl sat alone, wrapped in heavy sweaters, the wind tangling her dark hair into a thick mass behind her.

She held a letter in her hand, unopened. Around the edge of the airmail envelope was an intricate design of spirals and notches; she ran her finger over them. The postmark was Auckland, New Zealand.

But the girl was not ready to read the letter. She sat with her chin resting on drawn-up knees. Behind her, through the woods up the hill, classes were changing, and students walked among the bare trees that grew around the old brick buildings. But she was very far away — a whole world lay between her and those ivy-walled buildings. She threw back her head to escape the cold wind that was whipping her eyes to tears.

How had she come here? She barely remembered. She barely remembered, even, the wild run down through the woods that morning after finding the letter in her mailbox.

She had been sitting on these rocks by the lake a long time. She was very cold. The cold reminded her of another cold . . . a darker, more secret cold in a tiny clearing with a fire turned to white ash.

How had she come here? She struggled to calm her thoughts. The lake water swirled around the rocks and covered her with spray. She licked the water off her lips . . . sweet to taste, not salty. She looked around at the bare trees, the yellowing grasses. There were no soft-leafed ferns here. A bird called from behind her in the woods, but its song did not trill and linger in dappled light like the hidden bell-bird . . .

The girl shifted on the rocks, bumping against the pack that lay next to her. The hard edge of her flute case pressed against her hip. Slowly, she pulled it out. Her fingers were very cold. She held the gleaming silver instrument in her hands, turning it to see the light catch along the length of it. She lifted it to her mouth, arching her neck. The wind carried the notes out over the lake.

The bare November branches clacked and shook above her, and the lake water lapped choppily against the stones. Never before had these woods echoed with the strange, haunting song of a bellbird, never had the trees felt the whispery brushing of huge ferns against their bark. But the music was taken by the wind and flung out over the water and deep into the forest.

After a while, the girl stopped playing. Her fingers were white with cold. She put the flute back into the case. Now she was smiling. She pulled the letter from her pocket and carefully tore it open.

The handwriting was bold and dark; he had found a pen somewhere, she grinned to herself. No more smudgy pencils . . . Through her whole body a warmth was returning, a remembered warmth. His voice came to her as clear as if he were standing next to her. She looked out over the lake and at the low hills beyond. On just such a cold gray day, she had stood with the boy while an old woman was buried, and heard his voice speaking to her as it was speaking now . . .

She read his letter to her. On the last page was a poem. It was written first in Maori, and on the back, for her, in English. No longer was it scrawled in pencil on crumpled lined paper. It was typed carefully on thick creamy paper, and signed with a simple signature: *Mako*.

> "*Son, born in a winter's dawning,*
> *Climb, soar high, my son,*
> *To your countless ancestors in the sky.*
> *Will you triumph, my son,*
> *Over these evil times?*
> *My child, move quickly*
> *To reach the magic waters of your ancestors*
> *And free the black dogskin war cloak*
> *To camouflage you when the war party departs.*
> *For I have bound to my club of battle*
> *Feathers from an earth-bound albatross,*
> *And I have taken from the breaking waves*
> *Feathers of the sky-borne albatross*
> *Almost lost in troubled waters.*"

The girl sat for a long time with the poem open in her hands. Finally, she folded it carefully and slipped it back into the envelope.

A movement in the dark sky caught her eye. She squinted. High above her, caught on the edge of the clouds, a sea bird wheeled. Some bit of light caught on the tip of its wing as it curved out over the water, and for a moment the bird shone like a brilliant star.

The girl stared transfixed. Higher and higher the bird spiraled above her, until it was gone from her sight. She struggled to calm her breathing, shaking her head. Sea gulls often flew in over the lake . . .

. . . But something touched her cheek, a soft, drifting thing that fell from the sky into her lap. She picked it up and held it in her hand, a perfect white feather, bigger than any gull's. She drew it lightly across her cheek, and in that faintest whisper of sound, she heard the words as surely as if they had been spoken: "I love you, I love you."

She recognized the voice.

GLOSSARY

KAKA	A large black parrot with orange underwings
KIKIWA	A Maori word meaning "black"
KIWI	A New Zealander
KUMERA	A root, similar to an Amercian sweet potato, which was the Maori staple food before European occupation
MANUKA	A fast-growing tree that forms the bulk of "second-growth" forest — vegetation that grows back on land previously stripped of original forest
MARAE	A word that means both a building at the center of a particular Maori family or tribal group and a concept of community, religion, and ancestry
MOKO	An individual pattern of spirals and dots tattooed in blue dye on a Maori face. Men often tattooed the entire face, while women covered primarily the lower jaw area
MOREPORK	An indigenous owl, whose name is derived from the sound of its call

PA	The entire structure of trenches and stockades that surrounds and includes a Maori village
PIPI	A small clam with sweet meat, found in sand at low tide
POHUTUKAWA	A vinelike tree that can grow to great size; in midsummer it becomes covered in bright red flowers
PUKEKO	A marsh bird, with blue-black feathers, white underbody, and large red legs and feet
TAPU	Untouchable; sacred
TIKI	An image in the shape of a human fetus worn around the neck to ward off bad spirits
TOHUNGA	A chosen person highly trained and skilled in a particular aspect of traditional lore
WAITAPU	Sacred water (wai means "water")